Blood Loss

The Third in the Cycle of the Aphotic World

THE APHOTIC SERIES

Bad Blood
Out For Blood
Blood Loss
Blood Pact
Blood Relations
Flesh and Blood

Blood Loss

Tobin Elliott

Luminous Aphotica Publishing

ISBN 978-1-77826-298-2 (hardcover)
ISBN 978-1-77826-294-4 (paperback)
ISBN 978-1-77826-295-1 (ebook)

Cover Design by Camille Codling (Instagram: @codling.creations)
Interior Layout by Jennifer Dinsmore (jenniferdinsmoreeditorial.com)

This one is for all those crazy bastards I hung out with when I worked in fast food. You'll never get another first job, so you can only hope the ones you share that time with make the drudgery fun. Very few names remain in my memory – aside from Brian, Brian, Brian, Brian, Brian, and Bryan – but the laughter and the fun – both inside and outside the stores – still remain. And that's all you can really ask for, isn't it?

Also, this one's also for all those who I have worked with, and continue to work with, in both the bookstore and the comic shop. I don't have to work in retail now. But with friends and co-workers like these, I want to.

Acknowledgements

As with my note in the previous book, thank you to everyone in my life who keeps me sane. You are my family. To lose you would be to lose my blood.

To the Hickeys and the Longs. Both your families have taken mine in. That's a gift I can never repay.

To Patricia Flewwelling and A. L. Tompkins, who have poked and prodded and made damn sure I not only wrote, but finished what I started. I've always winced, but I've always appreciated it.

To Jennifer Dinsmore, who is shockingly good at finding out how shockingly poor I edit myself. If there's pleasure to be had from these books, it's because Jennifer made them make sense.

To my daughter Madison and her husband Devyn, and to my son Hunter and his fiancée Camille. And, of course, to my wife, who is mother to not just our kids, but to so many more.

Each and every one of you make me a far better person.

"Blood does not family make. Those are relatives. Family are those with whom you share your good, bad, and ugly, and still love one another in the end. Those are the ones you select."

– Hector Xtravaganza

PROLOGUE

JUST GIVE ME *the goddamn Geronimo, Billy.*

As Billy huffed and puffed, Sarah ticked off the various ways she wanted Billy out of her vagina and out of her life. Billy, for his part, existed only for the sex act, his body jackhammering into hers in a rhythm designed for his own maximum pleasure. Perfect hair over a perfect face. Billy enjoying the ride of his life. For her, it was simply a goodbye fuck, no more and no less.

The problem was, Billy just didn't know it yet.

♦♦♦

ITS EARS PRICK up at the unusual noises, so unlike the night sounds in this area. A slight, mechanical screech of metal stressing against metal. It doesn't think much in language when it's in a state like this, but it gets a barely recalled image of springs and shocks.

Yes, it knows this. *A car.*

It remembers them. Then, a more pleasurable thought: *Cars mean people.*

There is another sound, fainter, muffled, of heavy, rhythmic breathing.

Sex.

Then it's on the move, ears twitching, sourcing out the sounds, and nose enticing secrets from the cool night air.

They will have fun together, the people and it.

They just don't know it yet.

♦♦♦

SARAH'S HEAD THUMPED against the back seat armrest, Billy's thrusts keeping time like a bass beat to a heavy metal song. She tried to reposition her left leg a little and settled for draping it over the back dash. Billy continued to pump, ignoring—or simply not noticing—her discomfort. He'd never been particularly adept at noticing much that didn't directly involve him. During sex, it all came down to that thrusting five inches of muscle. Nothing else.

Billy could take a long time to come, having long ago fallen into the delusion that this was as good for Sarah as it was for himself. But really, after all this time, with the lack of care he put into this so-called lovemaking, she wished he'd just blast through it like some of her girlfriends always complained their boyfriends did. *No, I had to pick a guy who's all stamina, no compassion.* She envied her girlfriends' three-pump wonders right now. Not a lot of fun for her to have a guy who basically used her vagina to masturbate himself.

How the hell did I get here?

They'd been dating for over a year now, and she had always been a realist. Billy was a good-looking guy, and they looked good together, but even with that, she realized very quickly that arm candy simply wasn't enough. Not by a long shot. Oh sure, he had other points. He could be funny, some of his friends were nice…but overall, Billy missed the mark on more important things. And over the past few months, those missing important things had become more and more noticeable to Sarah.

She thought of her parents, married over two decades now and still happy. Sure, they squabbled and disagreed, sometimes they even fought. But mostly, they respected each other even though each still did things that irritated the other. Her father's damn coat, for one thing. An ugly navy-blue parka with an eye-wateringly repulsive orange lining and a matted fringe of fake fur around the rim of the hood. He'd owned the stupid thing so long that he had resorted to reinforcing the thinning elbows with duct tape. Small strips of tape also showed up haphazardly around the coat to repair the odd rip and tear. It was easily the most hideous thing Sarah had ever seen, and her mother hated it even more. But still, her father wore it every winter. He would pass over the stylish leather jackets or modern ski jackets her mother purchased in vain in favour of the hideous thing that had been outdated by the eighties.

And yet, for all of that, as much as she threatened to throw the thing out, somehow she never did. And Sarah knew why.

Because her mother respected her father.

That was something Sarah wanted for herself as well. The way Billy fucked her was just one symptom of his lack of respect. Sarah knew he'd finish, then go and have a smoke, leaving her alone. It's simply what he did.

And the sooner he does that, she thought, *the sooner I can get this over with.*

♦ ♦ ♦

THE WOODED AREAS and the hills play tricks on its senses. It takes longer to pinpoint precisely where the sounds originate.

It took longer than it likely should have for it to remember to equate cars and roads. It crossed three before it makes the connection and begins following them.

The additional time it spends searching only serves to build its anticipation of the sport to come from excitement to rage.

It wants to find them. *Now.*

But the small, human side of it that still held on in a corner of its brain makes it slow down. Sit and take a moment to both calm itself, somewhat, and to cast about for more sensory input.

And when it does, its nose immediately picks up the unmistakable musk of intercourse.

It stands, angles its ears this way and that, then lopes down the road. They are close. The sport would begin soon. They would be found.

The sooner it finds them, the sooner it will get this damnable hunger over with.

♦♦♦

SHE VERY DELIBERATELY started working up to her spectacular, and completely manufactured orgasm, hoping that he would take that as a signal to let go.

God, seventeen and I'm already faking orgasms. She knew it was wrong, knew it sent the wrong signal—that Billy was the greatest lover in the world—but if she didn't, he'd half-heartedly pump at her for another half-hour before giving up. Then the ego-massaging questions would start.

It was bad enough that she was letting him get his dick stroked one last time. She wouldn't stroke his ego as well. *Well, aside from the bullshit orgasm.*

She built up to an enthusiastic but not too over-the-top crescendo, then slumped, her head still pounding against the damn armrest. *Okay, that should clear the path for Geronimo.*

Billy worked up to his own, much more authentic release. She felt him tense a little more, felt his hands squeeze a little tighter. To be honest, this part wasn't bad, just as he approached his own finish. Though she knew it was completely reflexive, he held her a little tighter and she felt some passion from him, even if it was only a side effect of his own pleasure. It was for him, but she could, at least for a few precious moments, kid herself into believing it was for her instead.

Then his breaths changed to tight little Santa Claus noises—*ho! ho! ho!*—and he tilted his head back as though he would howl at the moon. She smiled, but kept it to herself. A small smile, because even after most of a year, she still could never predict when it would happen. She always tried to gauge from his twitching body and huffing, but whenever she figured it couldn't go on, it did.

Then finally, he threw his head back even more, his Adam's apple jutting prominently from his taut neck muscles. He stopped the huffs, holding his breath, pushing himself as deep as he could into her, gathering his strength, then, in a rush of air, yelled, "*Geronimo!*" and came in great bucking waves before dropping heavily down on her, his breath irritating in her ear, ruffling her hair. She could barely breathe.

His breathing slowed to normal as Sarah continued to take shallow breaths, doing her best to not push him off her. Finally, he lifted himself up and pulled out.

"Gotta take a piss, babe," he said. "Probably grab a smoke while I'm out there." She pulled her legs up to give him room to slip his feet into his crumpled jeans and pull his underwear and pants back up. She felt what he'd left behind leaking out of her, cooling on her buttocks.

He opened the door, letting the brisk October air in. She saw he'd left his pants low enough for his ass to show whitely above the waistband, like he was one of those idiots who wore those low-rider jeans that showed *way* too much underwear. For him though, she knew this was simply for expediency. No sense in doing the pants up only to undo them again for a piss.

He held the door open, letting even more cold air in. "While I'm out here, you wanna fold up the blanket before anything soaks through?" Sarah restrained herself from mouthing the next words along with him. "The old man'll kick my ass if anything stains his seats." It was the usual spiel and the cleanup was always left to her.

He closed the door and she sat up, the leather cold against her bare skin. She could see his blurred form through the fogged rear window and felt the small jolt as he leaned against the side of the car to take his piss.

She gathered up some of the ratty beach towel and wiped herself as clean as she could, then pulled her own jeans up as well. She folded the towel up to keep the wet deep inside and tossed it on the floor in the front where he wouldn't miss it.

Then, she sat and waited. She knew he'd be a while. He'd pee. He'd smoke. He'd fix his hair. He'd look at the goddamn stars. He'd make her wait.

She glanced out the rear window again and saw his outline, dim in the moonlight, a small red glare of a cigarette.

She turned back around and looked out the side window closest to her. The window was still fogged, so she brought a finger up and drew a circle. Two dots for eyes. A downturned line. Not a happy face.

That was her right now. Not happy.

♦♦♦

ITS TASK BECOMES easier as it gets closer. The sounds are more pronounced. The smells sharper.

Then there comes, just back from the road, the slight mechanical sound of a vehicle door opening, and someone speaking. It hears the words, but in its present state, it cannot understand them.

However, the story is very clear. The fug of sex drifting from the man's penis, then the sharper, acrid odour as he urinates. The patter of the liquid hitting the dirt. The sigh of release.

Then, more sounds, fumbling, before a flare of flame, and the point of red, a beacon for it to follow, as if the stink of the thing in the man's mouth isn't enough.

It treads more carefully now, predator stalking prey, but there's a lightness in its step.

This is what it is. Happy.

♦♦♦

SHE'D ASKED BILLY—still called William Stradlater Junior if his mother happened to be particularly pissed at him—if they could get together tonight to talk. She stressed the words *to talk*, but they seemed to whistle right by his perfect hair. "You lookin' for a little action?" he had asked, an expectant gleam in his eye.

"Billy," she'd said. "I'd like to *talk*." She was damn near tempted to bust out the *William Stradlater Junior* tag herself at that point.

"Okay, babe," he said, placating. "Okay. We can talk." A salacious grin twisted his lips.

Sarah had talked to her mother about Billy, about how he just didn't seem to be the one. Her mother had suggested she may be outgrowing him. She'd smiled when she told Sarah that women always mature faster than men. Smiled wider when she said some men don't ever mature at all.

Then she'd put her hand on Sarah's, resting it lightly over her daughter's. "You do what your heart tells you to do," she said. And Sarah had known what that was. Had, in fact, known it for months.

Her mother had just underlined it for her. So, she'd asked Billy to talk.

She'd had to talk him out of inviting friends. She'd had to make it clear she wanted to be alone with him. Of course, Billy being Billy, he'd read the signals all wrong.

He'd picked her up that night in his father's car. When she hopped in, he'd asked her where she'd wanted to go. She didn't have a destination in mind, and made a critical error in saying she didn't really care, instead of suggesting a fast-food place or a coffee shop. It wasn't until she realized he'd pointed the car toward the more rural area north of the city that she began to expect what Billy had in mind.

"Billy," she'd said to remind him. "I said I wanted to *talk*."

She watched that same small grin—a grin she'd first loved, then learned to despise—slide across his lips again as he drove, wrists loose on the wheel. "I know, babe. We'll talk. Promise." He kept the car pointed north. He took one hand off the wheel and placed it on her knee. "It's just that Little Billy needs some lovin', y'know?" His hand crept up her thigh. "Then we can have that little talk, okay?"

She stopped his hand's roving path mid-way. "Little Billy isn't getting a damn thing while Big Billy's driving."

That was enough for Billy to find a secluded spot, an old driveway that now led to nothing but a dense copse of trees. He drove through the trees, then past them to the other side. "So we can still see the stars," he'd said. She knew he'd had no intention of looking at the stars until after he'd gotten his dick wet and then had a cigarette. That was just how Billy rolled.

So now, here she sat. Billy had, as usual, gotten what he wanted while she still waited for the real purpose of the night to start.

When he finally got back in the car, she was going to tell Billy she didn't want to see him anymore.

She didn't expect him to take it well, but she also didn't think he'd be overly disappointed either. She'd seen the way he looked at some of the other girls in the school. With more than just a passing interest.

Then again, if she was honest with herself, she had to admit she was doing the same damn thing.

Lately, she'd been focusing her attention on one specific boy. He was the exact opposite of Billy. Nothing to really look at, but still there was something about him. A vulnerability. An openness.

And he'd caught her looking too.

Sarah wasn't the type to screw around on her boyfriend, no matter how much of a dick he was. Better to break it off clean and start fresh. That was what she wanted to accomplish tonight. A clean break from Billy.

Jesus Christ! What's taking him so damn long?

It was time to get this over with.

♦♦♦

IT WATCHES THE man as the red light at his mouth flares and dims, flares and dims. It will not approach while the man has the thing.

It can't remember what it's called, but it knows that thing is as hot as it is bright.

The man takes forever with the glowing thing.

Then, just at the point where it is about to go against its own judgment, it sees the man throw the glowing thing at his feet, hears the sizzle as it lands in the acrid pool of urine and extinguishes.

The man exhales a last, pungent breath of smoke, and then it is on the move.

It is time to get this over with.

♦♦♦

JUST AS SHE turned to look out the rear window again, the car rocked. It was likely Billy pushing hard against it, screwing around, but also letting her know he was done and they could have "that little talk" now.

Instead, the car rocked again. And she heard something. A squealing scrape, as though a screwdriver had been drawn down the side of the car. The car rocked again. Then again.

Then she heard Billy scream.

Goddamn him! she thought. *This is* so *not the time to be screwing around!*

"Billy!" she yelled. She pushed the seat forward to scramble into the front.

The car rocked again. A thunderous *boom* as something hit the car. Hard.

She wormed to the driver's seat and started the car to lower the fogged window. No way she was opening the damn door. The window cracked and she caught a glimpse of two glowing, yellow eyes. She pawed at the controls to get the window back up again.

Hyperventilating now. Something jumped on the hood of the car. Two legs. Dark. "Jesus!" she yelled.

Then the front window spiderwebbed as something hit it dead centre. The safety glass held, but the window bent inward. Another thunderous boom, this time on the roof. And another. The roof of the car pushed downward, bowing into the interior.

A high, keening whine. Sarah realized it was her. The roof boomed again, then again.

The front window, again.

Then the car jumped as the weight left it and Sarah caught movement out of the corner of her eye. Whatever was out there was back at the side window again. The window shattered, pebbles of glass showering her as she screamed. She spit them out as she frantically grabbed for the shift lever to put the damn car in drive.

She pulled at it, pushed at it, yanked on it, but it wouldn't fucking move.

Something splashed her. It was the taste, not the sight of the blood that woke her up. Her left side gleamed wetly, almost black in the cold October moonlight.

Billy?

She realized then that she needed to push the brake to get the car into gear. She slammed her foot down on the pedal as something shot through the window and raked her scalp from the back of her head to the front. She heard a wet ripping sound as flesh—her flesh!—pulled away from bone.

Tendons shrieked as her jaw flexed, her mouth opening as wide as it possibly could as she screamed, expunging every bit of the air in her lungs. Tears streamed down her face as she finally got the goddamn gear shift into drive. She lifted her foot and slammed it back down, a little to the right, pounding the gas pedal to the floor, doing everything she could to push it into the ground, her butt rising from the seat with the effort. The car jumped forward. The sound of the screaming engine and the thump of gravel and clumps of sod pounding at the rear wheel wells filled the car as the tires fought for purchase. Then the vile thing came back in the window again. This time in front of her face, reaching for one of her arms. She batted at it with a hand, pulling away from the feeling of—

Of what?

Hair?

Fur?

A bear. Goddamn bear attacked us.

Whatever it was, it grabbed the wheel and wrapped a meaty fist around it.

A fist. *Not a bear.*

She risked a look to her left, saw a sloping head that came down to a snout and thought *bear*, then *dog*, then gave up. It snarled back at her. The car careened back down the road Billy had driven them up just an hour earlier.

They approached the copse of trees again and Sarah wondered desperately how the thing held on. She looked again, saw the snarl again, saw the rhythmic rising and falling of that head, realized the thing was running—*It's fucking running*—beside her.

She did the only thing she could do. She cranked the wheel to the left to push the thing off balance. Its hand fell from the steering wheel, grabbed madly for her face, her arm, anything. It caught the rear-view mirror and tore it off and it was gone, no longer beside her.

The car hit a tree and Sarah saw the shattered window fly at her, realizing only at the point of impact that it had actually been her flying at the window.

♦♦♦

SHE WASN'T OUT long. But when she came to, she came back to instant panic. The thing now squatted on the hood and reached for her through the shattered ruins of the front window. She couldn't fight it off and it pulled her out like an infant from a car seat.

It held her, half in, half out, of the damaged vehicle and stared at her. She saw with some small measure of satisfaction that she had injured it. It bled from a wound on the side of its head and a deep gash on one arm.

Got you too, fucker.

It stared at her. Blood streamed into her eyes and she did what she could to blink it away. It pulled her forward and she caught its sharp, fetid odour as it opened its mouth to lick at the blood, its tongue long and moist and hot.

You're a dog? No, wolf. But, with hands?

The werewolf reared back, opened its jaws, then shot forward and she felt the jaws contract on her face. A brief shock of pain.

Then Sarah had one last thought. Absurdly, it was, *Geronimo.*

♦ ♦ ♦

It feeds well this night.

The bright moon above, its constant companion, looks on quietly until it has taken everything it wants.

And the moon watches as it finally rises, its tongue swiping away the last flecks of blood and offal, to find a place to hide and sleep.

It's been a productive night.

PART ONE
DISCOMFORT

"We live on a placid island of ignorance in the midst of black seas of infinity, and it was not meant that we should voyage far."

THE CALL OF CTHULHU
H. P. LOVECRAFT

First Interlude

SHE STOOD IN the backyard of the house that used to be hers. Her family's house. Now, instead, her husband's house, and her daughter's house.

Now, she had been subtracted from that equation.

She had tucked herself into the corner where the shed met the hedges. She could push back slightly behind the shed to hide, yet still see the windows. Thankfully, there was no snow yet. When there was, these surreptitious visits would have to cease. Her footprints would give her away.

She focused on the second-floor window. It bled pink light through the curtains in her daughter's room. The light had just come on. She knew then that Dave had finished giving April—her daughter—a bath. She knew that light would stay on now for a good twenty minutes while April dressed in her nightclothes, climbed into bed, and then read a story with her father.

She couldn't hear them. She couldn't see them. Still, it was enough to know they were there.

She could imagine her daughter's high, tinkling laugh as Dave tickled her or read in a particularly funny voice. God, she missed April's laugh most of all.

So, instead, she stood like a fool, with the cold biting at her fingers and cheeks, while she stared at a closed window and imagined how her life should have turned out. Imagined how different it would have been if—

Ah hell, what good was it to imagine? It would never come back. She couldn't undo those things. She could only remain very still and be content with the small gift of getting into the backyard undetected by one of the neighbours.

Or Dave.

Dave would freak if he caught her back here again. He'd already swore he would get a restraining order if she continued to stalk them.

Stalk them. That's what he'd said, the words he'd used. *Stalk.* Her own family.

Her old family.

Not mine anymore.

Was this stalking? Was that what she was doing?

Yes, Ray, of course it is.

She knew he didn't want to go as drastic as a restraining order, but she knew he would. She knew it was wrong, knew she should stop. Shoulda coulda woulda. All it really meant was she had to take even more care than she had previously.

She tried to see it more like visiting the grave of a loved one. She came, not expecting to ever get them back. She did it to remember the good times and grieve for the husband and daughter, the family she'd lost.

Still, they'd carried on living. *Maybe I'm the one who died,* she thought. She closed her eyes and pushed that thought away. That one hurt. It felt more true.

She was the ghost who kept coming back to visit the living.

I'm trying to move on, guys, she thought. *That should please you, Dave.* She smiled to herself. *I'm making the effort. Even if it doesn't look like I'm trying to move on. I know, I know, I shouldn't be here if that's the case, right?* Then the smile went away.

I try to stay away. I know I'm no longer welcome. I know this part of my life is gone. I get it. I know it's my fault. I know it was my obsession and my decision…but I can't just let go and not miss you. Both of you.

Anyway, she thought. *I just came by to give you some news.*

She took a slow, deep breath, as though the next thought would cause her some pain and she had to build up to it. Prepare for it.

I've bent my own rule. She smiled. *Okay, full disclosure. I've* broken *my own rule.*

I came to tell you both that I've got a date this Friday night.

Her eyes welled up and she angrily knuckled them away. She wouldn't allow tears. She'd get through this.

It was just a little tougher than she'd thought it was going to be.

I've got a date. His name is Zach and he seems to be a nice guy. And he seems to like me.

I can't say for sure if I like him yet, but I can say he's the first person who's even tempted me in...well...since you, Dave.

April, I'm sorry. Don't hate Mommy, okay? Try as she might, the tears came anyway. She pushed them away, warm on her fingers. She looked up at the window again, willing her daughter to hear her. *No matter where I am, or what I do, I'll always love you. You'll always be my baby girl.*

Except she knew that was false. April was Dave's baby girl now. Mommy was gone. Only Daddy remained.

Okay, this isn't going the way I'd planned it.

She looked back up at the house, at April's window. The light went out. Storytime was over.

She looked at Dave's window. It took a couple of minutes for his light to come on. Maybe he'd gone to the bathroom. Maybe down to the kitchen for a drink. No matter. He was in their bedroom—*his bedroom,* she corrected herself—now. All was safe in their world.

I'll make sure it stays that way. Safe.

She glanced up one last time. His curtains were drawn tight as well. She stepped out onto the grass, scuffed the ground to remove any traces of boot prints, then, staying close to the hedges, glided back out of the backyard.

She took care to study every lit window in the area until she was a few houses down. Only then did she relax slightly. She assumed a normal gait and walked away from her old life.

CHAPTER ONE

"YOU READY FOR this, Taylor?" Zero said, her voice hushed in quiet of the van.

Taylor was nowhere near ready for this, but he didn't have a hell of a lot of choice. When Zero asked him to integrate the new member, it was understood—Taylor integrated the new member. No fucking around.

"Yeah, I'm ready, Zee."

"You remember what's gotta be done?"

Taylor laughed a little, careful to keep his lips tight, showing no teeth. "It's not brain surgery, Zee. He kills the family, we get out, and he's in the club. You've been there. I've been there. We all know how it goes." Taylor didn't miss the weird expression that flickered across Zero's face.

Syd obviously missed it, because he just smirked. "Taught him well," he said, clapping Taylor on the back with a lot more force than necessary. "Kid can do it."

Zee glanced from one to the other. "Kid's *gotta* do it. The pack's getting a little thin."

"Got that right," Syd said. Taylor nodded his agreement, his mouth a grim, serious line.

"All right then," Zee said. "Go get him."

Taylor stepped away from the van they'd been sitting in. The vehicle, an old second-generation Econoline van—which meant it had rolled off the line no later than 1974, so it was thirty years old if it was a day—was a shit pit. Whoever owned it needed to learn a little about basic hygiene. Discarded food wrappers, long-dead fries, bits of burger bun, desiccated meat…all of it littered around the back seat and floor, pushed into the hard-to-reach crevices and corners. Made the van smell like a fucking fast-food joint dumpster.

Yes, it was old, but Jesus wept. Couldn't the owner throw his garbage out once in a while? Whoever owned it deserved for it to be stolen. Wherever it ended up after this, it would go to a better home.

Still, it would serve their purpose well enough tonight. An anonymous ride to get them to the house, then away again. But the smell assaulting his senses was enough to make his eyes water. Humans and their odours were disgusting.

Taylor glanced left, then right. No cars, not that he expected any at this time of night. He pulled out his cellphone and glanced at the display. 2:47 A.M. Hell, it was damn near morning. He walked across the road and straight up the driveway to the house like he belonged there.

It wasn't that long ago that Syd had made this same walk into Taylor's life.

Taylor didn't remember a lot of that night, to be honest. He remembered waking up in a cold sweat, his sheets soaked, his body maddeningly itchy, his joints aching, stabbing pains shooting up his cheeks, down his neck.

He'd tried to get out of bed, but it was like someone had replaced his limbs with strange, unfamiliar ones of different lengths and strength. He couldn't seem to make them work the way he needed them to, so he'd fallen to the floor. Tears blurred his vision, scents blurred them more. He smelled…so many things. His sweat. The stink of garbage. The musty fug of the carpet and the reek of feet. The soap fragrance on his clothes in the drawers. The plastic and the warm electronics in his clock radio. The burned dust on the lightbulb in his bedside lamp. So many smells.

Sounds! The regular deep breathing of his father as he slept. His mother's slight snore. The higher-pitched sound from his sister. The groans of the house, the pings of the warming ducts after the air conditioner stopped. The rustle of the trees and grass outside his closed window.

As he had tried to calm himself, on his hands and knees, he saw the individual fibres of the carpet weave. He saw the small, chipped spaces on the corners of his bedroom furniture. The imperfect line of the wall that had always looked straight before.

It was all so overwhelming.

But it went beyond that. If he could make his body work, if he could get to his bedroom window, he'd see the Earth spinning under the sky, feel it moving through the atmosphere.

And that thought freaked him out. Though he was on all fours, he had trembled so violently he thought he might fall over.

Then someone stood in the doorway. Of all the things Taylor sensed, that figure had not been one of them. Taylor stared up in disbelief, too stunned to even form words to ask who he was, what he was doing here, how he had gotten in. He could only sweat and shake, having no idea what was going on, who this person—Syd—was, or what he'd wanted.

Syd had come in and sat beside him, talking him down, talking him through it. Quietly, like an old friend getting a buddy through a bad bender.

And then, of course, he'd made sure Taylor did what he'd needed to do afterward.

Taylor stopped thinking about the whole thing, then. What he had done next. Wasn't that it bugged him so much as it was a waste of fucking time to even think about it. Who thought about chicken bones left over from a meal after they threw them away?

He brought himself back to the task at hand.

He'd need to be on the ball, like Syd had been for him. He'd need to talk this guy, this Eli, through it too.

And he would. But first, he needed to get inside.

Most of the houses in this area were nice enough, their owners doing what they could to show a little pride of ownership. Still, most of the fences needed a new coat of paint. The driveways were a little rough.

But this place. *Jesus fucking wept,* he thought. The place needed a little more than basic TLC, that was for damn sure. The garage door was more grey than white, the paint peeling in flaky, curling strips. The grass hadn't been cut in, probably, three weeks. Weeds poked up several inches between the concrete slabs of the walkway to the front door. Nails pounded into the veranda rail—likely to hold Halloween or Christmas decorations at some point—were now simply creating an ever-lengthening rust stain down the wood.

Taylor took it in, his senses unable to completely ignore all the input as he walked alongside the garage to the entrance to the backyard. A wooden fence, grey with age, blocked his way. He stopped for a moment, sniffed.

No dog. Good, makes it easier.

The lock was a simple rusted latch that he lifted without too much issue. He pushed experimentally on the door. It squeaked softly, but had the potential to be a lot louder. Instead, he pulled the door closed, stepped back, then jumped.

Easily clearing it, he landed softly on the grass on the far side, in the backyard.

Now to find a way in. No basement windows. He checked the main floor, but they were all a no-go, unless he broke one, which he'd prefer to avoid. He looked up.

Then he smiled.

A window was open up there. Either a bedroom or bathroom. Better yet, the screen was slightly pulled away. He looked around. All the surrounding houses were dark. He heeled off his shoes and pulled off his socks, positioned himself just right, crouched, focused, then leaped.

In mid-spring, his body came level with the window screen, his senses receiving input at a more frantic rate. Choosing his spots carefully, he hooked the window frame with his fingers just as his feet found purchase on the lower sill.

He used his free hand to first push the screen open, then he was in the room.

The bed was made, there was a basic chest of drawers with a mirror, and a couple of pictures beside the lamps on the end tables. Nothing distinctive, nothing to give it personality. It smelled slightly musty, as though rarely ever used. Probably a spare bedroom. Taylor guessed, from the disrepair he'd seen outside, that Eli and his family rarely received visitors. Which made Eli an even better target.

He replaced the screen, then padded lightly to the opened door. No sound. Funny. Usually the recruit was up and panicking by now. It was then that Taylor smelled the sharp tang of blood.

That can't be good, he thought. *Are we too late?*

He moved down the hallway, keeping to the side as much as possible to avoid any squeaks. The hall was carpeted, but it was worn and faded in the middle from years of use. The intensity of the smell increased exponentially. It had a lot of competition. The smell rising from the carpet, as well as the dust and rotted kitchen smells, tweaked Taylor's olfactory senses.

This place is as much a shit pit as the van.

He passed a bathroom that stank of piss and encroaching mildew. The next room was obviously used. The bed was unmade, the covers not just messed up, but crumpled on the floor. Shirts, socks, underwear, pants, and towels were all strewn around the room, enough that Taylor wasn't sure if there was carpet or just more layers of clothing. Plates, bowls, and glasses, all showing stains or food remnants, perched on a desk with a laptop and a desk lamp. More dishes sat precariously on bookshelves and on the seat of the desk chair, adding to the fug of smells.

Taylor knew Eli was up now. The smell was so intense it almost brought on the shift. The smell of blood and shit and fear.

The smell of food.

Abandoning caution, he walked ahead the three steps to the last door, what had to be the master bedroom. The door was closed. He placed his hand on the knob and slowly twisted it.

"C'mon in! It's open," he heard a rather excited man say. And he thought, *The fuck?*

He opened the door and then the smell smashed into him. The room was an abattoir.

"Ta-daaaaaa!"

Taylor didn't even follow the voice's origin, due to the unreality of the scene before him. He'd automatically dropped to a defensive crouch, his sharp gaze sliding around the room, lit by two small lamps on the nightstands. On the bed lay the old woman, the savagery of the tear in her throat so deep the vertebrae shone through. Worse travesties below the neck. Blood spattered the walls, the ceiling, the curtains. Pieces of the woman had been flung about the room. Great pools of blood soaked the carpet.

She'd been eviscerated, savagely, brutally. Left hollowed out, her flesh flayed from her bones, her ribs a cage arcing up from the hole in her body.

Taylor had seen a lot of carnage in the past couple of years, but nothing on this scale. This was Jack the Ripper shit.

Finally, Taylor tracked the one responsible for this insanity. After grandly opening the door, the guy had backed off to allow a full viewing of his deeds. Taylor, still crouching, finally saw him, standing, arms spread wide in a *ta-da!* pose.

"Eli?"

"The Fed," he said.

"Excuse me?"

"That's what the Fed goes by." He dropped his blood-slicked arms then, a tall, slimly built man. "The Fed."

The Fed looked like he'd been dipped in blood. He shone red-black in the dim lighting. Bits of gore clung to his naked body.

"Got it. Eli Federman. The Fed." Taylor looked around the room again. "You did this?"

"It's what the Fed's gotta do, right?" He stepped forward, his red arms out as though to hug Taylor. "The Fed's gotta kill his family to get into the pack, right?" He gestured around the room as though showing off new wallpaper. "Well, he did it." He looked at the old woman in the bed—his mother, presumably—spread his arms again, and said, "Ta-da!" He turned back to Taylor. "The Fed's only sorry he didn't have more family to kill."

Taylor watched the frown fall over the Fed's face. He would have taken anyone else, in any other circumstance, as joking, grim as that would be, but the seriousness of his expression told Taylor he was earnestly serious and horribly disappointed.

"He tried to make it epic. Hopefully his mama is enough."

Taylor looked around the room, now realizing it really *was* Jack the Ripper shit. What he'd taken as gore-soaked wallpaper earlier was actually the Fed's mother's intestines. They'd been strung around the room like Christmas garland, held up with nails. *Jesus Christ, we got a guy who plays with his fucking food.*

His thoughts were interrupted by the Fed. "Is the Fed in?"

Christ Almighty, Taylor thought. *What the hell did Zee get us into?*

"Yeah," he said. "The Fed's in."

Chapter Two

TWO DAYS AFTER she had visited her daughter and her ex-husband, Rainer was three hours from her old home, driving along mostly gravel roads north of the bedroom community of Laughlin. She was looking for someone.

The roads north of the city were essentially a grid, neatly dividing the rural properties like a massive checkerboard, old-growth trees lining the routes. She'd driven up and down these roads all day yesterday, looking for any signs, anything out of the ordinary. She stopped only once to first investigate an old, abandoned concrete grain silo, then to prepare it. There was no question she would find what she was looking for, and she wanted to be ready.

Once she had the grain silo the way she wanted it, she'd continued her careful, meticulous search of these roads until the dark made it impossible to continue.

She'd gotten up just before sunrise this Wednesday morning to do it again. She'd rose, scrubbed the sleep crust from her eyes, and greeted the sun in her normal way. When she was done, she dressed and clambered back to the front seat of her SUV. She then drove out from her hiding spot behind the abandoned silo and continued her search from the spot she'd finished at the evening before.

Two hours later, the sun having already burned the last of the night's dampness away, she finally saw something. Tire tracks, reasonably fresh, pulling off to a road that looked like it didn't get much use. The weather had been in her favour—damp a few days ago, then dry since—as had the lack of excessive traffic along these back roads.

She pulled the car off to the side, put on the four-way flashers, thumbed the button on the key fob to lock it, then crossed the road to investigate the tracks more closely.

She crouched and examined them. Followed them along their path with her eyes to where they disappeared in a copse of trees. Stood again, stretched, then walked the path.

Once she reached the trees, she didn't have to walk far. She saw the car off to her right. She saw the scene on the rear of the car, but decided to avoid it for now. Time enough for that later. She knew most of the clues would come from there, so she'd save that for the end. Instead, she focused on what the rest of the scene could tell her.

The vehicle had veered off the path and down a slight incline and straight into a tree. Fairly high speed at that, judging from the way the front of the car was wrapped halfway around the trunk. Hugging it like a drowning man on a life buoy.

She took a deep breath and stepped carefully down the incline, watching where she walked, not wanting to disturb anything. At the passenger side of the car, she leaned down and, resting her arms on the doorframe where the window would have been had it still been intact, she studied the driver's side. The first thing she noticed was that the airbag had not deployed.

Leaning in, she inspected the steering wheel. Four large gashes had been torn deep into the plastic at the centre of the wheel, where the airbag was stored. There was a large quantity of blood on the dash and the hood of the car.

Leaning further, she saw something on the floor of the car. Stretching, she reached down and pulled up a ratty beach towel. When she unfolded it, there was a crusted section in the middle that filled in the picture a little more for Rainer. Despite the display on the trunk of the car she was avoiding, she was pretty sure both the girl and the boy—Sarah and Billy, she reminded herself—had been attacked. The stained towel confirmed her guess as to why they had come out here.

That was enough to get her up and heading around the back of the car for more information. Even though she mentally braced herself, even though she had expected it, known it was there, what she saw there stopped her.

A young woman, or more accurately, what had once been a young woman named Sarah, was splayed out across the trunk of the car. Her head was turned to one side, as though she hadn't been able to face her attacker. Her face had been torn away, horrible slashes where the skin had separated from muscle, tendon, and bone. Her hair matted enough at the back to suggest serious injury there as well.

Rainer could find not a single square inch where the skin hadn't been scratched, slashed, or torn open. She saw something in the girl's left hand, a small tuft of something sticking out and shaking in the mild breeze. *In a moment.*

Rainer took her time, examined the wounds closely, confirming what she'd known anyway. Claw marks. Teeth marks.

She'd been eaten.

All her organs had been removed. Glancing around the area, Rainer saw spatters of blood, but no meat.

Turning back to the body, to the girl she knew was Sarah, she slid around the side of the car to examine her left arm, the one she'd seen something in. The hand remained tightly closed, even in death. Rainer took a deep breath, reached toward Sarah's hand with her own, but hesitated just before contact. Rainer looked back to Sarah's desecrated face.

"Please," she said.

She touched the girl's hand. She held her breath for the shortest of moments, then let it out, relieved. "Thank you," she said. Then she got her fingers under Sarah's and prised her grip open. Inside, there was a blood-matted tuft of fur.

Rainer breathed out slowly, as though trying to rid herself of what she knew.

She spent even more time going over the body, not touching, simply looking, but that handful of hair had told her everything she'd needed to know. She moved back to the driver's side door once again.

He pulled her out through the front window. Finished with her, then laid her out on the trunk like some fucking prize buck.

Rainer completed her examination of the area around the car and put some distance between her and Sarah and the vehicle. She stood, both fists on hips, the towel still clutched in one, and said, "So where are *you*, Billy?"

It didn't take much more searching to find him. She walked back along the path of the car, moving earlier along the timeline, until she found him. There was even less left of him to find. *Productive night. Fucker got his fill with this attack.*

After a slightly more cursory review of the area—really, she knew now precisely what had happened—Rainer headed back along the path to Sarah, rhythmically squeezing the towel still in her hand, almost forgotten until now.

She didn't want to use the soiled towel, but she really had nothing else to do the job, so she opened it up and covered as much of Sarah as she could.

Then she walked deep into the copse of trees, found a spot that seemed peaceful enough, sat down, and became very still.

She stayed that way for a long time before getting back up and leaving.

CHAPTER THREE

BO STOOD ON the corner of the street, waiting for the light to turn green. He needed to make a phone call and he needed a couple of quarters. He wondered why, with all that he'd done lately, he didn't have two damn quarters to rub together, but that was his goddamn life in a nutshell.

Hell, even if he got the change, the next challenge would be to find a phone booth. Everyone was getting cellphones these days. Shit, ten years back, the only ones were those monstrous bricks. Now everyone seemed to have one, even the one he had to call, for fucksake. Maybe he should just swipe a cellphone instead. Yeah, a nice flip phone.

Ahead of him, the light turned green and he started across the two-lane street. As he reached the middle, he noticed the car idling at the front of a line of three, waiting for the light. A young guy driving and a young girl beside him. *How fucking cute.*

Bo angled toward them and knocked on the driver's side window. The guy turned and stared at him as though Bo sported two heads. Bo popped a dirty index finger out, then made a wheeling motion with his wrist to show the guy he wanted him to lower his damn window. Instead, the guy shook his head.

Bo punched the glass lightly, getting a little pissed now. *How fucking hard is it to drop the window and toss me a goddamn quarter or two?* He made the motion again. The guy looked down as though for the button to drop the window, but now girly in the passenger seat was motioning at him. He dropped the window about an inch.

Bo stuck his face to the crack. "Gimme a quarter, Mack."

"Sorry?"

Great, got a dumbass who doesn't understand English either. Bo spoke slower and louder. "I need some change. To make a phone call. Can you. Please give me. A couple of quarters?" Keeping it polite. Saying please.

Now girly was bitching at him again. "Just close the window, Allan."

Allan. What kind of a pansy-ass name was Allan?

"Al," Bo said. "C'mon. Help a brother out. Throw me four bits, man."

"*Al*lan," girly said again. "Just drive." *Fuck, she's a whiny bitch.*

And then the guy behind Allan started in with the honking. A quick look at the lights told Bo they'd changed to green. *Shit. I need to make this call.*

He pushed his fingers into the space Allan had thoughtfully provided and, before he could squeeze the window shut, Bo pushed hard and the window groaned, then dropped into the door.

"What the *hell*!" girly bitched. "*Gawd!*"

Bo reached in, gathered up the front of Allan's shirt. "Dude," he growled. *Dammit, I shouldn't be growling at this point. Way too soon for growling.* "Some change. Fifty cents. That's it."

"I...I..."

"Just drive *away*, Allan," girly whined.

Fucking car behind Allan honked again.

"Fifty cents!" Bo couldn't believe this. "Two quarters! Five fucking dimes! Ten motherfucking nickels!" He reached across Allan's chest—Allan flattened himself back into the seat to avoid contact—and tore at the centre console. Girly slapped at his hand. "The *fuck* are you *doing*?" she said. The goddamn console was clean. Just some paper and old fast-food napkins stored against future spills.

"Leann," Allan said, almost in Bo's ear now that he was stretched in through the window. *Pansy-ass is finally finding his voice. He should thank me for that.* "Just dig some change out of your purse."

Bo turned and gave him what he hoped was a wide, friendly smile. "Now you're talkin', Al!" he said. Motherfucker behind Allan leaned on the horn.

"I'm *not* giving this *ass*hole *any*thing!"

The horn again. Bo looked past Allan's head to the car behind. *Fucker's playing with his mortal existence back there.*

"Leann—"

She slapped at Bo again. "Get *out*!" she said. "Get *out* of our *car*!" Slapped at his hand. At his face. *Bitch. My fucking face.*

Horn again.

Leann opened her goddamn mouth to bitch at him again and Bo couldn't do it, couldn't bring himself to listen to that whine any more. He shot a hand out—trying to ignore the distressingly dark, matted fur springing along his arm—and grabbed her by her chin. His fingers went inside her mouth and he felt her moist tongue recoil from his clawed fingers, felt her hard teeth tentatively bite down, then loosen again at the foreign feeling. His thumb wrapped under her chin and pushed up against the soft flesh underneath.

Her eyes were wide as she made an indignant sound, but he didn't even want to hear that so he squeezed, tightening his fist around her jaw, feeling his nails dig in, and watched with satisfaction as her eyes went even wider.

Then that motherfucker laid on his horn again, long and loud, and Leann made another goddamn noise and it was enough for him. He clamped down even tighter and pulled.

She was splattering noise all over the car and now Allan joined in as well and the horn added to the cacophony. Bo felt more than heard the sweet pop, first one side, then the other, as he pulled her jaw out of its sockets and, with a savage jerk, yanked his arm back toward him, her lower jaw and teeth coming along with it.

There was a satisfying gout of blood that splashed the inside of the windshield, but he couldn't stick around to enjoy it. He looked down between Leann's frantically spasming hands and saw her massively overstuffed purse. Perched right on top, like a ripe piece of fruit, sat her wallet.

He looked back at her, her hands wanting to come up to her face but somehow not finding the courage to complete the motion. Instead, they hovered a few inches away, fingers splayed, quivering. Jazz hands. "You bitch," he said.

He snatched the wallet with his clean hand, dropped her useless jaw into Allan's lap with the bloodied one, and, as he backed the upper half of his body out of the car, raked his now-empty hand straight across Allan's face. He felt at least one eye pop, which made him smile.

Teach that douchebag a lesson.

"And speaking of douchebags and lessons..." He stood up and marched to the car behind Allan. Horn still tooting away, he punched the hood of the car, buckling it severely, leaving some of Leann's blood behind. *That's some fucking modern art, right there.* It was enough to get the guy's hands off the horn. Without pause, Bo carried on, punched again at the side window, reached in, grabbed the douchebag's arm, pulled it out, then popped three fingers in his mouth and bit them off.

If he had had the time, he would have torn the entire goddamn arm from the socket, but he didn't. Instead, chewing furiously, he popped the wallet open, scooped out a bunch of coins, pocketed them, threw the wallet back at Allan's car, spit some finger bones at the douchebag's car, then loped away from the scene.

He just wanted to make a fucking call.

That's all he'd wanted to do. Make a call.

Just wanted to get a couple of goddamn quarters.

I really need a fucking cellphone, he thought.

Chapter Four

THE NEWLY EXPANDED pack sat naked around a small fire in a hollow well north of Laughlin, miles from any roads, any people. They'd left their clothes carefully stowed several miles back, before they'd gone on the hunt.

It was far too early to have a fire, but Taylor enjoyed them and had insisted on a small one. They hadn't gotten much time to talk after Taylor got the weird new guy back to the van. He'd exchanged some pointed looks with both Zero and Syd, and the Fed had rambled excitedly, but Zero explained that they would be heading back to the no-name motel for the night, and catching some sleep most of the day. So, this evening, they'd roused themselves and, starving, went on an early hunt. Pickings had been meagre, but it was still a chance to run under the moon and smell all the smells.

With the Calling coming up, they'd steered cleared of any jobs. They were picking up the new pack member, then heading to the Hole.

Now, after the hunt, their hunger somewhat satiated for now, they gathered around the small fire, the first real opportunity to get to know this new guy, the Fed. The firelight gave them something to focus on as they brought him up to speed on what had happened to him. Only, the Fed turned the tables on them.

"You kidding the Fed?" the Fed said. "He studied the lore like you wouldn't believe. He knows the rituals, he knows the rules, he knows it all." Turns out the crazy bastard had been waiting for his ticket to be punched for years. He'd done everything he could to increase his chances of being chosen.

In the meantime, he'd practiced his skills as best he could.

As far as Taylor understood, he'd experienced none of the difficulty Taylor himself had experienced when he'd first turned. He'd been *waiting* to kill his mother, for chrissakes.

But man, this guy talked. And he never said *I*. It was always *the Fed* this and *the Fed* that. Kind of creeped Taylor out.

The guy who's just been turned creeps me out? I'm a fucking werewolf. What the hell is that all about? The Fed was seriously fucked-up as far as Taylor could see.

Not that he could do anything about it. The Fed was pack now and would be until death. Taylor would defend the Fed with his life. And vice versa. Unless he pulled a Bo and got his ass shunned. There weren't too many shifters that had gone Rōnin from what Taylor knew, but Bo had been one of them.

Stupid fucker.

Taylor shut his introspection off and turned to look at Zero. She didn't like being ignored and he sensed her patience already had a shorter fuse with the Fed. Better not to rile her. She had found a break in the Fed's stream-of-consciousness ramblings when he'd finally—mercifully—stopped to take a breath, and she jumped in.

"With all your *research*," Zero said, putting a little more emphasis on that last word, expelling it from her mouth instead of simply speaking it, "you've likely already determined that we are more of a migrant pack rather than a—"

"Yes, yes! I know this!" the Fed said, looking up to the smoke-obscured stars as he drew upon the information he had studied as though cramming for a final exam. He glanced sideways, ignored the look from Zero, flicked his gaze back to the stars, and held up two fingers. "There's two types of packs. There's the stationary or non-migrant packs who typically engage in certain types of highly illegal enterprises such as drug manufacturing, stolen vehicle redistribution, and warehousing of various illegal products." He curled in one finger, leaving the middle on extended, obviously not realizing the sign he made to his pack leader.

"Then there's the migrant packs, such as ours." He looked back to Zero, then took in Syd and Taylor, utterly ignorant to their stares. "These packs tend to intersect with the non-migrant packs by muling their drugs and transporting their vehicles, weapons, or anything else that involves or requires a more mobile capability. Often, they run with, or create their own motorcycle gangs, though they are not limited to that mode of transportation or lifestyle." He finally curled that damned finger down and swung his gaze to Zero, obviously pleased with his performance.

Zero stared back at him, unmoving. A direct challenge that he missed entirely. *Obviously, there's still some gaps in brainiac's knowledge,* Taylor thought.

"So," the Fed said, "what does this pack do to earn money?" Not *our* pack. *This* pack.

Zero's stare continued. Taylor heard her breathing deep, slow breaths. He knew she fought to not do something to this fool. Glancing at her, he wondered if he could perhaps defuse the situation a bit. After all, he was the one who was the idiot's mentor. Lucky him.

"We kill," he said.

The Fed redirected his attention to Taylor. His mouth opened into a small circle and his eyebrows shot up in surprise. "The Fed apologizes. Say again?"

"We kill," Taylor said. "We're essentially a murder-for-hire pack. Assassins, if you want."

A small but widening smile slid distressingly across the Fed's face. "Really?" he said, like a kid who'd just been given the keys to the chocolate factory.

Zero said, "Really." Tone dry and flat.

The Fed broke his gaze from Taylor. It obviously cost him some effort to do so, as though Taylor may proffer more golden drops of sunshine from his mouth and the Fed didn't want to miss a one.

"You finished?" she said.

He glanced to Zero, shot back a glance at Taylor, scrubbed a hand over his mouth, focused back on Zero.

"Say again?"

"I said, 'you finished?'"

"Finished?" The Fed stared at her dumbly.

"Finished showing off your prodigious fucking research? Finished your fucking Yahoo or Google results? Finished—"

"Oh, the Fed had to dig a lot deeper than that. And while Yahoo is still quite popular, Google has gained some prominence." Taylor winced at the interruption.

Zero breathed slowly, deliberately. She cocked her head to the side. "Are you finished interrupting your *fucking pack leader*?"

"Oh," the Fed said. "Yes," he said. "Apologies," he said.

"Shut up," she said.

"Okay."

"Lovely." Zero stared at him for an uncomfortably long time, daring him to say something else. He didn't.

"Obviously you understand much of how the packs earn a living," she said. "Let's move on to something else. Let's talk about the Calling." The Fed squirmed where he sat, and Taylor thought, *Oh no. Don't do it, dude.*

"It only happens once a decade—" she said.

"Oh yeah, this is where—"

"Eli," she said.

"The Fed," he said, and Taylor heard the automatic response in it. He questioned whether the Fed even knew he'd said it.

Zero moved so fast no one had time to react. She'd been across the fire from the Fed, between Taylor and Syd, then she was over the fire with a hand—still a human hand, Taylor had time to notice—clamped around the lower half of the Fed's face, covering his mouth as his eyes grew wide.

Taylor had to give him credit. He didn't make a sound.

But he did hold up a hand, index finger raised in a question.

"Shut up and listen. Eli," she said, tightly clipping each word, ignoring him, ignoring the finger.

It took only a moment, but then the Fed nodded. Once. Slowly. Eyes down.

The Fed might not know a hell of a lot, and it obviously took him a while for any message to sink in, but it finally appeared that he realized when the pack leader told him to shut up, he should very likely shut up.

She released her grip on his face, stared at him for a long moment, naked in the light of the small fire. Then she walked around the fire and took her place between Syd and Taylor again.

All was quiet for a few minutes save for the crackling of the fire. The Fed fidgeted some, but mostly, no one moved.

Then it was over.

"It only happens once every not-quite-fourteen years," Zero started again. "Every five thousand days." She looked at him. He looked like he was going to explode if he didn't say anything, but he kept his mouth shut. Words were replaced by incessant squirming.

We just made a goddamn sociopath into a werewolf, Taylor thought.

"So every pack heads north to all meet at the same place." The Fed jiggled in place. "For about a week, we become one massive pack. We hunt together. We live together. We mate and howl and hunt and run together."

"We remember why we're werewolves," Syd added. Zero nodded.

"Now, this is all based on the belief that werewolves are special creatures that can bring through—"

There was an obnoxious tinny noise, muffled singing. Taylor heard the line about a sad affair when there's no one there. Zero's cellphone. He didn't know why she even bothered with the damn fanny pack. Aside from a thick wad of cash, the only other thing in it was her cell. She called it her insurance policy. Figured between those two items, she could likely get her ass out of most jams. It wasn't even the phone they got their kill calls from.

He knew what was next.

She dug the chirping thing out of the pack, glanced at the display, then tossed it to Syd. She never answered the phone.

Syd also glanced at the display, thumbed a button, and held it to his ear.

CHAPTER FIVE

"I SWEAR TO God, I'm going to kick your ass."

"Yeah, you and who's fucking army, bitch?"

Jake's face went slack-jawed with shock. "Samantha Lea Palmer!" She grabbed the girl by both arms. "I'm going to march you straight into the washroom and scrub that filthy mouth of yours with soap!"

"That before or after you kick my ass?" Sam said. "And before I go to bed?"

Jake released her grip and tickled the girl's ribs, making her giggle furiously.

"Seriously, your father's going to kill me, but if you promise to go get ready for bed, I'll let you stay up another hour." She looked at Sam, her eyes wide to show she was serious here, but she couldn't stop the slow creep of a smile. "One. Hour. Not a minute more."

"Make it an hour and ten," Sam said. "I gotta go drop a Cleveland steamer and it's a sphincter stretcher, I can just tell. It's going to take ten minutes to get the whole thing out."

Jake gave her another disbelieving look. "Are you sure you're only nine?" Sam nodded proudly. "And female?" Sam nodded again. "Where do you pick this stuff up? 'Cleveland steamer'? Really?"

"Dad's Tenacious D album."

"Do not ever tell your father you listen to Tenacious D."

"They're funny."

"They're filthy."

"Whatever," Sam said. She turned and headed down the hall. "All this yakkin's cutting into my stay-up time. 'Sides, I gotta drop a deuce."

Jake shook her head. *God, this kid.*

She heard the door to the bathroom close. She knew Sam would get ready. She was a good kid, she just liked to break Jake's balls. Well, both Jake's and Zach's, if she was honest. Still, the kid had at least managed to bring them together. Without Sam's mouth, Jake would never have picked up the babysitting job.

Not like she needed the money. But she loved Sam.

She went to the small kitchen and grabbed a Coke from the fridge. She closed the fridge door, stared down at the can, cold in her palm. Then she smiled.

♦ ♦ ♦

IT HAD ONLY been six months earlier. Jake had been washing her clothes in the laundry room downstairs. She'd been popping coins in the machine to grab a Coke when Zach and Sam had come in. Jake had given them a smile and a polite hello. She'd seen them around the apartment building. In the elevator, grabbing their mail, that sort of thing. But she'd never really interacted with them.

That day had been different. She'd had a few more things in the dryer to wait for. The little girl had been chatting her father's ear off. Jake pretended to read her book, but she mostly watched them, sneaking glances as she sipped her Coke. They were a funny pair, the girl asking incessant questions, her father's increasingly exasperated, yet still polite responses. Jake considered whether she had ever seen a woman with the two of them, a mother for the child, and decided she had not.

After the father got the clothes stuffed into the washers and got them going, he dropped into one of the uncomfortable plastic chairs that passed for amenities in their building. "You wanna play Go Fish or Crazy Eights?" he'd asked.

"When you gonna teach me poker?" Sam asked and Jake had gulped down the mouthful of Coke and guffawed slightly before she could stop her reaction.

Of course, the girl had noticed it. With no sign of shyness whatsoever, she turned to Jake and asked, "You know how to play poker?"

Jake smiled back. "Yes I do, but it's been a while."

"You wanna play poker with us?" she asked. "Dad's gonna teach me."

"I never said I was gonna—" he stopped, exasperated again. But smiling.

"I don't think I should," Jake said, lifting her paperback slightly to show she was reading. *Song of Susannah*.

"Dad won't let me read Stephen King," she said. "Says it's too goddamn *scaaaary*."

"Sam! Language!" her father said.

"Well, this one's part of a series. Doubt you'd dig it anyway," Jake said, trying not to smile at the girl's profanity and the father's mortification. "Besides, my clothes are almost done."

"Okay," she said, completely ignoring Jake's mild protests, "well, how about you and me play against Dad," she said. "Come on," she said, waving her over. "It'll be fun." She turned to her father. "Let's do *strip* poker."

Jake had been taking another drink and immediately backwashed the entire mouthful into the can, getting most of it in. Her resulting guffaw was loud. The girl's father sputtered out a shocked "ex*cuse* me?" as Jake went for some paper towels to clean up her spill.

"Seriously!" the girl said, then pointed to Jake. "She's got a whole buncha clothes. We have a bunch, too. Ain't that how it works?"

"Isn't," her father said.

"What?"

"Pardon," her father said.

"What? Jeez Dad, you're confusing the shit outta me."

"Sam! Language!" he said again. Jake now sat in the chair, paper towel clutched in one hand, shaking with silent laughter. How could she not love this kid?

Her father finally addressed Jake directly for the first time. "I'm so sorry," he said. "She's got a bit of a mouth on her. We're working on it." Turning back and bringing his face down so he was nose-to-nose with the girl, he said, "Aren't we?"

The girl smiled and said, "Hell yeah."

"Sam!" he said again. Jake now had tears rolling down her face. She put a hand to her mouth and turned away, her eyes squinted with laughter, trying not to show the girl. As she did it, she knew it was a doomed attempt. The father turned back to her again. "Seriously, I'm sorry."

She turned back to him. "Oh jeez," she said, pulling her hand away from her mouth. "No need to apologize." She wiped at the tears. "At the risk of encouraging her," she said, nodding at Sam, "this is the most fun I've ever had doing my laundry."

"See?" Sam said. "Come on over here, and let's play."

Jake set her book down on the table, careful to avoid any wet Coke spots, and rose. "Well, the way I see it, Sam…" Here she stopped and looked at her. "It is Sam, right?"

Sam nodded. "It's short for Samantha, but no one calls me that except my teachers," she said.

"Fair enough." She nodded. "The way I see it, is you have a problem."

"What's that?"

"Well, I got all the clothes. All yours are in the machines."

Sam looked at the empty baskets sitting beside her father. "Dammit, Dad."

"I guess you and your father are going to have to play with the clothes you're wearing."

"I don't *think* so!" Sam said. "What if I lose?"

"Then you'll have to walk around the building naked."

Now it was Sam's father's time to laugh. Sam was furiously shaking her head.

Jake smiled at her, stuck out her hand. "I'm Jake," she said.

"Jake?"

"Well, actually, it's Jacqueline," she said, "but no one calls me that except my teachers."

Sam took her hand and shook it once. "Pleasedtameetcha," she said, quickly, as though embarrassed with this adult act.

She turned to Sam's father and extended her hand again. "Zach," he said. "Zach Palmer. Sam's beleaguered dad."

"Whoa," she said.

"What?" Sam said.

"I honestly don't think I've ever heard anyone say the word 'beleaguered' out loud before. It's one of those words you just read, but not say, you know?"

"Is it a cuss word?" Sam said, her entire face brightening. "Is it bad?"

Jake shot a surreptitious look at Zach, then back to Sam. "It's a terrible one. I'm quite offended." Then she watched Sam nod, obviously filing it away.

Then there was the awkward silence that follows introductions. Zach gestured to a chair. "You wanna sit?"

Jake smiled gratefully and sat.

Sam looked at her arm. "What's that?" she said.

Jake looked down. "My tattoo?" Sam nodded. "Which one?" She was pretty much covered in them.

"That one," she said, putting her small finger on Jake's arm.

"Sam," Zach said. "You don't touch people, that's rude. And you don't point out things on their..." He faltered. "You don't ask about their..."

"It's okay, Zach," she said. "Your father's right, Sam. You should ask permission first. I could have torn your finger off with my teeth. But, luckily, I don't mind."

Though the girl had zeroed in on the one that she did sort of mind. It was just a large handprint, all black, angled as though grasping Jake at the shoulder. "It's just to remind me of a friend," she said, knowing she was not doing a good job of keeping the sadness out of her voice. "Someone who's gone now."

"What's their name?" Sam asked.

"Sam!" Zach said. Jake figured that was one of his most-said words.

She smiled and put out a placating hand. "It's okay." She turned to Sam. "Her name was Cassidy. She was a good friend of mine, but I...lost her a while ago."

"Were you two gay lovers or something? Lesbians, like?"

"Sam!" Zach said. "I swear to god..." But Jake, though not laughing, was smiling.

"No," she said. "I'm straight. Not that that's any of your business." She reached out a finger to lightly bop Sam on the nose. "But no. Just friends. Good ones." She looked down at her shoulder. "I got this to remind me of her. To keep her memory close."

"That's cool," Sam said. "My mom's dead, too." She said this without the sadness or wistfulness an adult would have injected into it. She just seemed to accept it. Her mother had died. It was fact.

Sam turned to her father. "Think I could maybe get a tattoo of Mom?"

"How about you ask me when you're older?" Zach said. Jake read the tone of his voice. She'd heard it before.

"Not crazy about tattoos?" She kept it light.

"I know they're quite popular right now," he said. "But never really had a desire to get one myself."

"Lots of people don't."

"Nothing against yours, though," he said quickly.

Jake laughed. "Don't worry about it."

They chatted amiably for a while, then Jake's dryer beeped. She rose and pulled the last of the clothes from the dryer, making sure to toss a couple of racier articles that Sam would likely ask about in one of her baskets off to the side. She brought the rest back to the table and picked the first one up to fold.

Sam reached over and grabbed at another article, a T-shirt, and laid it out to fold. Jake reached for it too late.

"Hey Dad, check this out." Sam pointed to the front of the shirt, where something was written in very small letters right at chest level. "It says, 'Nosey little fucker, aren't you?' That's hilarious!"

"Sam! Language!"

"Yeah," Jake said. "Sorry. You shouldn't have seen that."

Zach smiled. "No worries. She's said worse." Then Sam handed her the shirt, expertly folded.

"Hey Sam, you're pretty good at that."

"Better'n him," she said, casting a withering look at her father. "He sucks."

"Hey, I'm getting better," he said.

"He needs help," Sam said.

"I do not need help."

"Yeah well, you need a damn babysitter for me. You keep saying so."

"Okay, you got me there," Zach said.

"Hey, I got'n idea," Sam said, then turned to Jake. "You wanna be my babysitter?"

"Sam, I don't think..." Zach said. "I mean, she doesn't even know us."

"And you don't know me, either," Jake agreed.

"Okay," Sam said. "You ever been arrested?"

"Sam..." This time, Zach's voice went low and menacing.

Jake laughed. "No, Sam. Never been arrested."

"You a terrorist or anything like that?"

"No."

Sam narrowed her eyes. "You sure? Nothing to do with that World Trade Center thing three years ago?"

"No. I try not to fly."

"Cuzza 9/11?"

"Just don't like it."

"You like kids?"

"Not really, but I gotta be honest here, Sam. I'm really beginning to like you," Jake said.

"Done!" Sam said. "You're hired."

"Not so fast, little lady."

"Dad, seriously. You're harshin' my mellow here."

"How old are you, Sam? Like...twenty-five?"

"Almost nine," she said. "Two more months."

"Wow."

"Sam, how about you go flip the clothes to the dryers."

"You gonna interview her too?" Sam said. "Just to let you know, I'm good with hiring her. But I'll let you two work out the beleaguered money stuff."

"Sam!" Zach said. "You watch your mouth."

Sam preened.

"Thank you for the trust in my abilities, Sam," Zach said, smirking. "It's quite humbling."

"Welcome." She slid from the chair and went over to the washers. Jake saw her glancing over.

"Eyes front, missy," Jake said. "And make more noise."

Sam turned back to the washers and started humming. Loudly.

Jake looked from her to Zach. "Is that...?"

"'(I Can't Get No) Satisfaction,' yeah. She loves the Stones."

"Huh," she said. "Kid's impressive."

"Listen, I…" He looked back at his daughter. "I feel like I need to keep saying I'm sorry."

"Don't worry about it," Jake said. "She's adorable."

"Yeah, try living with it." He made a face, then rubbed his palms over it, as though to wipe it off. "Anyway, the truth is, Sam's only been with me a couple of years."

"Her mother died?"

"Yeah, same old stupid story. Started dating. Sheila got pregnant, but we knew we didn't really love each other enough to ever make it work." Jake nodded, encouraging him. "Long story short, I saw Sam as much as I could, then a few years back, she was maybe five, Sheila got sick. Cancer."

"Damn."

"Yeah." He looked at the table. "So, Sam started spending more time with me when Sheila couldn't handle the day-to-day stuff anymore. Then, a couple of years ago…"

Jake nodded again. "And now Sam's with you."

"Yeah. And I've got this shitty manager's job in fast food that's some weird hours at times. Four to midnight. Sometimes eight at night until four in the morning. Makes it hard to get a regular babysitter."

"I bet."

"And Sam's a bit of a handful." He smiled. Leaned in conspiratorially. "In case you hadn't noticed."

"Really?" Jake said. "I hadn't picked up on that." She let her smile go wide and dazzling.

"It's been a bit of a revolving door when it comes to people looking after her. Lost my last one two days ago. I've been scrambling to switch my shifts until I find someone else."

"Okay."

"Okay?" Zach looked confused.

"Okay, I know you don't know me, but I'd look after her."

"I'm sure you're just being nice, but—"

"I'm gonna fill you in a bit about me, Zach. I'm nice, but I don't really make a habit of 'being nice' just so I can look after a precocious kid. You're in a jam. You seem like a nice guy. Sam's an awesome kid, and my job's flexible enough that I can accommodate, at least until you find someone else."

"But—"

"But," she said, "you're concerned about leaving your daughter with a woman with tattoos and piercings. Can't blame you, but honestly, it's just me being me. No agenda other than that."

"Oh...kay," he said, drawing out the word.

"And I'm gonna drop one last bomb on you. I have a website, not sure if you've heard of it. Mom warned you dot com. And there's a second one called, About girls like me dot com."

"No, haven't heard of them."

"It's okay, I'm still growing them."

"So, these sites..."

"The first one is pictures of me."

"Okay."

"Usually undressed."

"Oh."

"The second one is...well...other women like me. Tattoos and piercings."

"Also...um...undressed?"

"Now you're getting it." She leaned in a little closer. "But I swear it's not porn. No sex acts. Just pictures."

"Well that's a relief," Sam said. "You were losing him there for a minute." Jake fought back any trace of a smile.

"Sam..."

"Yeah, got it. Eyes front, make noise, blah blah." The humming resumed.

Zach turned back from Sam, but seemed a little more reluctant to meet Jake's gaze. She knew he was going to look her up tonight. They always did.

"And…you make money off this?"

She did. She explained the membership process.

Zach said, "Huh."

"So, there's a little about me."

"Thanks." He shook his head, then did meet her eyes. "Thanks for the honesty."

"Welcome."

"And you really want to look after the mutant?"

"Sure. I think it'd be fun."

He took his time. Folded a couple of shirts. Badly. She gave him the time he needed, shocked at herself because she found she actually wanted the job. Finally, he said, "Okay."

"Okay? Yesssss!" Sam did a fist pump over the washer.

"Sa—"

"Eyes front. Make noise. Blah blah. Been there. Done that. Got the beleaguered T-shirt."

♦♦♦

AND NOW, SIX months later, standing in Zach's kitchen sipping a Coke, things were still going well. Better than that. Jake loved Sam, and Sam loved her as well. She knew Zach had likely looked her up, but he never mentioned the sites again.

To be honest, though, she did this as much now for Zach as she did for Sam. Something about him…

Sam came back out in a nightgown that reached just above her knees but that should have been ankle-length. "Think you could have found something a little more not your size, kiddo?"

"I like it."

"Good enough."

"When's Dad getting home?"

"Should be soon, unless the date goes better than expected."

"Think it will?"

"Dunno, kiddo. Maybe."

A sly smile. "You like him, don't you?"

"Your father?" Jake said. "Of course I like him. You know that."

"No, I mean, you *liiiiike* him." Sam swung her upper body first one way, then the next. "You *liiiiike* him."

"And just what's that supposed to mean, you little mutant?"

"You know exactly what I mean. You *liiiiike* him. You wanna be his *giiiirl*friend. You wanna *kiiiiiss* him. You wanna *smoooooch* him."

"I so do not," Jake said, indignant.

Sam moved to the couch, her arms crossed in front of her, a self-satisfied grin spread maddeningly across her face. "Yes you do. I got a knack for figuring that shit out."

"Oh, you do, do you? Listen, I *like* your Dad," Jake said. "But I don't *like* like him."

Sam threw up a hand, palm out. "Whatever, girlfriend."

"Your dad's right, you know. You really are a little mutant."

Then the phone rang. Jake glanced at the display but didn't recognize the number. They looked at each other and both said the same thing.

"Dad."

CHAPTER SIX

"WHAT?" SYD SAID, not a hint of warmth in his voice. Then he listened.

Taylor watched his eyes roll. He breathed out audibly, the phone a tiny thing in his hand.

"No," he said. "You know that's not possible." He met Zero's gaze. A slight nod. Taylor had witnessed this particular interaction enough times to know what was going on. It was Bo.

Same old story. Bo calling to beg for his position back in the pack. The pack shutting him out. By rights, they could kill him, but Zero had always refused. Instead, she made Syd deal with it. She hadn't talked to Bo since the excommunication.

"No," he said again. Then, more firmly, "I said no." He listened briefly, his other hand moving to a scar that ran raggedly along his jawline.

"Lose this number." He listened for a second. "Bo?" A beat. "Bo?" Then, "asshole," and he snapped the phone from his ear. To Zero, he held out the phone. It sat in his open palm, fingers splayed wide. "Can you get a different number?" he said. "Please?"

"No," she said, mimicking the dry tone he'd just used. "The right people know this number."

"Yeah," Syd said. "So does the wrong one."

"Which brings us to the next point," Zero said, looking back to the Fed, who'd watched the entire exchange intently.

"Which is?"

"The prime rule," she said. Her eyes flicked to Syd's, then back to the Fed's. "No wolf knowingly harms another wolf without just cause. Not ever."

"The strictest code we have," Syd said. "Pack does not turn on pack. Wolf does not turn on wolf. Not a lot of rules with us, but this one's sacred." Again, Taylor watched a finger trace the scar.

Fucking Bo, Taylor thought.

Chapter Seven

Rainer pulled out a gun and levelled it at the large bleeding man on the ground.

"Rainer," Zach said. "What the hell?"

This date wasn't going quite the way he'd intended.

The movie, *Collateral* had been pretty good. He'd kind of been hoping for either *AVP: Alien vs. Predator*, or even *Van Helsing*, but Rainer made it pretty clear neither was in her realm of interest. Zach found himself constantly having to work to pick up the thread of the storyline. He spent a significant portion of the time in the theatre trying to decide whether it was too forward to put his arm around the back of her chair, and if he did and his arm went numb, what he would do next. Then he'd moved to maybe just reaching out and holding her hand, but that seemed a little too presumptuous. It wasn't a horror flick, and besides, she'd already proven she was more of a man than he was.

He wasn't used to this damn dating thing. He'd never been good at it in his teen years, barely managed to catch Sheila's attention in his late teens and, a decade on, he was even more out of practice now.

When they'd left the theatre, he again considered holding her hand back to the car, but that struck him as too…what? Teenybopper? Whatever. Rainer didn't strike him as a cuddly type.

Instead, he tried to salvage the night by suggesting a late dinner. She'd agreed and he told them that he'd have to hit a phone booth on the way to call and let the sitter know. He tossed it out there in hopes that Rainer might have a phone that he could borrow, but she didn't offer one up. He thought about saying something about his being broken, but he didn't want to lie to her and get caught out later. But he also didn't want to highlight the fact that he couldn't really afford one of the damn things, so he just left it at finding a phone booth.

It had taken less time than he thought to find one. And it was a legitimate, honest-to-god phone *booth*. The kind that was actually like an upright, glassed-in coffin, instead of one of those stupid stations open to the elements and the surrounding noises.

He'd pulled in, but there was a guy in there using it, so he parked and left the car running to keep the heat flowing. "We'll just wait for him to finish up?" he suggested.

"Sure," she said, but weird and slow. She watched the man in the phone booth intently.

Then they fell into an awkward silence.

This was a bad idea, Palmer, he thought. He knew Rainer was likely bored to tears and probably just humouring him until dinner was over and she could make her gracious escape.

"So, what'd you think of the mo—"

He'd never finished the question. Instead, a big Dodge Ram pickup lumbered into the gas station and a big man in an old, navy-blue parka got out quickly. He shut the door, never taking his eyes off the man in the phone booth. He walked to the box of the pickup, reached inside, and pulled out a large piece of wood, something like a four-by-four, maybe three or four feet long.

Then he strode purposefully over to the booth and, with no hesitation whatsoever, he pulled the door open, raised the wood like a battering ram. The man in the booth had just managed to turn his head slightly when the wood cracked into the side of his ear, edge on, with enough force to bounce his head off the back glass wall. The man blinked quickly then, dropping the phone, staggered out. Zach sat, stunned and rooted to the seat, his breath fogging out in a cloud, but Rainer was out of the car and running toward the two men. Much larger men.

Running *toward* them.

There was no way someone wasn't calling 911 right now. Had to be. But when Zach looked around, he saw one man at the pumps, steadfastly looking in the other direction as he squeezed the handle of the gas nozzle. He looked in the little booth where the attendant sat, but he had visored his hands over his eyes and angled his head down to stare at the floor. Again, steadfastly refusing to see what was happening.

The phone booth guy fell to the ground, clutching at the damaged side of his head, his other hand still holding the handset, torn from the cord. The big guy stood over him. Zach saw something peel off the end of the end of the piece of wood and fall to the cold pavement.

Was that his fucking ear?

The parka guy raised the wood up as though to bring it straight down, piledriver-style onto phone booth guy's head. Zach saw strange, jagged shapes at the elbows of the man's parka and realized they were duct-taped.

Rainer pulled up short in front of them. "Hey!" she yelled. Zach figured he'd better get out there. He didn't know what he could do, aside from possibly getting injured or killed, but maybe he'd at least save Rainer from the same fate.

He came up behind her, but loudly. He didn't want to surprise her. She never turned. "Put it down, man," Zach said.

"No!" the man said. Zach got a better look at him now. Unshaven, hair all askew. Guy was a mess.

Still not as bad as the guy on the ground, though. Zach went to bend down to check on him, but Rainer reached out and touched him lightly on the shoulder. "Don't," she said.

"But he's—"

"He's fine for now." Zach got it. *Get the wood-wielding guy talked down first, then deal with phone booth guy. Good plan.*

She turned back to the man. "Please," she said. "Put it down."

"No," he repeated. "You don't know what he..."

Unbelievably, Rainer stepped around the bleeding man on the ground and touched the parka guy, just lightly, on the back of his hand. It was as though she'd sent a command and he dropped the wood. It made a loud clatter as it hit the ground.

"I know what he did," Rainer said.

"No you don't," the man said, but his tone said he believed Rainer. His voice caught and tears slipped down his cheeks. "How could you know?" His voice was the barest whisper.

"Walter," she said and the man blinked at looked at her as though seeing her for the first time. Zach thought, *Walter?* Then Rainer was talking again.

"I know what he did to Sarah." The man now stood, arms at his sides, the tears flowing freely but his eyes never left Rainer's. His mouth made a horrible shape, but no words came out.

"Your little girl," she said. "I know. I've been looking for him, too. You need to get into your car and get out of here."

Walter shook his head weakly.

"The police will be here soon. Then they'll take you away and take him to a hospital. You want that?"

Another weak shake of the head.

"You get away from here. I'll take care of this. Take care of him."

That same horrible shake. "My little girl."

"Yeah," Rainer said, her voice soft. "Yeah, your little girl. I can't help her, Walter, but I can, at least"—and here her finger stabbed down to point at the man on the pavement—"make this bastard pay."

He looked at her a long time, as though taking her measure. The tears still came, the mouth kept its shape, but somewhere in there, he judged her worthy. He raised a hand to the side of Rainer's head, lightly touching her cheek. *Like a father would with his child,* Zach thought. Then, without a word, he nodded once, turned, and went back to the truck. He climbed in, started it. Zach watched him wipe at both eyes, then put the truck in gear and leave.

"Wow, Rainer," Zach said. "You make a habit of saving people's asses?"

"Not everyone's."

"Okay, I got his plate number, so we can give that to the cops."

"Forget it."

"Pardon?"

"Forget the plate number."

Zach was about to ask why, but the guy on the ground made like he was about to get up. That's when Rainer reached around behind her and pulled out a large freaking gun.

"Rainer," Zach said. "What the hell?" *Wait. Has she been carrying that gun the entire night?* About the same time, it struck him that this date was not going anywhere near the way he'd intended. He'd had much higher hopes than endless confusion, violence, and handguns.

"Don't move, you piece of shit."

"Ray," Zach said. "I think you're a little mixed up. This is the guy who got attacked."

"Yeah," the guy agreed. "I'm the victim." Zach was shocked at the deep rumble of his voice, like an idling muscle car.

Rainer pointed the gun at the injured man's face. "You. Shut the fuck up."

Zach tried to ignore the gun.

"We gotta get him to the hospital," Zach said. "We gotta call the police."

"No, we have to get him into your car."

Zach eyed the bloodied side of the guy's head. "No offence, Rainer, but wouldn't an ambulance make more sense?"

"No."

"Okay," he said, resigning himself to an even longer and shittier night than he'd even envisioned. "Fine. We'll get him to the hospital ourselves."

"No," Rainer said. "No hospitals."

"Then what are we going to do with him?"

"We're going to kill him," she said. "But we're going to do it right."

Zach couldn't decide if it was the coldness of her voice or the deep rumbling laugh from the injured man that scared him worse.

Chapter Eight

"YOU'RE REALLY PLANNING on killing him?"

"I'm really planning on killing him," Rainer said from the passenger seat.

"She only *thinks* she can kill me," the bleeding guy said from the back seat.

"What's your name?" Zach asked.

"I don't give damn," Rainer said.

"Bo," he said.

What the hell kind of name is Bo? Zach thought. *Boris? Or is it Beau? Like Beauregard?* Normally, Zach would have asked him, but the mood was a little tense right now.

"Rainer, you gotta level with me here." He watched the road, but he was very conscious of her gun. "What the hell's going on here?"

"You're the Chatty Cathy here tonight, Bo," Rainer said. "Why don't you tell him why you're going to die?"

That rumbling laughter again. "Well, it might be because Van Halen hasn't gotten their shit together for years now, or it could be that she's just angry with who's in the White House—"

"Bo," she said.

"What?" Bo said amiably. "You asked me to speculate. Dubya's a dick. And Van Halen ain't toured since the '90s."

Zach said, "Um…they toured all last summer, dude. Where you been?"

"What?" Bo said, genuinely shocked. "David Lee Roth, or Hagar?"

"Hagar."

"Oh, for fucksakes. Everyone knows Roth's the only—"

"Don't say it, man," Zach said, totally forgetting the situation for the moment. "Don't go there. Hagar's—"

He happened to look over at Rainer. And instantly shut up.

She gave Zach the stink eye, then turned back to Bo, rolling a hand to get on with it.

He sighed, muttered, "Hagar. Fucksakes," got the stink eye again, and said, "All right, all right. It's more than likely because I'm a shifter."

"The hell's a shifter?"

"You'd know me as a werewolf." Zach watched him in the rear-view as he locked eyes with Rainer. "Like someone else we both know."

Rainer's eyes flashed menacingly, but she said nothing.

Zach let out a little *heh* noise. Werewolves. "So, Warren Zevon? Piña coladas? Trader Vic's? Like in that 'Werewolves of London' song?"

"Yeah, something like that," Bo said. His tone said it was nothing like that.

"Okay," Zach said. "Nice." He flicked a glance in the rear-view. "Just gotta say, your hair ain't perfect."

They drove on in silence for a good five minutes. Rainer told him where to turn and he looked at her. "When you gonna tell me what this is about?"

Rainer looked at him, eyebrows raised slightly. *She's really a beautiful woman,* he thought.

"He just did," she said. "You heard him."

"Heard him tell me he's a werewolf. A shifter." He glanced over at her quickly again. "Now I'd like to know the real reason."

"That is the real reason," she said. "Minus the 'Werewolves of London' part."

"Fine," he said. "Don't goddamn tell me then."

Another few minutes passed. Then he remembered. *Shit! I never called Jake.*

"I don't know what you've got planned, but I need to call Jake and let her know I'm going to be late." Rainer's eyes never left Bo's. She dug into an inside jacket pocket and pulled out a phone. She glanced down quickly, flipped it open, then handed it over to Zach. "Phone," she said. The phone she hadn't offered to him earlier.

Now he was getting pissed.

"How late?" he asked, his voice tight.

"Ooo, boy's growing a pair," Bo said.

To Bo, "Shut up." To Zach, "Late."

"Do I have a choice in this?"

"Not anymore."

His voice got tighter. "How late?"

"Depends on how easily Bobo here gives me what I want." She glanced back at him, her mouth in a grim line. She and Bo locked eyes and she stared at him for a moment, considering. "Early morning," she said.

Zach stabbed at the numbers with his thumb. He glanced at Rainer, not happy with what he saw. He looked in the rear-view and liked the smiling eyes reflected there even less.

In the close quarters of the car, the tinny buzz of the ring tone was audible to all. Rainer hefted the gun slightly at Bo and said, "Not. A. Word." Bo mimed zipping his mouth shut and smiled at her.

Zach waited for the connection to go through. Then he heard some giggling, then Jake saying, "Hello?"

"Hey Jake, how you guys doing?" He kept his voice light. *Nothing bad going on here. Nope.*

"Oh, we're good," Jake said and Zach heard some jostling. Sam giggled in the background, likely responding to Jake's giggles. "How goes the date?" More giggles.

"S'okay," he said as noncommittally as he could. "Listen Jake, I may be a little later than originally thought. You cool to maybe sleep over?"

In the mirror, Bo dabbed at the space his ear had occupied earlier. He inspected the blood on his fingers, then popped them in his mouth.

He tried to ignore the man behind him, focus on the call. "Of course," she said. He heard something there, some quality of her voice change. He couldn't place it, as she was still just as bright and happy as she normally was.

"You can take my bed if you want," he said, knowing she wouldn't. "The sheets are clean, just changed this morning."

"No," she said. "That's your bed. The couch is good."

"You know you're welcome to it."

"I know."

"Thanks, Jake," he said, trying to convey all the gratitude he could through the ether. "If I can get home earlier, I will."

"Don't rush it, Zach," she said. "Sam and I are good."

"I know. She loves you a lot, y'know."

Bo raised his hands as if in prayer, then canted his head, placing them to a blood-flecked cheek. He mouthed, "How cute." Zach shot an awkward finger.

"Feeling's mutual."

"You wanna put her on the line? Let me say good night?"

"'Course," she said. More jostling, then Sam was on the line, her voice a light shining in the darkness.

Zach said his good nights quickly, fearing Bo was going to be able to handle only so much before his assoholic tendencies reared up again. He ended the call and handed the phone back over to Rainer. She had maintained the same hard glare throughout the entire call.

She took the phone and pocketed it.

"Thanks," he said, his voice gone cold again.

"'She loves you a lot, you know,'" Bo said, his voice high and girlish.

"Bo?"

"Yes, sir?" There was no respect in the tone.

"Fuck you."

"Like I said," Bo said, looking at Rainer. "Boy's growin' a pair. Gonna be a shame that it took all this time and I'm just going to tear them off and eat them."

Rainer said nothing, except to direct Zach where to turn.

Chapter Nine

SAM LUNGED FOR the phone, but Jake's longer reach won out. With her other arm, she held the squirming, giggling kid at bay.

"Hello?"

"Hey Jake," Zach said, and with those two syllables, her radar went on alert. Something was wrong. "How you guys doing?"

Sam was making kissy faces, still breaking Jake's balls about Zach. She trapped the phone between shoulder and ear to free up both hands. "Oh, we're good," she said and pinned Sam to the couch and tickled her in the ribs. She called this making her bone music. Sam erupted into a gale of giggling. Into the phone, she asked, "How goes the date?" More bone music, more giggling.

"S'okay," he said and now she knew there was something going on. As she was about to ask him about it, he said, "Listen Jake, I may be a little later than originally thought. You cool to maybe sleep over?"

Okay, maybe I'm wrong. Maybe it's going better than I think. Maybe…

Oh, fuck what she thought. She just needed to answer him. "Of course," she said.

"You can take my bed if you want," he said. And Jake thought about the promise she'd made herself. *I'm not going to sleep in your bed unless you bring me to it yourself, Mr. Palmer.* A silly promise, but still.

"No," she said. "That's your bed. The couch is good."

"You know you're welcome to it." She only wished she was. At least in the way she wanted to be. But obviously Zach wasn't interested in her that way. He wasn't into the tattoos and the piercings and the soft porn website shit.

"I know."

"Thanks, Jake," he said, and she heard probably the first genuine emotion there. She knew how much he appreciated her helping him out. "If I can get home earlier, I will."

"Don't rush it, Zach," she said, doing what she could to keep it light. *You're really staying out all night? That really isn't you, Zach.* Well, hell, even he needed a little fun once in a while. She just wished he'd consider it with her. Just once. "Sam and I are good."

"I know. She loves you a lot, y'know."

Jake felt an unexpected rush of emotion. She blinked away the extra moisture in her eyes before Sam could see it and break her balls some more. "Feeling's mutual."

"You wanna put her on the line? Let me say good night?" It struck Jake that Zach wasn't saying anything about his kid being up past her bedtime. Not that he'd care, but he'd normally say something about it.

"'Course," she said, not able to get out much more than that single sound. She put Sam on and left her alone to say her good nights.

Jake took her empty glass back into the kitchen, rinsed it out, and put it in the dishwasher. Then she turned and leaned her butt against the counter, her arms crossed, and stared at the floor.

Okay, if she admitted the truth, Zach's date was fucking killing her. She'd thrown every subtle signal out to the man that she was more than interested in him. She hadn't met a lot of good guys in her life, and in the past year she'd been exposed to some real scumbags. Showing your tits and vag to the world will bring them knocking on your door. So, when a guy like Zach came along, a good guy, a nice guy just trying to do right by his kid, well, that pulled at something deep down inside her.

Zach wasn't brilliant, but hell, he wasn't a stupid guy. He might be insecure about himself, and working well below his station as a manager in a fast-food place, but she had no doubt that his responsibility and devotion to his daughter would spur him to greater achievements.

And she wouldn't mind being around when he really found himself. She liked him a lot now.

She could love him if that happened.

Could love him pretty damned easily.

But he was out all damn night with this Rainer chick.

Fuck.

CHAPTER TEN

AN HOUR AFTER they left the gas station, Zach pulled off a gravel road onto a two-rut laneway, the long grass brown and pulled down with the weight of the frozen moisture.

He followed the path for another five minutes, twice bottoming out over a particularly rough patch—the added weight of the guy in the back not helping—before coming to a rise and the remains of an old farm silo.

The roof was long gone, leaving only the tubular concrete structure. Zach brought the car to a stop with the headlights pointed at the silo.

"Here?" he asked.

"Yes," Rainer said. She stayed facing Bo. "Okay, here's how we're going to play this. Zach, if you walk inside the silo, you'll find a plastic tub. Open it up and bring back the handcuffs."

"Come on, Rainer."

"Zach, seriously. There's reasons I brought you. This would be one of them."

"Mother*fuck*." Zach opened the door, the cold night air shocking him. He leaned down, faced her. Her eyes never left Bo, but she was listening.

"What the fuck would you have done if I wasn't here?" he said. "Huh?"

Her eyes remained fixed, but her mouth tightened into a thin line. Bo said, "Man's gotta point, toots."

Zach stared a moment more, but got no additional response from Rainer. He pushed the door closed behind him. Huffing up the hill, the stiff, frost-rimed stalks of grass pushed against his pantlegs. His Chucks were absolutely the wrong footwear for this area, but still, he trudged on—not truly understanding exactly why he was doing so—and into the darkness of the silo. There was enough reflected light from his car to easily find the plastic tub, one of those sturdy Tupperware storage bins. He went over and pried the lid off. *Jesus*, he thought. There was a lot of stuff in here that made him uneasy.

He fished out the handcuffs, shiny in the crisp moonlight. They made a cold, metallic noise as he gathered them. He pushed back along his already-broken trail back to the car, the grass the only thing making sound in the night.

Just as he came back into the glare of the headlights, he heard one sharp crack.

The gun, he thought.

Most of him wanted to run away, but his logical parts got him moving again, heading down the hill to the car. As he approached, he heard a stream of cursing coming from the vehicle.

She shot him. Then, *She shot him in* my *car!*

He opened the door, leaned in, and immediately smelled a sharp odour. "You shot him?" *Is that cordite? No, they stopped using that after World War II. Gunpowder, then. Is that what it smells like?* On the heels of that, he thought, *Why do I know so much stupid, trivial shit?*

"Give me your hands," Rainer said, ignoring him.

Bo held his hands out, resting on the front seats. "Zach," she said, "would you?"

"Yeah, Zach," Bo said. "Will you please be her bitch?"

Zach kept his mouth shut and put the handcuffs on first one held-out wrist, then the other. Bo's hands were thicker than his own, and calloused. His nails were too long, ragged, broken, and dirty. Rainer came after Zach and pinched them tight. "Kill the lights." Zach hit the switch and the darkness rushed back in.

"Okay Zach, get out." Zach backed out and shut the door again.

He heard her giving Bo commands, then she came out of the car, gun still levelled at the man. She tilted the seat forward and he came out, but with some obvious difficulty. It wasn't until they both made their way around the front of the car that Zach saw why.

"You shot him in the balls?" He felt his own contract up tight in sympathetic reaction.

"He wasn't behaving," she said. "Were you, fucknuts? Sorry. Fuck*nut*."

Bo winced in pain, but that was all. Guy lost a 'nad and he was only wincing? Zach would have been curled in the fetal position, crying like a bitch. If this guy could take losing an ear and a nut, why was he even listening to Rainer? He didn't seem all that concerned with the gun. "Kill you for that," Bo said.

"Many have promised, none have delivered," she said. She waggled the gun. "Get moving or I'll take the other one." Bo moved.

He walked by Zach, who remained out of arm's reach. "Pretty sad when your date's tougher 'n you." He snorted out a huff of derision. "Maybe you like being the bitch, huh? Maybe she's got more balls than you?"

Though Bo scared the shit out of Zach, he couldn't let that one slide by. "Dude, keep talking, she's going to have more balls than you soon, too." Bo snarled, showing a mouthful of teeth.

"Oh, for chrissakes, Bo," Rainer said. "You're wasting your time. He doesn't even know what you're doing."

"What?" Zach said. "What's he doing?"

"Showing his teeth." She sighed. "It's a direct challenge for superiority."

"What, I'm supposed to roll over and show my belly or some shit?"

"Kind of."

"Then he'd take his shirt off and impress me with his abs or some such shit?"

Bo didn't exactly lunge at Zach—he was too aware of the gun behind him—but he did stare a little more menacingly at Zach. But with handcuffs, a gun, and only one testicle, a lot of the menace drained out of it quite quickly.

They got to the silo.

Once inside, Rainer made Bo face the wall. She got Zach to pull out a small, but bright, lantern from the storage bin. When he turned it on, he noticed the lengths of shining new chain fastened to the wall. Six big bolts had been fastened directly into the concrete. He saw handcuff-like manacles at the ends of four of them, and also loops of something thinner. From the last two bolts, a bigger loop, like a collar.

"Okay Bo, we're going to do this nice and easy, okay?"

Bo remained silent.

"You're going to put one leg in the cuff and fasten it up nice and tight. Do the zip cord, too."

Bo looked like he was ready to do damn near anything but that, but he went over to the chains, bent, slipped the plastic zip cord loop around his ankle, then attached the cuff. He cinched both tight.

"Now do the same for the opposite arm."

He had to reach, but he got both the loop and the cuff around his wrist and pulled them tight.

"Zach, here," she said, tossing him a small pair of keys. "You can take the first set of cuffs off him. And could you check the ones he put on, and the zip cord?"

"Why me?"

"No, you're right. I can do it if you'd prefer," she said. "You gonna hold the gun and shoot him if he needs shooting?" She proffered the weapon. Zach went to Bo.

He had to get uncomfortably close to the bleeding man to check on the cuffs and zip cords. He heard the man's deep, rumbling breaths, sounding like the inner workings of a blast furnace. He imagined he felt a heat off him. The feeling intensified when he came in close enough to reach up and unlock the cuffs from his wrists. There was a power to this man. Zach saw it in the striated muscle at his neck, in the way his jaw worked. He saw it in the tempered wildness of his eyes. He could smell it on him. Zach let the handcuffs fall to the ground and stepped carefully and quickly around Bo to his other arm. "Lift it up to the cuff," Zach said, shocked at how calm his voice was.

Bo lifted his hand, then, like a shot, it was up and around Zach's neck, pinning him to the concrete wall. Zach would have yelled if he had been able to pass breath from lungs to lips.

"Fucksake," Rainer said, and shot Bo in the shoulder. His hand released Zach's neck, and Zach slid down the wall, gasping.

"I've got all night, Bobo. And a metric fuck-ton of bullets. Even ones made of silver if you prefer."

"Fuck you," Bo said.

"Good one. Fuck you too." Then, keeping the gun on Bo, she turned to Zach, who was pulling himself back up the wall, one hand massaging his neck. "You good?"

He nodded. "I'm okay."

"I could have killed you, boy," Bo said, showing his teeth again.

"Many have promised," Zach said, his voice rasping. "None have delivered."

"Yet."

"True enough," Zach said. "But it won't be you, asshole. Now get your fucking hand up."

Bo complied, if slowly. As he attached the cuff to the man's other arm, Bo looked at him from less than six inches away.

"I'm going to rip the top of your skull off and suck out your brains." He smiled again, and this time Zach recognized the challenge for what it was. "I'll tear your heart out and eat it as it beats its last."

"You need to see a dietitian," Zach said.

Bo's rumbling laughter sounded again. "Okay, maybe you do have some balls."

"Now the collar, Zach," Rainer said. "And don't be kind. Nice and tight." Zach did as instructed, snugging the collar tight. Finished, breathing a sigh of relief, he moved away.

"Okay," Rainer said. "Now we can get down to business."

♦♦♦

"I WANT TO start with who you were talking to."

Bo said nothing.

"Really? This the way you're going to play it?"

Bo stared at the wall.

"You trying to call your pack? Maybe get them to reconsider your membership?"

Zach saw him stiffen slightly. Didn't need to be a genius to see she was getting to him.

"You're essentially a Rōnin, now, right?"

"A Rōnin?" Zach asked. He'd read the Frank Miller comic, but wasn't sure she was using the term the same way.

"Yeah. A warrior, a samurai without a master." She pointed to Bo with the gun. "That's what happened to Bobo here, not that he's anywhere near as classy as a samurai. He got tossed from his pack. Doesn't play well with others apparently.

They used the term Rōnin, probably, to salve the sting of excommunication a bit."

"How did he get tossed?"

"He attacked another wolf. Didn't you, Bobo?"

Bo remained silent.

"And…that's a bad thing."

"Oh, hell yes," she said. "The pack is all about brotherhood. It's all about the group need, not the individual need. You get infighting amongst the wolves over who's top dog, well, then wolves are gonna get killed. Wolves get killed, the packs get thin. That's not good for business." She smirked as she said, "This is their evolutionary step beyond the animal. Or it's the shit they'll feed themselves to stop from killing each other."

Turning back to Bo. "So, my guess, Bobo, is that you're desperate for a pack sponsorship. Isn't the Calling coming up?"

"Fuck you, bitch."

Rainer turned to Zach and smiled. Zach read that as "see what I did there? I got him."

"Where's your pack, Bo?"

"You can ask all night. I'm not telling you anything."

"I'm just asking out of politeness." She sighed. "Okay, let's get down to what we're really doing here," she said.

"That is a good question," Zach said. "What *are* we doing here?"

Rainer looked at Bo, then at Zach. She answered with one word: "Information."

"What kind of information?" Zach asked.

"I need to know where his Alpha is."

Zach saw the man stiffen slightly yet again, but remain silent. Yet again.

"What the hell's an Alpha?"

"The shifters can make others into shifters as well. The maker is called an Alpha."

"Okay, a werewolf is a shifter and a shifter is a werewolf, right?"

"Yeah, they're similar. Shifters are humans that can shift into wolves. All werewolves are shifters, but not all shifters are werewolves. Though I haven't run across them myself, I've heard claims for bears, tigers, birds, dolphins, sharks. Even squirrels, for chrissakes. Maybe they're not lying, maybe they are. The only ones I've seen are the wolves. They call themselves shifters. And when they decide to play god and turn an innocent into one of them, they are known as that one's Alpha. Basically, it's a power trip for them."

Zach decided he didn't want to know any more.

Turning back to Bo, Rainer raised her chin and asked, "So. You gonna make this easy, or hard?"

"Listen, bitch," he said, addressing the wall. "You know about shifters and Alphas, you know damn well that I can't tell you who my Alpha is. That's the one crime that al—"

"That allows one wolf to kill another, yeah I know," Rainer finished. "Been there already. Try to imagine how little I care."

"What makes you think I'm going to tell you anything?" He snorted as he laughed at her. "Whaddya gonna do? Threaten to kill me? Yeah, it can be done, but if you kill me, you're no farther ahead. So, me? I ain't worried."

"No?" Rainer asked. "You should be. Because I'm not going to even put the threat of death out there. I know how hard it is to kill vermin like you. You're worse than goddamn cockroaches." Bo seemed to get a chuckle from that one.

"No," she said, facing Zach. "I'll admit, this was a tough nut to crack, Zach. I really had to think long and hard about how to get a shifter to talk. I mean, I could shoot a hole in him, I could take his arm off, no big deal, it'd eventually grow back. And I didn't want something that would make him pass out, however attractive suffocation sounds. It wouldn't kill him, but the oxygen deprivation would definitely fuck him up for a bit." She crossed her gun arm in front of her, set her other elbow into it, and rested her chin in her free hand, as though pondering the secrets of the ages. Looking back up, she said, "Eventually, I came up with it."

She stepped over to the storage bin and pulled out another couple of containers. Zach looked at her and didn't know what to feel. Fear? Respect? Disgust? All had slid through his mind in the past couple of hours. He felt he was meeting the real Rainer for the first time, and she was nothing like he had imagined. With what he knew of her, he'd imagined a lot, but nothing like this.

"Here's what I came up with," she said, dropping a red plastic container and a white bucket on the ground. Bo turned his head this way and that, trying to catch a look, but it was directly behind him and out of his view.

She turned again to Zach and, leaning casually against the concrete, gave him the explanation as though it was as dull as balancing a chequebook. "The thing you've got to keep in mind, Zach, is that shifters can't really be permanently hurt. They can contract the odd disease, but a gunshot won't affect them for too long, nor will any other physical trauma. It's an annoyance, but they can grow back damn near anything, given the time."

Even a testicle, Zach thought as he stood quietly, his back to the wall. He truly didn't know which of the other two was the more dangerous one, and wasn't taking chances at this point.

"So, in the course of my travels, I began tracking the duration of the wounds. A gunshot will take a day or two to heal. The wound stops bleeding fairly quick, but the hole stays open until the body can expel the bullet. It usually pops out in a few hours." She huffed out something that could have been a laugh. "Amazing to watch, actually," she said.

"Bigger wounds, like a shotgun blast to the gut, can take a week or so. Losing a limb might take a month before it's fully functional again—and I'm talking an arm or a leg here. And during that time, they are down and out. I mean, a *leg*. That's a major injury." She used the gun to point vaguely in Bo's direction. Zach stepped quietly to his left.

"The other thing I found was, it's not painless," she said. "They'll feel the pain for most of that time, right up until the final healing takes place. Nature's way of telling them not to fuck up quite so spectacularly next time."

"What's with those?" Zach asked, pointing to the canister and bucket.

"Oh, the gasoline?" Rainer asked sweetly. "Well, that's the idea. There was one night when I was going through a magazine, and there was this article on photographs that changed the world."

"Okay," Zach said.

"Ever heard of Thích Quảng Đức?"

"Can't say I have."

"Everyone should know his name. Unfortunately, they only know him from one photo. He was a Vietnamese Buddhist monk who, on June 11, 1963, set himself on fire to protest the persecution of Buddhists by the South Vietnamese government. He was willing to die for his cause."

"Okay, I know who you're talking about," Zach said, recalling the horrifying photograph.

"Right," Rainer said. "I saw that photo and it got me thinking…I can cause our buddy here a lot of pain for a long time." She looked down at the items, then back to Zach. Her eyes were cold. "I'm going to burn every square inch of skin right off him. He won't die for the cause, but how long do you think it'll take for his hide to grow back? A month? Six weeks?"

She smiled. "I'm betting it'll take him at least three weeks before he can even blink again. Probably twice that to actually see."

♦♦♦

RAINER PICKED UP the gas can as she headed toward the chained man.

"What's it gonna be, Bobo? Talk, or tan?" Zach was horrified by her calmness. It was the same sense of peace he had seen back at the restaurant the day she'd saved his ass—the day they'd first actually spoke to each other—but it was in the context of *his* reality then. Now it was hers.

The man chained to the wall said nothing, apparently finding something incredibly interesting in the concrete inches from his nose.

"Hey," said Rainer. "Have it your way." She lifted the can and poured some gasoline on Bo's right arm. "You should be grateful. Had I had more time, I would have mixed this with Styrofoam, give you a nice napalm body lotion." Had Zach's mind not already been overwhelmed, he knew he should have been horrified by everything Rainer had done up to now, and what she was getting ready to do.

The smell of gasoline hung fetid and heavy in the cold night air, and Zach felt his eyes watering. Rainer set the can back down again and held up a cheap plastic lighter.

"Last chance, Bobo."

No response.

Rainer didn't hesitate. She cranked the little wheel with her thumb and touched the flame to the man's arm. He barely had time to flinch. His arm came alight with a *whump*. Zach found it incredible that *he* reacted more than the guy on fire. Bo simply rotated his head enough to look at Rainer, and smiled through the flames.

Rainer smiled back. Zach realized he was stuck in a silo with two mentally unbalanced people. His fear mounted and his flight instinct kicked in. He edged toward the silo's opening, trying to keep his feet silent on the dirt floor.

"Stay here, Zach," Rainer said, not taking her eyes off Bo. "I'd rather not have to shoot you. I'm gonna need you again soon, and besides"—and here she stopped and looked straight at him—"I really like you."

Zach stopped moving. *Fan-fucking-tastic. I find a girl I like, take her out, find out she's some kind of unhinged freak from a Hannibal movie...*then *she decides she really likes me. And somehow, I find her attractive by the light of a burning man. Fuck my life,* he thought.

But still, he stopped moving.

"Thanks, Zach."

"Yeah," he said in a breath. "Don't mention it." He ran his hands through his hair and stayed still. The smell of burning material soon gave way to the heavier odour of burning flesh.

Looking up, the two were locked back into their stare down. Most of Bo's sleeve was burned away, and the flame now directly attacked the meat of his arm. The gas had burned away, and the flame fed off the skin and muscle now.

The odour was far too reminiscent of barbequed pork, and his stomach lurched.

Jesus H, he thought.

"Ray, for god's sake!" Zach cried.

Rainer broke contact with Bo, glanced at Zach, and grabbed a blanket from the other bucket. Water and small sheets of ice streamed off it as she lifted it to the burning man's arm. She hesitated, then dropped the blanket on his burning flesh.

The smell of burned meat was thick as cotton in the circular area. It got so much worse when Rainer pulled the blanket back off Bo's arm. A large, viscid slough of blackened skin came with it. First it was the sight of the skin, the ruined arm, then it was the smell that hit Zach.

He had no choice—he turned and puked where he stood. Liquefied popcorn and Coke. The smell hit him again, and so did the heaves. Finally, there was nothing left to come up.

"You finished?" Rainer asked, not a trace of sympathy in her voice.

"Yeah, for now," Zach answered, swiping at his mouth with his sleeve.

"There's bottles of water in the bin."

"Thanks," he said. He moved slowly, avoiding the puddle of sick, and grabbed one. Cracking the lid, he took a mouthful, swished it, and spat.

At the risk of restarting the heaves, he raised his eyes to check out the damage Rainer had inflicted. He wiped again at his mouth, mainly to have the material of his shirt and jean jacket block the smell. Bo's arm was a mess, the flesh blackened and smoking. In other places, the flesh gleamed bright red and shiny in the pale moonlight. The man had to be in agony, but said nothing.

Rainer still kept a respectful distance, but checked out her handiwork as though checking a child's homework for errors. Apparently she was happy with the result. She tossed the wet blanket to Zach. He caught it gingerly, his ass scooching backward to prevent any of the blanket or the skin from hitting him. Small bits of blackened cloth or flesh still clung to the thick material.

"Put that back in the bucket, will you?" she asked. Zach nodded and walked the blanket to the bucket. When he dropped it back into the water, Zach saw the large strip work itself lose and float to the surface. He turned away, his eyes watering.

Rainer was watching him, but turned back to Bo when she saw he would be okay.

"So," she said, addressing Bo. "You're holding up quite well, but we aren't anywhere *near* done." She reached down to one booted foot and pulled out a knife. "Now I'm gonna skin you."

Holy fuck. She had a gun and *a knife?*

Bo started to sweat. Zach imagined he could smell the man's fear.

Seriously, was he really standing here watching a woman torture an already-injured man?

And yet, Zach had thought Bo had held it together too well—but hell, anyone who could stand there while his arm was barbequed and not say anything was impressive as shit as far as Zach was concerned.

But still, he'd had enough. His brain and his moral centre had been completely overwhelmed. "Ray," he said, "I know I can't run away screaming like I want to, but I'm going to stand in the doorway here. You'll still be able to see me, but I can..."

"Yeah," she said. "I understand." Some humanity crept back into her face. "I'm sorry," she said. "I really didn't expect the night to go like this." She flicked a disdainful glance at Bo. "But needs must."

Zach nodded stupidly, not sure exactly which part he was agreeing with, and moved to the door opening. Thank god the air was fresher here.

Ray turned back to her captive. Zach listened as she described how she was going to peel the burned skin off to expose the raw flesh underneath. Then she described in great detail how she was going to do that to the rest of his body. Burn and peel.

As she spoke, she reached out with the knife and scraped a section of Bo's raw arm. Zach watched as charred bits of flesh fell to the dirt floor of the structure.

"Do you have any idea how long it will take to heal?" Rainer asked Bo. "You're going to be in constant agony for weeks. And you know you're going to scar from this. You'll grow back that ear that Walter tore off, but your arm'll always be a mess. You might not even have fur when you shift."

♦♦♦

IT TOOK A while longer, but Rainer got the information she needed. She'd kept scraping at the raw flesh and telling Bo how she would do that to his full body. As she scraped, Zach saw him go from relatively calm to shivering and shaking. Sweat blossomed on his forehead and eventually matted his hair tight to his skull.

And then, something incredible happened.

Zach had been looking away, out the door and across the dark fields, sickened by the events he had witnessed, but then he heard Bo shout "*Enough!*" in a voice far lower than he'd used to that point. Throatier. Growly. Then came the noises, sickening noises, and Zach looked back. The sound of creaking and popping bones and the soft hiss of muscle sliding under skin. The wet sluice of organs roiling and twisting upon themselves. The low moan of air exchanging through reshaped passages.

Zach heard the sound of a one-eared man shifting from human to wolf.

All told, it seemed like it had taken a couple of minutes for him to shift, but in reality, it had taken only a few seconds. The massive wolf tried to shake its head, but it was still locked within the collar. The wolf's arms, now its forelegs, had easily slipped from their cuffs, and the links around its ankles fell to the floor. But the dragging of the forelegs and the thrashing of the hind limbs pulled the zip cords tighter, capturing three of his four limbs, keeping him trapped. The clothes Bo had worn were still on the creature, but threatened to either fall off or rip open like they'd always showed on that old TV series, *The Incredible Hulk*.

Rainer had backed off immediately at the transition and stood a healthy distance from the straining animal. Zach watched as it tried to spin on its leash, the one free leg scrabbling wildly but never reaching the ground. Hacking, the beast turned itself back around to face the wall and planted its paws so it stood upright, like a dog begging to be let out. It wobbled, horribly off-centre.

The right foreleg of the animal was burned and shiny with pink, stretched skin. The wolf only had one ear, and a ragged hole where the other should have been. Presumably, it only had a single testicle as well. Zach didn't want to check.

Rainer looked over to her date. "You can close your mouth, Zach," she said.

Zach's mouth worked, the jaw went up and down, up and down, but no sound came.

"I told you he was a werewolf," she said nonchalantly. "Hell, so did *he.*" She gestured toward the animal that had, just seconds before, been a man.

Zach stared, dumbfounded. This was no Lon Chaney makeup job, basically a hairy man. No, this was a massive, powerful animal. Thick fur covered most of its body, but underneath, where the muscles bunched and corded, there was power. He—it?—was mostly black, with a golden-white belly. Its paws were huge things, the width of his own hand, but tipped with thick black claws. *The better to tear you with.*

Its head above its thick neck was marked with golden-white slashes of colour. But it was its eyes, deep blue and intelligent, sharp and focused, missing nothing, that first caught Zach's attention. *The better to see you with.*

The next thing he noticed was Bo's teeth, particularly the fangs. *The better to eat you with.*

Zach stood away from the animal and tried to understand what exactly it was that made him tremble. Was it the fact that a man just turned into an animal? Literally changed physical shape, grew fur and fangs, and—yes, *shifted*—from a man to a wolf? Because that was impossible, literally against all physics.

And yet, it had happened.

Or was it the claws? The teeth? The eyes?

Or was it simply that he knew that this beast, this animal, was simply a shell of the man Zach had been scared of before the change? That, within those blue eyes, there burned a seething, psychotic intelligence that no ordinary wolf would ever possess.

Yes, he decided. It was the intelligence and the malice in those eyes that scared him most of all. Those eyes, now in a form that could tear him apart. *The better to kill you with.*

Bo, for his part, stood on his hind legs, still facing the wall, his head now turned back to Rainer. Zach, seeing the look on the animal's face, backed up even further. No way he was going near that.

I'm going to rip the top of your skull off and suck out your brains. I'll tear your heart out and eat it as it beats its last.

Nope. No way in hell.

Rainer turned back to the werewolf, unconcerned by the fact that the thing facing her was no longer a man, but a massive beast that was eager to tear her throat out at the first opportunity. To Zach, she actually seemed pleased.

"Now we're getting somewhere," she said.

"Can he even talk now?" Zach asked.

"Oh yeah, he can talk," Rainer said. "But it's a series of growls, barks, and whines. Nothing you or I would understand."

"Can it understand you? Does it understand English anymore?"

"It can kind of catch the vibe," she said.

"Then how...?"

"I've got my ways," she said.

♦♦♦

RAINER, ONE HAND firmly grasping her gun, approached the creature slowly.

"Okay," she said. "I'm still giving you the choice: the easy way, or the hard way." She pointed to the gas can. "You already know how the hard way's gonna go." Bo looked at her and bared his teeth.

"Yeah, exactly," Rainer said. "The easy way will take a lot less time. And a lot less pain." She paused, allowing the animal to take in what she was saying. "Now, I'm going to have to get a little closer to you than either of us is comfortable with, but it'll be quick. You gonna be a good doggie?"

The animal stood a few seconds longer, then lowered its head. Zach saw the ripple of the muscles under the thick coat. Rainer nodded back and approached the animal. She put the gun right up to the animal's ribcage—Zach thought he might have seen the animal flinch slightly—and slowly, reverently, she placed her other hand on the sweat-beaded fur.

Her eyes closed tight, like she was in pain. Her head cocked to one side, and Zach saw her teeth bare in imitation of the animal she touched. Her hand, initially open on the hide of the wolf, as though petting him, clamped down, bunching the fur in her fist. Her mouth opened and her brow furrowed and she emitted a soft *unh* sound.

Through it all, the gun never wavered.

Bo stood still, though he would twitch every so often. But after a few seconds he started to shake. A spray of urine from the animal darkened the wall, steaming as it ran to the ground and melted the frost.

Rainer, still concentrating, brought her head down and swiped the sweat from her brow by rubbing it on her outstretched arm. It was then that the wolf made his move.

The huge animal, already facing the wall, *pushed*. Zach heard metallic *pops*, like gunfire, and the beast came down on all fours, the collar still hanging from his neck, with a length of chain and a small chunk of concrete from the silo wall trailing it. The zip cords had snapped under the pressure, though it had cost him. Zach saw the ragged flesh where the plastic had torn away. Zach watched as the werewolf turned his massive head to attack. There was a flash of teeth and saliva, and then a thundering *BOOM*.

Rainer stood as the animal dropped to the ground, a small hole in one side of it, a large crater-shaped chunk missing from the other. Zach looked up and saw bits of flesh and fur splattered on the wall of the silo. He looked back to the beast and noticed the original entry wound had burned fur around it and it still smoked.

Without slowing, she placed the muzzle under Bo's long jaw and blew his brains out the same way.

Zach couldn't hear for shit.

Rainer wiped dog fur off her one hand, and blood off the other, with the wet blanket she had used to douse the flames. Her gun was gone, presumably holstered back wherever it had appeared from so many hours previous. She looked up as Zach approached her.

"What now?" he asked, not hearing his own voice from the loud pinging sound reverberating in his head.

Zach didn't hear her reply either, but he thought he made out the word, "Floored."

Whatever the hell that was.

CHAPTER ELEVEN

THE PACK STOPPED for the night. With no pressing contracts for killings, it was yet another night to run, another night to feed, just for the fun of it.

They found a quiet, nondescript place to park the car where it wouldn't look suspicious and afforded them the privacy to shed their clothes without being seen.

They ran the wide areas first, finding small game, rabbits and raccoons to whet their appetite. Soon, they found themselves on a stretch of field where the streets ended abruptly. In the distance, the smell of wood smoke and beer. The sounds of strong, young bodies without a care in the world.

They might even find another suitable pack member, though it would be tight to wait the three days for them to turn and still make the Calling.

They'd just started moving toward the field party, their mouths already salivating in anticipation, when Zero suddenly stopped. Even the Fed stopped.

Taylor looked over, concerned. The pack knew, if Zee stopped, something was going down. He was about to say something to her, ask her what was going on, when he saw her drop. She didn't lie down, she dropped from a standing position to belly on the ground. Taylor moved cautiously over to her. She looked up at him, but he saw she was in distress, tail tucked between her legs, sides heaving from the panting. Eyes closed and rolling.

Then she started digging.

Taylor knew what was coming. He'd never experienced it. Syd had, he knew, but he himself had not. The Fed, still intent on their quarry, had started inching forward again, but Syd, several yards away, caught his attention with a growl and the Fed stopped. Taylor let a low, quiet whine go, a warning.

He saw Syd lift his head, trying to get a look at Zero…

Then it hit them all.

Every one was different, but every one was horrible. That's all Taylor had ever been told about losing a pack member.

Light exploded behind Taylor's eyes, dropping him to the ground. Pain shot from his skull to the tip of his tail. His muscles collapsed and left him prone on the ground. He felt his bowels loosen and though he wouldn't discover it until later, he shit himself, the feces squeezing through the space under his tail tightly coiled under his balls. He pissed all over his tail, his belly, the ground under him. The air felt toxic as it slid along the ravaged nerves in his snout, and it was this that started the impetus to dig.

With each stroke of paw to earth, pain sang up his forelegs in bright white arcs. Still, he dug until his muscles gave out. The air was more painful. The moonlight, normally their guardian, now seemed treacherous. Its light tore at his eyes, scraped along his fur and dug into his muscles. Everything hurt, everything was sharp jabs and serrated edges, the grass now razor blades, the ground sandpaper flaying his skin, the ripples of breeze flensing knives of pain on fur and hide.

He dug, the need to escape beyond logic, beyond control.

Then he lay in the shallow grave he had made, completely defenceless.

It went on forever. Taylor wanted to die. Felt as though he was dying. Felt like he'd died a hundred times.

Then, an interminable time later, as quickly as it came on, it finished.

One of their pack was gone.

♦♦♦

TAYLOR GOT TO his feet, muscles stiff, bones aching, still unsteady, fur matted with old shit and piss, but at least he was okay. He looked around. Zero was up. Syd was rising.

The Fed? "Where the hell is the Fed?"

The Fed came bounding across the field. "What happened?"

"One of the pack died," Syd said.

"Who?" said the Fed. "We're all here."

Zero said, "Bo." She turned and headed back to the car.

The hunt was over for the night. The field party got a pass.

♦♦♦

EACH ONE MOVED tentatively, with the exception of the Fed. He was possibly too new, or too stupid, to understand the gravity of what had happened. Each had been in their own world, recovering from the effects of Bo's death in their own way.

Quick flashes of sensory input flashed through Taylor's mind, illuminating fragmented scenes for the briefest of moments, like lightning. Pain. A screaming woman, her mouth wrong. Pain. A phone booth. Pain. An old silo, lit by headlights. Pain. A man. Pain. A woman. Pain.

He knew the others were getting similar flashes.

He couldn't get a handle on the images. They were nonsensical. Confused. Insane.

Still, if he could just release them from their cage of pain and emotion, he knew he could likely pull something from them.

But each image, each sound, each feeling carried a dragging, painful weight with it. So, like the others, he simply pushed them away.

Zero reached the car first. Then Syd. Taylor dragged in just behind him.

They waited for the Fed.

They waited a long time.

CHAPTER TWELVE

IT TOOK SOME time for Zach's hearing to come back to normal. In that time, he got to watch Rainer produce a large knife—Zach didn't know if it was a hunting knife or any other type of knife, as he was just as knowledgeable about knives as he was guns—and remove Bo's head from his body.

Zach learned two things. The first was that the movies were wrong. The dead wolf didn't revert back to its human form in death. A dead wolf was a dead wolf.

The second was that it took a lot of time and effort to separate a head from a body. None of this one swipe and gone stuff.

"Was that necessary?" he asked. "Cutting his head off?"

"I can't take any chances," she said. "I've seen these things come back from the most catastrophic injuries you can imagine. The one thing I do know for sure is, they cannot regenerate a new head. But, even still… Well, come here," she said. "Look at this."

Zach bent closer to the body.

"What?" he said. I don't see—"

"Here." The blade touched the large exit wound on Bo's side. "Look at it. Just watch this area for a second."

Zach stared. At first, he saw nothing…

But then, he did.

"Holy shit! It's knitting itself back together!"

Rainer said nothing, just nodded. Then she stood and moved over to the head, toeing it. "This works, cutting the head off. So yeah, it was necessary."

"Anything else to complete this ritual?" he asked, meaning it sarcastically, but then thinking, *If the body's knitting itself, there has to be.*

"Three more things," she said, not seeing, or simply ignoring, his look. "One of the many legends I've read states you should separate the head from the body, burn both separately, mix the ashes with holy water and garlic, and bury the two sets in different locations, preferably with running water between them."

"A little overkill, don't you think?" Zach asked, then looked back at the wound again.

"I don't think so," Rainer replied. "But in this case, even though you may think it's bullshit, it doesn't hurt."

"Seriously, Ray," Zach said. "What do you think holy water and garlic are going to do to something that's already ash? I mean, you really think there's a chance it'll come back from that?"

"If I had asked you two hours ago if a human could change themselves into a wolf whenever they felt like it, would you have said yes?"

"No."

"Why?"

"Because..." And then he ran out of words. "I don't know. Because it's ridiculous."

"Right. About as ridiculous as mixing the ashes with holy water and garlic?" She prodded the body with a booted foot. "About as ridiculous as having this discussion over the dead body of a wolf I just decapitated? A wolf that used to be a man a couple of hours back?"

Zach nodded once, a quick jerk of his head. She'd made her point.

"Right. So, the garlic and holy water and different locations thing. I try to do it as often as possible, but we really don't have the time for that."

Try to do it as often as possible, Zach thought. *How often has she done this? Killed someone?* He wasn't going to ask.

"You listening?"

He nodded.

"Okay, we're going to drag the body over that way," she indicated to the left of the car, "soak it with gasoline, and burn it for as long as it takes to dig a grave for it. And we'll do the same for the head over that way," she said, pointing in the other direction.

"Really?"

"Really."

"Still with the garlic and holy water?"

"Yes, of course."

Zach looked at his watch. It was almost one. Figure an hour to get this done, then an hour to get back home again. Three in the morning at the earliest. More like four.

"Fine," he said, pissy now. "It's your party, you get the biggest gift." He pointed to the headless body.

"Fair," she said agreeably. "First, let me do something," she said, reaching into her pocket for what looked like two jackknives pushed together. She did some pulling and twisting and somehow the damn thing turned into a pair of pliers.

She bent to the head, pried open the mouth, and prised out about six teeth.

"You take souvenirs?"

"I tend to look at them as conversation starters," she said.

She pocketed the tool and the teeth. "Okay," she said. "Ready." She felt around in the pocket, then pulled out a small, flat packet about the size of a cigarette pack and held it out to Zach.

"What's this?"

"Something to make the flame burn hotter. A lot hotter."

"What is it?"

"It's something to make the flame burn hotter, Zach. Do you really need to know its chemical makeup? Put it under the head, get some gas on the head, light it up, then step back. Way back. It'll get crazy hot."

"Okay."

Rainer and Zach dragged the body a ridiculous distance away and he left her to barbeque the body. Zach came back and gingerly picked up Bo's head by the least-bloodied section of fur, shocked by the weight of it, scooped the gas tank and walked it to the spot Rainer had indicated, then dropped it. He added the packet, then toed the head over top of it.

He poured what he assumed would be an ample volume of gas on Bo, then added that much again before throwing a match to it. The head exploded into flame and a small mushroom cloud rose from the initial burst.

Jesus! thought Zach. *I nuked him.*

It took about thirty seconds, but then the flame went from reddish orange to a searing white, so bright he couldn't look at it. It burned with a sound like ripping canvas and, through sidelong glances, Zach watched the head disintegrate.

Rainer's right, he thought. *I don't want to know what's in those packets.*

While he stood monitoring the flame, he became aware of the pain in his lower abdomen and realized that he needed to piss with an urgency he hadn't felt in years. Turning from the flame, he unzipped his fly and let loose a stream that steamed in the cold night air. He let out a long sigh and his body involuntarily shuddered from the sheer joy of the release. He flashed back to Bo releasing a jet of piss while Rainer touched him. *What had she been doing?* Then he thought, *Forget it, Zach, you don't wanna know.* He closed his eyes and just enjoyed the feeling only a good long piss could bring.

"Make sure you don't piss on the flames." Rainer's voice was close. Too close.

"God, Ray!" Zach blurted, trying to stem the flow. It was like trying to stop Niagara Falls. Unsuccessful, he turned a full one-eighty degrees from Rainer and continued to go, uncomfortable as it was. "A little privacy?"

"You don't think I've seen a guy pee before?" she asked. "I was married once. I know what it looks like."

Ray was married?

Before he could compose himself long enough to ask about her marriage, she had moved on to other things.

She walked over to the fire, apparently feeling no discomfort even though Zach could feel the heat ten feet further back.

"I didn't come to spy on your penis," she said. "I need the gas can." She inspected the burning head and nodded. "Looks good."

"Thanks," Zach said. *Isn't this weird,* he thought. *Getting complimented on my body-burning skills. But not on my penis.* The penis comment stung, though, in a low-level, non-specific way. He finished off, very conscious of the last few squeezed-out squirts. Rainer didn't seem to notice. She was all business.

"Back at the silo, there's another gas can with holy water in it, and shovels around the back. While this burns, you can get a hole dug. Go as deep as you can. Once this has burned to ashes, pour a good portion of the water—say, a quarter of the can—on it, then shovel it into the hole."

"You've got this all figured out, don't you?" Zach asked, amazed. *Okay, I gotta ask.* "How many times have you done this?"

"You don't want to know."

"How the hell do you get a gas can full of holy water?" Zach asked.

"Connections," she said in reply.

"Same way you get the supernova packets?" he said, pointing to the still white-hot flame.

"Same way. Different connections."

Zach sighed, tired of this night, wanting only to get home to Sam. Rainer seemed to notice.

"Look, Zach," she said. "I'm really sorry you got dragged into this—I really am—but you are now, you're in deep, and I need the help. After this thing is buried and we're on our way home, we'll talk, okay?"

She seemed sincere enough, though Zach had never doubted her sincerity. Not wanting to commit to anything more at this point, he just nodded to her and turned back to the flames.

He never heard her leave, but a couple of minutes later, when he decided to fetch the shovel and the holy water, he found them both neatly arranged not five feet behind him.

She moves like a friggin' cat, he thought, turning back to the burning dog.

I just hope I'm not the mouse.

♦♦♦

BECAUSE IT WAS only October, the surface frost hadn't gotten its icy fingers into the soil yet, so the digging went fairly easily. Zach finished his hole and, seeing Rainer's fire still going strong, decided he could wait for the head to burn down a bit more.

No fucking way he was going to go and talk to Rainer, so he instead headed uphill, away from the fires.

As he rounded a small knoll, he found Rainer sitting on the grass facing the large flattened ball of the setting moon.

Zach couldn't decide what was hitting him harder: the fact that his date was sitting calmly on a hill after killing someone, or the absolute beauty of her framed by the moon.

"Ray?" he said, more tentatively than he had intended. All objections to talking to her fell away. "What are you doing?"

No response, but he could see her chest rising and falling, her back straight. Her face was lifted to the delicate light of the stars and moonlight. He stepped back a few feet from her cross-legged form, giving her privacy, but also a little concerned to let her get out of sight.

She sat with her eyes closed for a long time, not moving. He looked back at the fires, both still burning, lower now, but still under control.

It took maybe fifteen minutes. He'd sat down on the ground, several yards away, and felt nothing but the cold. He was about to get up and warm himself up by the heat of burning wolf when she finally stirred, opened her eyes.

She turned and faced him.

"What…?" he began.

"This is how I…cope," she said. "This is how I recharge. Feeling the quiet of the sky, the stillness of the Earth…it centres me. Makes me realize what's important." She trailed off a bit and Zach wondered if there was a hint of embarrassment there, but looking at her face, no. She was just trying to frame her thoughts.

"I guess I've learned to be still," she finished.

There was silence between them then. A long silence. *But,* Zach thought, *it is time to get going*. He stood. "Ray," he said, wiping the dew from his hands. "You're a complex individual, aren't you?" A small, crooked smile crossed his face. Then he went back to his cremation duties.

♦♦♦

ZACH SHOVELLED THE last of the earth over the ashes and tiny fragments of skull—having sprinkled garlic from a jar Rainer had provided him with—then went down the hill to meet her, studying her as he approached.

He was sure she was firmly on the crazy side, and what he had previously taken for mystery or an interesting eccentricity now seemed more like mania, or an obsession.

But he had seen that guy transform—shift?—into a werewolf. He'd *seen* it!

And Rainer. He didn't know much about her, but some of the statements she'd made in the past few hours.

I know what he did to Sarah.

I was married.

I've learned to be still.

And the big one: *It's what I do.*

It's what I do.

This is what she did. She took on werewolves…and won.

Zach covered the last few steps to meet her, seeing her with fresh eyes. A good eight inches shorter than him, and Zach wasn't tall by anyone's standards. Short, bed-head hair. Not beautiful in the conventional way, but attractive on a deeper level. In their short time as friends, Zach had noticed how men looked at her, almost as though they weren't sure why they found her attractive, but that they did. A combination of lust and curiosity.

She'd have a beautiful smile if she ever smiled, Zach realized.

They finished up with Bo's burial, cleaned up the area, got back to the car, and stowed Rainer's tools.

Zach opened the driver's side door and, with the weak interior light on, checked out his back seat. *What a fucking mess.* Blood across the fabric, and a decent sized hole. *A bullet hole,* he thought. *How do I explain that to Sam?*

Rainer opened the passenger door, ducked her head in, saw the expression on his face, saw the blood, saw the hole. "We can make it look like someone jacked your car, went joyriding, and burned it," she said. "I'll buy you a new one."

"Burning doesn't solve everything, Ray," he said. *You shot someone in my car.*

She didn't reply. They just regarded each other for a few long moments. Zach had to admit she did appear genuinely sorry, but still.

With no additional dialogue, they both got in. Both put on their seatbelts. Zach started the car.

He gave it a good ten minutes to get the car warmed up before he put it in drive.

♦ ♦ ♦

AS HE BUMPED the car back along the rutted lane, he said, "Okay, you said something about talking. Let's talk."

"Okay," she said. "I'm just going to throw it out there. Will you come with me?"

"Excuse me?"

"Come with me. You and Sam." She sighed. "You're in danger now. I've put you in danger." She hooked a thumb at the back seat for emphasis.

Zach became quiet. For a long time. He drove.

"You're hesitating," Rainer said in observation. "Goddamn it, of course you are." She pounded a fist softly into her thigh, staring down at it as though the answer of the ages would be found there. "This is why I don't date. This is why I don't let anyone in. This is why I didn't want to go out with you."

"So why in the hell did you?"

She stopped the thigh punches, turned to look at him. "Because I like you, Zach." She put a hand on his arm. "I like you a lot. More than anyone else I've met in the past while."

"And yet, you held a gun to me. Threatened me."

"I did. And, though it's nowhere near adequate, I'm sorry about that." She sighed. "You realize now it was to save your life, right?"

He didn't want to admit to that, but he did see it.

"And now I'm asking you to drop your entire life and run."

"Yeah. Run away with the girl who kills wolves and carries guns, knives, packets of...something...that burns white-hot, and holy water by the gallon. Who the fuck are you? Batman?"

"I know. I get it," she said. "I'm so deep into this now, I usually forget what I look like from the outside. I forget how...*unreasonable* my life is."

"Unreasonable?" Zach said. "That's the first word that comes to mind?"

"I've been doing this so long now, been chasing wolves so long, I guess I'm starting to lose what it is to be human. I don't know how to act around my own kind anymore."

"And you question why I'd hesitate to throw my life—my human life—and that of my daughter's away to be with someone who doesn't know how to be human anymore?"

"Makes sense. I'm a bit of a whack job. And this is your life, your child. I'd hesitate, too. Hell, three years ago I would have run screaming." She stopped, stared out the window as the miles tumbled under the car. Her brows knitted together. "Zach, you have to understand this. You're in danger. You and Sam. And whether you know it or not, you're on a ledge now. If you jump, that's it. There's no going back."

And there they were, at the crossroads. While Zach still thought he couldn't continue on with her, a big part of him—a part embarrassed at his own selfishness and stupidity—was screaming at her to give him a reason, just one good reason to go.

They got as far as the first paved road. Zach stopped at the sign, but didn't move after that. He felt locked up, like he could see no good way to proceed.

Rainer let him take the time, but then she said, "Zach, what's it gonna—*shit!*"

"What?"

"My eye," she said, rubbing a finger around her eyelid. "I got something in my damn eye."

Zach put the car in park and turned on the roof light. "Here," he said. "Let me look."

"No, I'm fine," she said, shrugging him off.

"Hey, you wanna be Dirty Harry, that's fine with me," Zach said, irritation finally breaking through. "I was just trying to help."

Wrist cocked, Rainer wiped at her eye with the back of her hand, unsuccessful at removing the irritant. Zach sat watching her, a small, sarcastic smile bending his lips. With a shake of his head, he popped the car back into drive, but kept his foot on the brake. He could hear her snuffling beside him. He knew she was still working at her eye, but he wouldn't look at her.

"Y'know," Zach said, "I thought we were friends. I trusted you—even through all this shit, when I normally wouldn't trust anyone—I trusted you. As far as I was concerned, what you did for me at the restaurant that day allowed you to earn my trust. You held a gun to my head and I still helped you. You killed a man—okay, a wolf, but he *was* a man—and I still helped you. You made me burn and bury his fucking head and I did it. Through all that, my ideas about you changed." He huffed out a breath, watched it fog in the car. "Now I find out you aren't anywhere near what I thought you were."

"Zach," he heard her say. He didn't turn to look. Let her wait for a change.

"Zach," she repeated, drawing the name out.

"What?" he finally answered, the sound coming out short and sharp. He turned to face her. She still had the back of her wrist to her eye. As she looked at him, she dropped it to reveal her eye, red and puffy.

"Help me?" she said, then, after a pause, "Please?"

His breath came out in a long sigh. "So you aren't invincible then, huh?"

Back to park again. She raised her head up to the roof light. She was close, very close. He could smell the smoke on her clothes, saw a streak of ash lightly marking one high cheekbone.

I was wrong, he thought. *She is beautiful.*

Zach cupped her chin in one hand, angled her head. "I see it," he said. "I think it's a piece of ash."

"You mean I've got a werewolf in my eye?" she asked, a small smile creeping in.

Zach paused and stared into her eyes. Of all the things she had done in the past few hours, this was the most shocking. "Did you just crack a joke?" he asked.

"Just get the damn ash out, okay?" she said, a small grin turning the corners of her mouth. "It hurts."

"Then you gotta learn to be still." Smiling. She smiled back.

He went back to his task. He pinned her eyelid open and whisked the black spot off her eyeball. She blinked away tears.

"How does that feel?" he asked. "Better?"

"Yeah, much," she said. His hand still cupped her chin. He liked the feel of her smooth skin under his hand.

"So," he said. "You aren't this warrior goddess with mystical powers and a deep, dark secret? You can bleed?"

"Yeah, I can bleed," Rainer said, the smile coming back again. "Sometimes I can bleed a little too well. Sometimes I could use some help." She made no move to remove his hand.

He dropped the humorous tone. "Are you trying to ask me something?" he said. Zach dropped his hand from her face. "Because, y'know, you've been pretty damn good at ordering me around for the past few hours, and I'm not really liking it too much."

"I'm sorry," Rainer said, dropping her eyes. "I know I keep saying that, but really I am. And I know I keep saying that, too. I guess what I'm trying to say is, will you help me? Will you come with me? There's a lot of travelling on my plate, and I could use a co-pilot."

"It's nice to hear you ask, for a change," Zach said.

"Part of me is asking," Rainer said, and her face changed, went all serious. "Part of me is still telling you."

"What do you mean?"

"We've killed a shifter. I don't know that there won't be some retribution."

"You mean they may come after us?" The thought of another Bo anywhere near him—or his daughter—terrified him.

"Yes," Rainer said. "May come after us. May come after you. That's what I meant when I told you I put you in danger." She sighed. "I like yours and Sam's chances better with me than on your own. I can protect you."

Zach killed the roof light, put the car back into drive, and pulled onto the paved road and turned back home.

"I'm going home to my daughter, and you're going to have to do some explaining. I need to know exactly what I've gotten my family into here."

CHAPTER THIRTEEN

SOMEONE WAS IN the apartment.

Sam rolled out of the bed silently and padded to the door. She heard the television on in the living room, volume low.

Something wasn't right. Sam left her room, keeping quiet as she came down the hall. Did she smell something different? A musty smell, maybe?

Something. A disturbance in the Force, something like that.

She entered the living room. Jake was asleep on the couch, the television flickering and her laptop on the coffee table. Sam knew it was late because *The Exorcist* was playing on the screen. Jake would never watch something like that. She was too pussy. And on the laptop?

Yup, Jake's nudie pics.

Sam didn't know how she felt about those. She thought it was kinda gross, especially when Jake showed her vajayjay, but some of the other ones were kinda cool. She left the computer alone though. Jake got all weird when she knew Sam saw her porn pics.

Whatever the feeling was that had worked her up was fading now. Whatever it had been, it was gone now.

Still, she couldn't shake the feeling that something had been in the apartment with her and Jake.

She went into the kitchen and, quiet as she could, opened the cupboard door, pulled down a glass, then turned and eased the fridge door open, grabbed the carton, and poured a glass of milk, then drained it in one long gulp, bathed in the refrigerator light. She shut the door and Jake stood behind it.

"Hey," Sam said.

"Can't I ever scare you?"

"Nope."

"Why you up?"

"Duh." Sam held the empty glass up, jiggled it. "Thirsty." She decided not to mention the real reason. Jake freaked easy over shit like that.

"Why didn't you wake me up?"

"Why would I?"

"Because I woke up and heard someone moving around in the kitchen, saw Linda Blair's scabby face talking nasty shit, and I freaked."

"Man!" she said. "Jake, you're such a pussy."

"Yeah, I might be, but I'm still your babysitter, not the other way around." Jake smiled. "So...shut up..."

"Oh, weak. *Weak!*" Sam scrunched up her face. "'Shut uuuup!'"

"It was the best I could come up with, okay?" Jake couldn't help smiling. "Cut me some slack, I just woke up."

"It was still weaksauce, bitch."

"Asshat."

"Meat garage."

"Ooo, good one. Geek."

"Internet slut."

"Okay, that's just below the belt!" Jake laughed, her eyes wide. "You're goin' down, missy!"

Sam shrieked and ran for her life. Bouncing off the walls, she skittered, slipping in her socks on the hardwood floors, into her bedroom, giggling all the way. Jake mere inches behind her, getting better traction in her bare feet, but not catching her until they both fell onto Sam's bed. Jake tickled her until they both just about wet their pants.

When Sam finally settled back down in bed, she'd forgotten all about the feeling that got her out of bed in the first place.

CHAPTER FOURTEEN

"WHERE THE HELL did that psychopath go?"

Taylor, exhausted and shaking after the death of Bo, wearily followed Syd back along their trail, right back to the pathetic holes they had all dug, reeking of their piss and shit. Taylor smelled it in the holes, he smelled it on Syd, smelled it on himself.

It sickened him, this weakness of their kind. Others, he knew, saw it as a sign of respect for the dead, grieving their loss. He saw it as a period of time when they were simply vulnerable.

What if it happened in the middle of a kill? What if, as he was about to take an upright down, about to sink his teeth into the soft meat of their neck, this happened? Maybe somebody got lucky, got to Syd. Or Zero. Either way, he'd be helpless, and his intended kill could turn the tables and kill him and whomever was left of his pack as they were stuck, hunkered down, shitting themselves.

He never wanted to be that weak.

"Anything?" Syd said.

Taylor didn't know what the hell he was saying, then he shook more of the fogginess from his head.

The Fed. That fucked-up weirdo who was now his pack brother. *We're looking for the Fed. Get your head in the game.* "Nothing yet."

They fanned out, tracking his movements as they had each found their way from their pits of despair, both with tails low, brushing the tall grass, choosing their steps slowly, carefully, smelling all the rich and varied scents as their noses scanned the area.

Taylor trusted Zero and Syd. He knew they were tough to kill. Hell, up to now, he'd been the weak link. But now, they had this goddamned psychotic lunatic in their pack. And he'd gone fucking AWOL, so maybe he was the one someone would get to.

Maybe the Fed's will be the next death that has me pissing on myself. He probably wouldn't mind that one so much.

Then Syd made a noise and Taylor knew he'd found something. Syd said nothing, but veered off, excited, shit-crusted tail up now, his movements more animated, his head almost bobbing as he followed the scent. Taylor followed close behind, catching the scent himself, not so much a smell as a sensory tag of the Fed. Taylor didn't so much smell him as see a full-blown image in his mind. Something in this particular collection of smells carried a unique marker, a *Fedness*.

It was one of the many things about being a wolf that didn't translate, having no human equivalent.

As a human, Taylor had memories of people. His parents. His sisters. Friends. Relatives. But they were broken up images. Even if he accessed them now, they were fragments of sensory input. If, as a human, one of them had a particular smell, usually a heavy, artificial scent of cleaning agents or sprays that masked their true odours, there would be a faint slap of recognition. A trigger that told him this smelled like someone he knew. He knew someone who had once smelled this way. It was more an association. And not just a smell. An image of his mother, laughing. The sound of his father's snoring. His baby sister handing him a birthday present, the paper crackling softly at his touch, his older sister wrapping him in a hug.

All quick, sensory recollections, brief and incomplete.

But as a wolf, it was a tag. A marker. A unique signature that no one and nothing else had. A collection of smells, the sweat, the musk of the fur, the funk of digested meat on its breath, the rich aroma around its anus, the sweet bite of its urine. It was the particular huff of its breath and the rhythm of its heart and the particular cadence of its step…it was these and a thousand other details that formed an indelible image, a unique signature, in Taylor's head.

And right now, they had the Fed's. Well, his scent tag.

But they only had it for a moment, until it ended.

The bastard had veered off to a nearby creek. It was small and very shallow, but it was enough to mask his path. He had deliberately obfuscated his trail.

They crossed the water, Taylor lapping at it half-heartedly as he crossed. They scanned up and down the far bank, careful at first, but, as they separated, Syd following the twists and curves east, Taylor west, became less and less meticulous.

Hell, for all they knew, the Fed was still running right down the middle of the damn creek, miles away.

They wasted another hour, and, in the way that they had, even several miles apart, both decided to end their search at the same time and loped back to their separation point. The Fed hadn't been around long enough for that connection to form yet. Probably the only reason he'd gotten away.

"Fucker's gone," Syd said.

"That a bad thing?" Taylor said, thinking again of weak links.

Syd said nothing, only swung his head in the direction of Zero. Taylor got it. They needed to tell her what was going on.

♦♦♦

"YOU'RE SURE?" ZERO said.

"Completely," Syd said, and looked at Taylor for confirmation.

"I agree," Taylor said. "No sign of a struggle. No shenanigans. He left of his own free will."

Zero and Syd stared at him.

"What?"

"'Shenanigans'?"

"It's an expression, okay?"

Syd turned away and Taylor knew he was hiding a grin. But Zero was pissed at the Fed, so now was not the time.

"Zee," he said, trying to get them back on track. "I know you chose the Fed and all, but seriously, he's a freakshow."

Syd spun back around. "Taylor," he said, his voice low and warning.

"I'm serious. You didn't see what I saw in that house. What he'd done to his mother."

"We all had to—"

"Not like that, Syd." Facing Zero again. "Zee, seriously, the guy's a hot mess. We should be happy he's gone."

"And if the situation was turned around?" she said.

"What do you mean?"

"If it was you who was gone, and one of your pack was trying to convince me to drop you?"

"That's the difference, Zee," he said. "The other two in your pack—*us*, Zee—wouldn't be gone unless it was on your say-so."

Zero stared at him.

"And if it wasn't on your say-so?" Taylor continued. "Then I'd expect that conversation to happen. And I'd expect to—"

"Taylor," Syd said, his voice coming down like an axe, cutting his words off. "Enough."

"I—"

"Unless you intend to directly challenge Zee's position as pack leader, I suggest you shut up."

Taylor opened his mouth to speak once again, to make Zero understand, but chose instead to close it again.

Zero looked between the two of them, her expression unreadable. After an uncomfortably long silence, she dropped her head, turned, and, swinging her head back toward them, said, "We'll wait for him."

Taylor wasn't going to say anything, and the look on Syd's face told him that was the right decision.

♦ ♦ ♦

WITH NOTHING LEFT to do but wait for him, the three of them loped to the creek and cleaned themselves. No one spoke. Then they headed back to the van, shifted back to human form, and got dressed.

The cold didn't bother them and there didn't seem to be anyone around who could see them, still, they needed to appear like other, normal, non-shifting humans. Which wasn't the easiest thing to do, sitting three in a van in the middle of nowhere, not even a working radio in the vehicle to occupy their time.

They couldn't leave. Taylor hated the fact, didn't agree with it, but knew it was right. They couldn't leave, not right away, not for a few hours. Not until they knew what had happened to the Fed.

Syd sat up front in the driver's seat. Zero took the passenger seat. Taylor took the back seat. Then they sat. Taylor initially tried to fill the time with small talk, throwing out lines carefully crafted to start conversations, but Syd only glanced at Zero, taking his cue from her. And Zero never took the bait. Instead, she became withdrawn and sullen and refused to issue any orders other than to tell them they'd wait until she didn't want to wait anymore. It could be days or it could be minutes.

Syd and Taylor knew better than to say anything and, instead, traded glances in the rear-view mirror.

Taylor wanted to lay his head down and sleep, but he needed to remain awake and vigilant for any sign of the missing pack member.

Asshole.

♦♦♦

HOURS LATER, IT was very silent, very cold.

Initially, Syd and Taylor engaged in some small talk. Nothing serious, both of them obviously skirting the elephant in the room—their missing pack member. But Zero remained silent throughout, only watching out the front window, occasionally twisting her head to look out the sides. Her hands remained in her lap.

In the face of such stoic silence, Syd and Taylor eventually fell quiet as well.

Any movement in the van was too loud. The shifting of position forced a creak of vinyl, the scrape of boot on dirty floor.

With nothing better to do, Taylor sighed, made up his mind he would make some noise, and found a comfortable position to wait for his sociopathic pack brother. It also afforded him a better view of Zero. He observed her only from the furthest periphery of his vision, knowing she could easily sense his gaze and call him on it.

She was a pretty woman, pleasing to look at, with long brown hair, usually pulled back into a sloppy ponytail, as it was now. She had dark, intelligent eyes, but those eyes always struck Taylor as sad. They'd seen…something…that had broken her in some fundamental way.

This was just his impression. She was a confident pack

leader, and made definitive decisions quickly, and they always seemed to be right.

But there was this other side to her. The side that remained walled off from everyone else. The side that kept her quiet. The side that made Syd answer all their calls and deal with all their shit. The side that—in the face of a missing pack member—locked her down to the silent, staring figure he watched now from the corner of his eye.

Taylor had been with her and Syd for a couple of years now. She kept her pack unusually small. Most, he knew, ran more to six, or even as high as ten pack members. It had been the three of them for most of the past year.

Taylor had, in the first year, questioned Syd and, on occasion, Bo, about her, but it soon became apparent that neither, despite Syd's almost decade with her, and Bo's almost five years, that neither knew much more than Taylor did now.

Which was fuck all.

Zero never spoke about herself, never talked about the past, about anything prior to the change. Granted, it was never a favourite topic for any of them, and most of them treated their time as an upright as a dream-like memory, but still, occasionally the past would creep in. Syd, Taylor, and Bo had once spent most of an evening remembering the candy they ate as kids. Pop rocks, man. Another evening was spent talking about bands. Van Halen had been Bo's clear winner.

However, in none of the many discussions they'd had, not once had Zero joined in. Instead, she would sit off to the side, as she was doing now, and stare her thousand-yard stare, as she was doing now.

And it was this utter refusal of her past that often made Taylor wonder. It was as though she didn't exist, pre-wolf. As though the forces of life that had shaped each of them into the people—and ultimately the wolves they were now—had never had an impact on her.

Now, his life was owned and ruled by someone who rarely spoke, who rarely showed an emotion, who was, for all Taylor could see, mostly robotic, silently making her way through each day, allowing nothing in, allowing nothing out.

Cold and silent.

Like this van. Like the night.

Like the moon.

♦♦♦

JUST BEFORE DAWN, Taylor, now sitting sideways in the seat to stretch his legs, saw movement.

"Guys?" Syd and Zero turned, then saw it as well.

The Fed, still shifted, slinked back to the car, but slowly, ears flat, hunched.

Defeated.

Zero cursed and popped the door. She met him about fifty yards out. Syd said, "How much shit you think he's in?"

Taylor snorted. "You know what Zee's like. She can't hurt him, but she can still fuck him up."

The Fed approached Zero, lowering himself until, with the final few feet, he crawled on his belly. Then he stopped, put his snout on his paws.

Zero stood over him, arms crossed. They stayed like that for an uncomfortably long period of time. Syd and Taylor waited for the Fed to break, for Zee to lose it.

Instead, she bent, wrapped her hands around his snout, pulled his face up. Taylor saw her say a few short words to him. Then she shoved his snout away again, roughly.

He lowered his snout to his paws again, stayed in that position. She straightened, stood over him a few moments more, then turned and came back to the car.

She opened the door, got in, pulled the door closed again.

Taylor spun, sat forward. Syd looked out the window to the Fed, back to Zero. "What's the plan, Zero?"

"Let's go."

Taylor knew Syd was smart enough not to question Zero, but he still wanted to determine what was going on.

"We still headed to the same place?"

"We are."

"And…"

"And if Eli can make it there before we leave, he comes with us. If he doesn't, we start looking for another pack member."

"Fair enough."

Taylor wanted to ask where he'd gone, what he'd done, but watching Zero yank the seatbelt across and snap it into place, seeing the quick, jerky movements, the tightness of the muscles, the set of her face, there was no goddamn way he was going to ask her.

They'd find out eventually. He'd have to be content with that.

Syd dropped the car into gear and drove away.

Taylor watched the Fed until he disappeared. He didn't move a muscle.

CHAPTER FIFTEEN

JAKE SCRAMBLED UP from sleep as the key ratcheted in the lock. By the time the door swung open, she was upright and trying to fix her hair with one hand while furrowing the sleep from her eyes with the other.

As Zach walked in, sheepishly glancing over in Jake's direction, she realized it had to be almost morning. The sun wasn't up yet, but a fuzzy glance at her watch told her it was just after five in the morning. She reached over and turned on a light, squinting against the brightness. With the light on, Zach couldn't hide how embarrassed he obviously was, and she couldn't help the smirk that slid across her lips. He was cute, she couldn't deny it.

"Jake," he said, in a hushed but fervent tone. "I'm *so* sorry I'm so late. I—"

"No need to explain, Zach," she said, the smirk becoming a big smile. And there really wasn't. She knew what had happened. The poor guy finally got lucky for a change. "It's nice…to see you get out for a change," she said, lying through a fist-covered yawn.

Zach looked a little shaken, but she put that down to his embarrassment at showing up so late. She was about to say something about it, but then the woman walked through the apartment door.

Shorter, with a wild tangle of hair and a confident way of walking, she entered the apartment as though she owned it.

She rolled into the room, glancing sideways only to toss her jacket on the back of a chair. Jake didn't like the way her eyes scanned the entire room before settling on her.

"Hi, I'm Rainer," she said, extending a hand as a man would. "You're Jake." More a statement of fact, as though there was a challenge put out to tell her she was wrong. Jake put out her own hand and felt an unusual warmth in Rainer's confident handshake. While she'd had an instant dislike for Rainer as she came into the place, it faded fast, only to be replaced with…what? She still didn't really like her, but Jake found her magnetic. She couldn't not watch her. Her eyes were electric, her body thrummed with an ancient rumbling energy like a large, ornate church. Jake found herself staring at Rainer's mouth, just to see if it would move and grace her with more words. She realized she *wanted* this woman to talk to her.

She still didn't like her, and it wasn't lust she was feeling—though it almost felt that way in some peculiar, non-sexual manner—so Jake settled on respect. If she was a dog, she guessed this would be the point where she would roll over and offer up her belly, her throat.

As that thought sparked across her mind, she noticed Rainer's eyes widen briefly, then a smile rolled across her face, instantly transforming her. *She's really pretty when she smiles*, Jake thought. Then their hands released and Jake began breathing again, not realizing she had even been holding her breath.

"I'm just gonna…go…uh…" Zach sputtered.

"Yeah," Rainer said, as Jake watched her mouth, watched her perfect teeth flash behind expressive lips. "Go check on Sam while Jake and I chat."

Zach disappeared down the hall.

Rainer looked at Jake and said, "I'm sorry."

"For?"

"I'm not going to beat around the bush here. We have very little time, so I'll get right down to it. I didn't know you, so I didn't know you have feelings for Zach. If I had, I wouldn't have agreed to the date."

"I don't..."

"You do." It was a statement of fact, so clear and plain that there was no disputing it. "It's fine. He's a good guy. He likes you a lot too." She hesitated a moment, then said, "And you should know, what you're thinking happened between us?"

"No, I—"

"It didn't happen, Jake."

Jake, feeling like she'd been strapped into a rollercoaster, could only nod. But there was a big sense of relief, and even a measure of gratitude she now felt for this incredibly odd woman.

"A word of advice?"

Jake, still shocked, could only muster another nod.

"Don't hint to him, don't beat around the bush. Zach's the type to who you need to actually say the words. Make it clear. You can't leave it to interpretation with him or he'll always interpret away from himself. Explain it away."

Then she smiled and Jake felt like she'd just made a new friend. "Uh, thanks, I guess."

"You're welcome."

Zach came out and the look on his face instantly killed her good mood. He covered it quickly with a big, guilty smile that sat on his face like a mask, and under it was misery. There was a lot more going on here than him feeling guilty for choosing wild monkey sex—no, she reminded herself, Rainer said they didn't do that, and Jake believed her, so something else, something unexpected, had happened last night. Whatever it was, it was driving him nuts at having not come home to his daughter as usual. Wild monkey sex would be a lot lower on the Richter scale than he was currently running at.

"Hey, Jake," he said. "Thanks again. I'm really sorry about the—"

"Don't worry about it," she said. "No biggie. You know that."

"Listen, Jake," Zach said. "I'm going to…" She watched his eyes flick to Rainer's, as though Ray had been motioning to him. Jake imagined her doing the big, showy thumb-across-the-neck thing. *Ixnay on the alkingtay.* "I'm going to be taking a few days off work," he said. "So I can give you a break from the mutant."

"Zach, is there something going on?"

Again, he glanced over at Rainer. *What the hell is going on between these two? She's telling me to go for him but there's some deep shit happening between these two.*

"No," he said, obviously lying.

Jake knew she wasn't going to figure it out today. He'd tell her in his own time. "Okay, I'm just going to let myself out then, go grab a shower."

Then, without really knowing why she did it, she flipped her long hair over her shoulder, reached out, and hugged Zach, allowing herself one squeeze. He hugged her back, to her surprise. "Thanks for everything," he whispered in her ear.

They broke apart and Jake turned for the door. Glancing at Rainer, she mouthed a thank you. She snagged her keys from the tray by the door and left without looking back.

It wasn't until she was going down the elevator that she became aware of the stink of smoke from Zach, and suddenly she was very worried about him and Sam.

That last exchange had been more permanent than just goodbye.

♦♦♦

SAMANTHA WOKE UP smelling smoke and wondering if the apartment was on fire. Or maybe it was the guy in the next apartment trying to cook again?

Either way, she didn't like waking up to smoke. Smoke said danger. There was a small but demanding part of her that whispered it was going to happen again. Someone else was going to die.

She heard her father in the shower, and traced the smoke smell as coming from his room. Bed still made. A vintage suitcase from the sixties, all faux-leather and snaps and probably weighing a ton, sat yawning on the bed, like a patient in a dentist's chair. The smell came from a small pile of clothes tossed to the corner. The same clothes her dad had worn on his date last night.

Sam didn't know how she felt about that yet. Her dad made it clear that it was just a casual thing, nothing serious, and that Sam was the most important woman in his life. Had actually said that. *You're the most important woman in my life,* and that had made her feel a little better.

But his bed was made.

She hadn't met the girl he went out with, and figured that Dad was waiting to see if there was going to be a second date before he put Sam through the trauma of an introduction. That was cool with her, she really wasn't interested in having to deal with some bim—

Somebody walked by the bedroom door. Her dad was still in the shower. Who the fuck…?

Jake?

Had to be. Jake had been up in the night, the whole milk and *Exorcist* thing—and her dad's bed was still made—so Jake stayed overnight.

But Jake would have said something to Sam, would have noticed her standing in her father's bedroom. Whoever walked by her dad's bedroom hadn't even looked in.

Sam padded silently over to the door and angled her head to peek out. There was a woman squatting by the doorframe to Sam's bedroom. She seemed to be unaware that Sam wasn't even in the room, though the door was now open. She just rocked back on her haunches, fingers lightly caressing the frame of the door, her other hand to her lips, as though deep in thought.

"You must be Samantha," the woman said, jolting Sam a little. She hadn't moved or changed position in any manner that would give away she had noticed Sam. Yet, obviously, she had.

"Call me Sam," she said, stepping out into the hall. "Everyone does."

As Sam approached, the woman turned and stood. She wasn't much taller than Sam, and she didn't seem big or anything, but Sam got a feeling of *power* from her. She had a calmness about her that said to Sam that she wasn't afraid of anything. The woman held out her hand, and Sam took it. That feeling of power increased with the contact of skin on skin.

"I'm Rainer," the woman said, then paused slightly. She squinted her eyes down a little, as though Sam had been hiding something from her. "You can call me Rainer, Ray, or anything else you want to. I hope we can be friends. You're a very interesting girl." Sam watched Rainer frown, as though puzzled.

"I mean, from the stories your father's told me, you seem like an interesting girl." Then Rainer smiled and the world lit up. Sam found herself liking this woman, even though she really didn't want to. Couldn't trust her yet, though.

"That's an interesting poster for a young woman to have," Ray said, pointing.

"It's the Periodic Table. Atoms and shit. Dad says every question I ask him goes back to that. Kind of a joke thing."

Ray nodded. "Got it."

The shower dribbled to a stop, and the familiar sounds of Zach towelling off echoed out of the room.

"C'mon," Rainer said. "We don't want to catch sight of your dad's cheese in the wind." Sam wasn't exactly sure what Rainer had just said, but it was funny enough for her to smile. It also seemed to reassure her, that, even though Zach's bed was made, maybe nothing happened last night. Her guard slipped a few more notches.

♦♦♦

ZACH CAME OUT of the bathroom trying to wrangle his hair into some stylish shape. Though he had towelled himself and put on fresh clothes, he still felt damp, but so much cleaner. Things seemed much more in perspective now. He could adequately explain all the reasons he couldn't go with Rainer.

He passed through the living room and into the kitchen, where he'd heard Sam and Rainer chatting.

Actually chatting, like old friends. Sam could talk anyone's ear off, but she was a lot more territorial at home, and when the person seemed interested in her dad.

Sam looked up from her cereal at him. "You *so* need a fuckin' hairstyle, Dad," she said. Following right behind it was Rainer's throatier laugh.

"Sam! Language!"

Figures, he thought. *I finally find a woman who Sam likes, and she's the one who's going to leave. The Palmer luck, true to form.*

Then again, the one she likes is Buffy, the werewolf-hunting terminator. Zach smiled, as much at the last thought as at the two of them sitting at his kitchen table eating Frosted Flakes.

"I made us breakfast, even though it's still the middle of the friggin' night," Sam said. "Your shit's on the counter. All you gotta do is pour the milk on it." She dropped her head back and shovelled more crunchy flakes into her mouth. Rainer scooped the cereal to her mouth, smiling all the while.

"Thanks, Sam," Zach said with a sigh as he pulled the milk from the fridge.

Sam finished her cereal with some rapid-fire clinks of her spoon against the bowl.

"Done!" she said. "Gotta piss!"

"Sam!" Zach said, his eyebrows furrowing. "We have a guest. Watch your mouth!"

"Sor-ree." Sam drew the word out. Then softer, "Christ!"

"That's okay, Sam," Rainer said as she angled her head toward Sam's. In a stage-whisper, she said, "I gotta piss, too."

Zach rolled his eyes, and frustration tempered his smile. "Let Rainer go first. Then you have a shower while you're in there, honey."

"M'kay," Sam said, turning to Rainer. Her face scrunched up as she said, "Can you make it fast?"

Rainer placed her bowl in the sink and Zach watched the two of them head down the hall, their conversation too low to hear. Seconds later, he heard the toilet flush, and the faucet run as Rainer washed her hands. More low conversation, then Sam scooted into the bathroom. Zach saw Rainer stand at the end of the hall, a small smile on her face. Zach heard the toilet flush again.

"She's really seemed to tak—"

Rainer's smile fell from her face and her hand came up, palm out. *Just wait*, it said.

She stood like that for another half-minute. The shower started up, but still, she waited. Then, when they both heard Sam singing Alice Cooper's "I'm Eighteen," Rainer quietly twisted her hand around, palm up, and waggled her fingers, beckoning. "Come here," she said.

Zach rose and walked down the hall, one hand nervously patting his damp head. *She's in that mode again.* The same one he saw a few hours ago when they killed something.

Rainer's eyes never left him as he moved down the short hall, and as he got close, she crouched on her haunches.

"What?" Zach said, knowing enough to keep his voice lowered. It wouldn't penetrate the white noise of the shower.

Rainer said nothing, but Zach followed her eyes as her hand lightly caressed the doorframe to Sam's room. About two feet up, under Ray's calloused fingers, the paint had been scraped off, the wood slightly splintered in four straight, close lines.

Claw marks.

"They were here last night," she said. "They know who you are." Her eyes seemed to apologize as she spoke the next words.

"I don't know why they left Jake and Sam alive, but we all need to leave. Today. Now. And we have to take Jake with us."

Chapter Sixteen

"IF YOU CAN make it there before we go, I'll consider letting you remain with the pack."

That's what that self-righteous bitch had said to the Fed. As though the Fed was a child.

She expected the Fed to get all the way to the Farm just for the slim chance of a damn *maybe*? The Fed didn't think so. The Fed was not going to be the next Bo. Bo was a moron. The Fed was destined for great things. The Fed knew it. The Fed's mother had even said so.

Still said so, as a matter of fact. The Fed heard her talking to the Fed incessantly. Just like she did in life. Only, she obviously understood why she needed to be sacrificed, because now she was completely supportive and absolutely committed to helping the Fed succeed.

In fact, it had been the Fed's mother who had whispered to the Fed to do something to help bring down Bo's killers.

The Fed knew it was her. She was the only one who ever called the Fed "Ly-Ly." Over the years, others had called him "Eel" and "Eely" and "Oily" and "Elijah," but only the Fed's mother called the Fed Ly-Ly. She once joked that she called the Fed that so the Fed always told the truth. Her Eli wouldn't ever be able to Ly-Ly to her. Bad joke, but it had worked. The Fed always told his mother the truth.

So, as the other ones showed how weak they were, pissing themselves and rolling in the dust and dirt, the Fed had hunkered down. Yes, the Fed had felt it too, but it didn't seem to impact the Fed emotionally like it had the others. Hell, nothing impacted the Fed emotionally. Not when the Fed's father died. Not when either of the Fed's grandparents died. Not when the Fed's first and only pet dog died. Not even when the Fed's best friend Corey died.

Then again, the Fed had been the one to kill those last two. Corey had been his first person.

None of it bothered the Fed. None of it.

Didn't ever seem to bother the Fed's mother either. The Fed had told her everything and she only told the Fed what a perfect, special boy the Fed was.

When the others were rolling around like worms, the Fed had hunkered down and rode out the initial shot of pain. Then the Fed's mother had whispered in the Fed's ear. *You feel that, Ly-Ly? You feel that connection?*

The Fed had. Images, snatches of conversations, faces.

Names.

This connection between the wolves, it was a pain in the ass most of the time, but now, this time, it had done the Fed a solid.

Somehow, not only were the wolves connected, but seconds before Bo died, he had somehow connected with this bitch. This…Rainer.

Rainer.

Like they'd been…joined or something.

The Fed got frustrating glimpses inside her head, like a tightly focused beam of light, illuminating only small sections of a great room. Again, those frustratingly small hints.

But one of them was a gem. An image of a young girl. That one was a spotty, staticky connection. She knew of the girl, but had not met the girl, only knew her through some strange, weird image thing she'd gotten when she touched this guy she was with when Bo died.

But the girl, that was gold. The Fed knew she had a boy's name, but the actual name was one of the missing details. Though it wasn't really details, was it? It was more…impressions. Feelings. Wisps of knowledge, often without reference.

Still, the Fed had an image of the girl. She was connected to the guy Rainer was with. Important to him. And this guy, he had a name, Palmer, which always struck the Fed as a good name for someone who jerked off a lot. The connection between the two was a vague familial presence, but with the girl so young and the sense of the age of this Palmer person, it had to be a parent or a teacher. The sense of emotion removed the teacher element, there was too much attachment there. The Fed went with the assumption of parent.

And finally, the Fed had a scent. Or rather, a mixture of scents. A fast-food place? Yes!

It was slim, but it might be enough to find out how this girl might lead the pack to Bo's killer. And if the Fed could pull that off, he'd have Zero in his pocket. The Fed would be Zero's go-to. Syd and Taylor would be the Fed's subordinates.

With the Fed's mother whispering encouragement, the Fed ran off before they knew where the Fed had gone.

♦ ♦ ♦

BUT THEN, IT had all gone so wrong.

The Fed had found the restaurant, broken in, located a record of a Zachary Palmer, got the address, got to the apartment, and, after a harrowing—harrowing for anyone who wasn't the Fed—climb up the balconies, found the right one. This high up, the sliding door wasn't locked, though the Fed would have broken the window had the Fed needed to.

The Fed had paused briefly before the sleeping woman on

the couch, weighing if she might be this woman with a man's name, wondering if the memory was an older one, but no. Not her.

The Fed bypassed her, gliding down the hall like smoke.

She was in the first room the Fed checked. A small bookshelf above her bed held a bookend, cartoon balloon letters surrounded by small teddy bears. It said *SAM*.

The girl with the man's name.

The Fed would kill her now, kill the other one, find more information, and return to the pack as the conquering hero.

Except…

Except when the Fed went to make a move toward the girl, the Fed could not. Willing, demanding, *commanding* the Fed's treacherous body to carry out this death. And the Fed could not move forward to do it.

The Fed could move backward, sideways. The Fed's control resumed, as long as the intent wasn't to harm the girl.

The Fed's brow furrowed. The Fed thought, *Touch the bed.* The Fed touched the bed.

The Fed thought, *Touch her hair.* The Fed touched her hair, careful not to wake her.

The Fed raised the Fed's hand and brought it down to tear out her throat. The Fed's hand remained suspended above her, immobile.

No.

This couldn't be.

Then the Fed's mother was screaming at the Fed to get out get out get out. Still, the Fed needed to leave some sort of warning. The Fed needed to mark them as the Fed's.

Concentrating, the Fed shifted the fingers of one hand into a hybrid paw, enough to get the job done, then, slowly, deliberately, the Fed left a mark.

The Fed could have killed the woman on the couch—at least, the Fed thought the Fed could—but if the Fed was being honest, the Fed was too freaked out to even think about that until the Fed was back outside the apartment.

It took everything in the Fed to get back out again with the same care it took to come in.

The Fed's mother must have been angry and disappointed with the Fed. She hadn't said anything all the way back to Zero.

But Zero had.

Oh my, yes she had.

♦ ♦ ♦

NOW, HERE THE Fed was, in trouble with the pack leader, in danger of excommunication. The Fed needed to fix this. The Fed needed to make this right.

The Fed needed to find a way to kill that little bitch.

The Fed knew her now, had the scent of her. The Fed knew where she lived.

The Fed would watch her every move and find an opening.

The Fed could do this. The Fed *would* do this.

Part Two
Driven

"Life is a hideous thing, and from the background behind what we know of it peer daemoniacal hints of truth which make it sometimes a thousandfold more hideous."

The Call of The Cthulhu
H. P. Lovecraft

Second Interlude

SHE CAME IN one night and ordered a vanilla milkshake. Nothing else. After paying, she went to the back of the restaurant to the corner stall, as though she wanted to be able to see the entire place at a glance. Zach watched her every now and again because, well, she was attractive. She nursed the shake for a couple of hours, then left.

The next night, she was back again. Vanilla shake again. Same seat.

Then again the next night. And the next. And the next.

Just like that she became a regular.

Zach never heard her say any more than, "Vanilla shake, please," and "Thank you." Her voice was soft and silken, but Zach sensed there was something hard buried under it. He liked to watch her move to her regular booth, her movements spare and lithe. She didn't walk so much as prowl, moving with an easy grace. He'd never seen anyone move like that before.

She was small, maybe a few inches over five feet, and her hair was cut short, almost mannish, but it suited her. What hit Zach the hardest were her eyes. Big lashes framed deep-mahogany eyes. Those eyes took in everything at once, and flashed with an intensity Zach had never before encountered. He knew he could look into her eyes for hours.

Those eyes were not the eyes of a regular. Those eyes had purpose. They had a goal. Those eyes carried sadness like an old scar, healed maybe, but still visible, still itching every so often.

Zach found he was anticipating ten p.m. every evening he was on shift, because she would usually show then. And she did, every evening for two weeks.

Then, as abruptly as she had started, she stopped coming.

Zach found himself uncharacteristically worried about her. About someone he didn't know but, while he didn't actually know her, he felt he did. At least the part of her he made up in his head.

Then reason stepped back in and he chided himself. No one, not even the most diehard regular showed up three-hundred and sixty-five days a year. When she didn't show for the next couple of nights, he found himself trying to write her off. She was just in town on some business. She was gone now, and he would never see her again. Zach knew he would think about her for a few days, until the old routine crept back in, pushing the thought of her further and further down. One day, maybe a month, maybe a year from now, some word or thought would dredge up her memory long enough for him to wonder, and place her in the "whatever happened to…?" file.

But that's not what happened. As the days passed and she continued to be a no-show, Zach found himself thinking of her more and more, wondering what she did, where she was, what her name was. At home, in bed, he would lie awake for hours running different names through his head, never finding a proper match of name and face for her. He began to think of her as Vanilla, because Shake-Girl sounded too tawdry, too…slutty.

Then, Vanilla came back.

It had been two weeks since he had seen Vanilla last, but today was Friday, and his thoughts were more on getting through the close tonight and enjoying a rare weekend off. It was looking pretty good because the restaurant was dead this

Friday night. Shitty for business, but great for working. That all changed with the hiss of the pneumatic door opener.

Zach was in the back, balancing the cash drawers in the office—which was small by closet standards, let alone office parameters. Crammed into the four- by five-foot area was a filing cabinet, several cardboard file holders, a safe, and a desk mostly taken up by a decrepit, wheezing, ancient computer slightly more powerful than an abacus. Papers—week- and month-end reports, schedules, tally sheets, order forms, invoices, Post-It Notes, napkins, sandwich wrappers, and other things that could have been as old as the computer—littered every inch of available space. Paper cups with half-consumed pop and coffee lined the back edge of the desk like enemy troops waiting for their chance to topple over and destroy whatever document dared approach them. The room smelled of paper, grease, coffee, sweat, and cigarettes. Zach hated it, but company policy stated all cash drawers were to be counted in the office with the door closed.

Zach had finished with the last of the eight tills he had been left with, noted the proper form—steadfastly keeping it away from the enemy cups—and carefully tucked it into the tiny safe. He shut the safe door, but didn't lock it yet. He still had two more cash drawers and the final deposit to make out, but that could wait. He needed a breather, so he grabbed the three-inch ring of keys, clipped them back onto the bungee-clip on his belt and locked the office door behind him.

He hated carrying the keys on his belt because it was dorky. Dorky like a pocket protector with a calculator and fifteen pens was dorky. But it looked a hell of a lot better than having a three-inch metallic bulge in your pants pocket.

Zach was just approaching the front counter when he heard the door hiss open. Though it was a subtle sound, it immediately brought him to alert status. Customers were entering, so he stood a little straighter, and fixed his best customer-friendly smile on his face.

It fell off just as fast. Zach always thought of the restaurant as his when he was on duty. His office, his kitchen, his lobby. He was sure this was how Riker felt whenever Picard left him in charge of the bridge on the Enterprise. He had the conn.

His lobby had been invaded by a pack of teenagers. Most looked like they were under the influence of something, which meant there was probably going to be some puke to mop up before the night was over. There were at least fifteen of them, strolling in—into *his* lobby—like they owned the place, plunking down on the orange vinyl seats, laughing uproariously when the friction between ass and seat made a farting noise, putting their feet up on the bench seats, pounding on the tables. No, this wasn't good at all. In the back of his mind, he praised himself for locking the office door. If any of that money went missing, it would come off his paycheque.

Zach turned to Brian Turbenchy, his unofficial second-in-command, Riker to his Picard.

"Turbo," he asked, "where the hell did these guys come from?"

"I don't know," Turbo answered. "I thought I heard one of them mentioning getting turfed from a party down the street. Something about breaking a picture window or something."

"Greaaaaaaat," Zach said.

Another customer entered the store. He was more cartoon than human. Stick thin, with a shock of clown-like, shrieking red hair, the teen walked across the lobby, oblivious to the noise and antics around him as he headed for the washrooms. As he passed Zach and Turbo, his head swung around to face them and his expressionless face suddenly twisted up as a hyena-like laugh exploded from him. Then his head swung back around and he continued on his way as though nothing had happened. Zach watched as he hit the entrance to the washrooms. As the door swung closed, Zach heard another muffled hyena laugh echo off the tiles.

His palms flat on the counter, Zach dropped his head. "Damn," he whispered. He knew what he had to do. Zach was one of the more popular managers in the restaurant, and one of the reasons for that was that he never forgot what it was like to be the guy who had to do all the shit jobs. When Zach was promoted, he swore he would never ask anyone to do something he himself wouldn't do. He'd always stuck to it, and earned the reputation as a fair manager.

Well, now he was going to have to go into the guy's washroom and kick out the hyena boy. None of the people in the restaurant had ordered anything so, technically, they were all loitering. That meant he could turf them all.

Well, let's start with the guys in the can, Zach thought. He would have to do it because there was no way he was going to send anyone else in. He unhooked the big, dorky ring of keys, twirled them around his finger a couple of times.

"Turbo, take these," he said, tossing the keys to the boy. "If you see any fur flying, go back into the office, lock the door behind you, and call the cops." Turbo nodded his almost too good-looking head, and held the keys in a firm grasp, as though showing how up to this task he really was.

Zach tried to keep it light, but he really didn't want to go into the shitter. "Okay, boys," he said in a bad John Wayne. "Awm jis' gonna go in thar and kick the shit outta the can. Y'all stay back and cover me. Got me a king-size can of whoop-ass t' open." He swiped at his nose and moseyed to the door. It got a couple of chuckles from the guys back at the sandwich prep counter, but it didn't really fool anyone. It didn't bolster his courage as much as he'd been hoping it would, either, dammit.

Zach passed through the door and was in an alcove with a door on every side of him. Behind him was the door he had just passed through. To his right, the door to the lobby. Straight ahead, the women's washroom. To his left, the men's washroom. He could hear a few voices in there. Maybe he should get someone to come with him? *Nah, how pussy would that look?*

Taking a deep breath, Zach pushed on the door to the men's washroom and entered.

The washroom wasn't big. One urinal, one toilet just beyond it. On the other wall, a sink, a stained and cracked mirror, and a paper towel dispenser. Below it, an overflowing garbage can.

Currently, there were five people taking a leak in Zach's washroom; one at the urinal, one at the toilet, two at the sink—Christ, Zach had seen people brushing their teeth in that sink!—and a final one using the drainage hole in the middle of the tiles on the floor. He wasn't too successful with his aim, and the sheer volume of piss was both breathtaking and a little concerning.

Two hands on the thing and he still can't hit the target! Zach thought.

Not having encountered a situation quite like this before, Zach was at a loss for words so he stupidly threw out the first phrase that popped into his head.

"What the hell is going on in here?"

The cartoon hyena-boy looked at Zach from his position at the sink and spewed his manic laugh yet again. Zach was really beginning to wonder if that one was capable of coherent speech.

The other guy at the sink, dressed all in black and made up with black, chunky eyeliner, addressed him in the mirror. "We're takin' a piss, genius. You really need to step up the number of shitters in here."

Jesus, didn't The Cure go out with the eighties? Zach thought, looking at the macabre figure's back.

"You guys really need to learn a bit more bladder control." Zach turned to the pimpled-faced kid pissing into the drain. "And you! Stop pissin' on my floor, for chrissakes!"

With any normal customer, Zach's language would have been much more passive, but these weren't customers, and normal customers didn't piss in his sink or on his floor. Then again, he rarely had customers looking like a reject from *The Crow* movie, either.

Zach desperately attempted to keep his anger in check, and he was trying his best to abide by the unspoken men's washroom rule of not looking at anyone's penis. Drain-Boy wasn't making that easy, standing there with his camouflage pants and frayed, greyish underwear pulled all the way down to the tops of his Doc Martens, his hairy legs gleaming white in the sickly fluorescent glow. His back was arched forward like a little child, and he had both hands on his dick as though it needed that much control to miss the target by half a fucking foot. Being a typical male, it was taking forever for any of them to finish draining the vein.

Drain-Boy simply stared at him with the blissed-out look of someone who really needed to go bad. The kind of piss that's so joyous in its release that it's almost a religious experience.

The look was so unabashed and comical, Zach never saw The Cure come at him. It happened so fast, Zach didn't have time to register anything other than the fact that he could no longer breathe. The Cure had his hands on Zach's neck, much like Drain-Boy's hands encircled his own cock.

Aw fuck, I bet he never washed his hands after that piss, Zach thought, and immediately wondered why that was his chief concern at present. He was jammed up against the wall, standing on his toes, the tiles cool on the back of his head and the hands tight about his throat.

Why the hell did I give Turbo those keys? Why did I walk in here empty-handed? He could have grabbed the key ring like brass knuckles, or pushed keys out between each finger in his fist. One punch with either of those and they'd know who was boss. Hell, he knew of one of the other managers who always brought a clipboard with him. "One shot to the ribs with this thing, edge on? Yeah, they reconsider real fast," he always said.

But me? Empty-handed. Then again, he hadn't seen the four early arrivals, and had come in expecting one hyena. He hoped fervently that the cops were on their way. *I'm an idiot.*

"Listen, fuckface—"

The Cure never got to finish his thought, because the door to the washroom opened.

"Hello boys," Zach heard a voice say. He couldn't quite place it, and without being able to turn his head, he could only see the faint blurred shape reflected in the beige tiled wall. A dark blob and...Converse running shoes? Black-and-white, going by the amorphous tile image. "Zach, is there a problem here?" The voice was calm.

"Get the fuck outta here," The Cure spit. "Ladies is to your right. Now fuck off!"

"Aw, now, didn't your mama tell you it's not nice to swear in front of a lady?" the owner of the running shoes asked in a soft voice. "And learn your right from your left, Dracula. It's on my left when I'm walking back toward it. Dumbass."

By now, everyone in the room was finished and zipped. Even Drain-Boy had his pants pulled back up to mid-hip. Zach figured he knew who was standing there, but really didn't want to think about it. He didn't want to be right, because she was going to get herself killed.

"Din'tjoo hear me? FUCK! OFF!"

"I got a better idea," the soft voice said. It had to be her. "Why don't you, me, and your dumbass friends take a walk around the back so I can kick all your asses?" Her voice was soft and sweet, and commanded more attention because of it.

Zach heard an underlying strength in there, like a hammer wrapped in silk, that told him it would be unwise to cross her.

"You an' us out back?" The Cure was incredulous. "You with my dick in your mouth? Yeah, I can deal with that." He dropped Zach and he fell to the floor, sucking in big whooping breaths, his hand to his own throat. He looked up and, yes, it was confirmed.

It was Vanilla. She stood relaxed in the doorway, one hand holding the door open, the other fisted and resting on her hip. She had on a pair of black, loose-fitting jeans and black T-shirt. And yes, black-and-white Converse running shoes. A long black coat covered the ensemble. One of those non-shiny, oiled leather ones with the split up the back like the movie cowboys wore. The long riders. The split was for the horse. Zach briefly wondered if Vanilla had a horse. Nothing would surprise him at this point.

Nobody moved.

"What, are you scared of me?" Vanilla taunted. "What about you, army guy?" she said, addressing Drain-Boy. "You pull your pants down so all the boys can get a good look at your pimply ass? Or are you really that proud of your three inches?"

Drain-Boy blushed and hiked his pants up another inch. He looked as though he was about to retort, but she dismissed him with a wave. She turned back to The Cure.

"And you! Dracula! What's with the eyeliner? You making up for"—her left hand shot out—"a needle dick, too?" The Cure went white. In Vanilla's hand, Zach saw something long, thin, and shiny. It looked like a car antenna. Before they started building them into the windows of cars. When she had shot out her hand, it had extended and slapped up against the crotch of The Cure's pants, impacting his scrotum.

"You, you, you, you, you, and me," she said, pointing to each in turn. "Outside. Now." Then she turned and ran.

The door barely began to swing shut when Drain-Boy was on his way, hitching his pants up with one hand. The others followed, one lashing out with a booted foot and catching Zach in the ribs on the way by. The Cure hobbled out, still holding his tender nuts, bringing up the rear.

The door finally did swing shut as Zach fell to his unkicked side. *Oh, there's at least two broken ribs there.* He took a shuddering breath. *Oh yeah, at least two.*

Turbo burst into the room, keys jangling. "Holy shit, Zach! What happened?"

"Tell ya...later," Zach answered. "Call cops...'Nilla's gonna get killed."

Turbo moved to get Zach to his feet. "No!" Zach barked. "Cops...first!"

Turbo hesitated. Dipped as though to pick Zach up, stood back up, dipped again, then rose and ran for the phone. Zach watched the door swing shut yet again, and did his best to keep his feet out of Drain-Boy's pool of piss.

♦♦♦

FIVE MINUTES LATER, Zach was up and back behind the counter. He was getting sharp pains every time he walked, or even took a breath, but at least he was up and mobile. When the rest of the teens in the store heard the police had been called, they vanished.

Zach yelled—as best he could with his ribs—at Turbo and a couple of the other employees to get their asses out of the store and try to save Vanilla. Then stopped when he heard the pneumatic hiss of the door opening, and a higher-pitched keening behind it.

Vanilla came in, calm as could be, dragging The Cure by his hairsprayed tangle of crusty hair. His feet kicked, trying to get traction, trying to lessen the tension on his scalp, but the girl's—*the woman's*, Zach corrected himself, *the woman's*—pace was just that much too fast for him.

She stopped in front of the counter as though she was about to order up a combo meal and, with only her left arm, cranked up on The Cure's hair until he spun around on his knees, his chin level with the rounded orange curve of the counter.

"Myron…" She smiled as she hesitated. She was looking at Zach with a bemused expression that made her remarkably attractive. "Myron has something to say to you, Zach." She gave a vicious yank on his hair. Zach saw the scalp lift at least a couple of inches off his skull, looking like a tiny circus tent with all the spires. "Don't you, needle dick?" Her eyes never left Zach's.

Tears streamed from his eyes, mascara streaking his cheeks. Blood flowed from his nose, snot smeared his lips. His dyed-black hair stuck to the mess, adding to the overall ambience.

"Apologize." Still her voice was soft and sweet, but both Zach and Myron jumped at the sound.

Myron's mouth opened, showing a remarkable lack of teeth, but he hesitated as his tongue explored the newest excavations.

"I. Said. Apologize." But she never gave him the chance. Her left arm pistoned forward and slammed his abused face into the counter, leaving a reddish-black smear on the surface. Her expression never changed, not even a tightening of the mouth.

"Ahh…" said Myron, outright crying now. "Ahh…aaahm thorrreeeee!"

"Good boy." She smiled again. "Now. Get lost." Her arm arced out straight from her side, and Myron tumbled to his side, got his hands under him—Zach noticed two of the fingers didn't seem to quite touch the floor, preferring to point up at strange, awful angles—and he slipped, running for the door.

Watching his sorry departing ass, Zach said, "Geez, I…" as he ran his hand through his hair, not knowing what to say.

"I'm Rainer," she said. She reached for a couple of napkins, wiped her hands, clearing most of the blood, and stuck one out.

Zach reached out his own and shook her hand. She had a firm, pleasant grip. Her hand felt much larger than it really was.

"Thank you, Rainer. I owe you."

She nodded once, economical. *Yes you do*, that nod said.

"I'm going to leave before the police arrive. I'd prefer you didn't mention me if you don't mind, Zach."

Zach looked around at his staff. They were all nodding their heads. Every one of them seemed to be awestruck by Rainer. He turned back and nodded himself. "No problem. You were never here."

"Thanks. Listen, can I get a vanilla shake?"

"Absolutely!" As Zach poured the shake, Turbo went to work on the bloodied counter and the others brought out mops to clean the floors. Zach handed her the cup and watched as she grabbed a straw, then calmly walked out the opposite door to the one Myron had vacated.

Zach looked down at the counter. "Jesus," he said.

There was the exact change for the milkshake stacked neatly beside the cash register. He shook his head as he scooped the change.

"Rainer," Zach said, rolling the syllables over his tongue, enjoying the feel.

It didn't strike him until much later that he'd never actually told her his name.

He figured she must have heard one of the employees use it.

CHAPTER SEVENTEEN

RAINER MADE ZACH leave his car behind. "No way we'll make it where we need to go in your shitbanger," she said. "No offence."

"None taken," Sam said. "Dad's craptacular car is lucky to make it back and forth to work every day. I keep telling him he needs a new set of beleaguered wheels."

Rainer instead offered up her SUV. "It's a pig on gas, but it gets me where I need to go."

"And where's that?" Zach asked.

"Florida."

So that's what he'd heard after Bo had died. *Florida* not *floored.*

Sam just said, "Yes!"

♦♦♦

IT TOOK A fair amount of convincing for Jake. They called her back to Zach and Sam's apartment to talk to her. In the end, it was Sam who convinced her.

"Remember last night?" Sam said. "When I got the drink?"

"Yeah," Jake said. "Of course."

"Well, I didn't tell you last night, but I figured someone—well, some*thing*—was in the apartment."

"What?" Jake said. "You didn't tell me that!"

"Well duh, that's what I just said."

"Why didn't you say something?"

"You freak too easy with that shit, Jake, it's a given."

Jake didn't respond. Sam knew she had her there.

"Besides," Sam said. "By the time you woke up, the feeling was gone and I thought all was cool." She reached over and took Jake's hand. "Then Rainer found this." She pulled and Jake rose and followed her to the mark.

"Rainer and Zach say we have to go. They said it's important for you to come, too." Then Sam pulled herself in to hug Jake. "I already had something bad happen to my mom. I don't want anything bad to happen to anyone else." She looked up at Jake.

Jake met her gaze, then leaned down and kissed her forehead.

"Nothing's gonna happen to me, mutant." She sighed. "Okay, I'll go with you guys."

Sam smiled and hugged her again.

Then Jake pulled back. "Just remember, though. I have a new photoshoot booked in a couple of weeks. We need to be back by then or someone's gonna get their ass kicked." She turned to look at Zach and Rainer standing at the end of the hall.

"I'm looking at you, Zach," Jake said. But she was smiling.

♦♦♦

TWO HOURS LATER, they were packed and on the road, heading south. A day later, they checked into adjoining rooms in a hotel near Jacksonville. Sam immediately begged to go for a swim.

Zach said, "Aw, honey, I don't know if that's such a good idea."

"Of *course* it's a good idea," Sam said. "We're in beleaguered *Flor*ida, Dad."

Jake said, "I could take her down, get her out of your hair for a couple of hours." She looked at Rainer. "I'm guessing we needed to come here for a specific reason. I'm guessing you guys need to discuss some stuff..."

"Without the little kid around," Sam said. "Works for me, as long as Jake promises to keep at least some of her naughty bits covered. For. A. Change."

Jake threw her the hairy eyeball. Sam shrieked delightedly and Jake chased her into the adjoining room, then closed the door so they could get changed. Five minutes later, Jake popped her head back through the door. "We're heading down now. You need us, we'll park our stuff right below the balcony." Their room looked out on the pool, three floors below.

"Sounds good," Zach said.

Jake closed the door behind her. They heard Sam's excited jabbering fade as they headed down the hall.

"So, what do we need to talk about?" Zach asked.

♦♦♦

A HALF-HOUR LATER, Rainer rolled her sweating, naked body off Zach's and collapsed beside him on the still-made bed.

"Goddamn," Zach said. "What brought that on?"

"Did you not want to?"

"You see me resisting? Complaining in any way?"

"I guess I just...I needed to be close to someone again. It's been a hell of a long time, Zach."

"What made you like this? Can I ask that?"

"Yes, you can ask that. You can ask anything." Rainer let out a long breath. "It just... That's a long story."

"If it's too personal..."

"No, it's not that. It's...well...I've never really told anyone but my ex about this before now. And, well, now he's my ex."

"That bad?"

Rainer turned on her side, propped her head up on a hand. "It involves werewolves, Zach. Mystical, mythological shape-changing feral creatures that shouldn't exist, but do. Yeah, it's bad."

She told him a story about her family. Her mother, her father, her younger brother and sister. She'd been an early addition to the family unit. A mistake, she'd always assumed, though her parents denied it. Still, they waited almost eight years before they had her brother, another three for her sister.

Rainer had been long out of the house and married when the attack came. It was about three years ago.

"The cops told me the prevailing theory was that a pack of dogs, or maybe wolves, had somehow gotten into the house and managed to kill everyone inside." She had been staring out the window, but now she turned to Zach. "They said there was no way a person could have been responsible for the wounds they found on my family."

"Jesus," Zach said. "So—"

"So, that's how my entire family was wiped out in one horrible night. Erased, Zach. Gone."

She was silent for a long time, her fingers picking idly at the comforter on the bed. She looked almost casual, bored, but Zach saw the tight line of her mouth. He gave her the time she needed.

"The story never sat right with me," she said. "And it didn't help that I had this thing that I do."

"Thing?" Zach asked.

"You've seen it in action. I know you have." She smiled. "It's funny, the lengths some will go to, trying to explain it away logically."

"What thing?"

"I can"—she reached out, lightly touched Zach's chest with her fingertips—"touch people and, when I do..."

And just like that, it clicked for Zach. "You pick up things about them," he said. "Names and things?"

"I can pick up more than that, but yes."

"That how you got my name that time you beat the snot out of those guys?"

"I knew that a couple of weeks before. You put change in my hand, your fingers brushed my palm."

"Huh. Cool." She looked at him. "So that's how you knew that guy's name was Walter? The guy at the gas station? And what he was talking about?"

She nodded.

"You get all that stuff just by reaching out"—he raised his hand—"and touching someone?" He lightly brushed her breast. Her eyes closed for a moment, brought her own hand up over his, moved it to a better spot.

"What do you get"—she saw his smile, slapped his hand lightly—"I'm being serious here," she said. His smile dimmed slightly, but stayed. "What do you get when you touch me? I don't mean any images, but more, I don't know, feelings, emotions, information?"

"I get that you're very guarded."

"No, I think you're getting that from what you already know of me." She paused. "Aside from dropping change in my hand, and picking something out of my eye, you never touched me before an hour ago. Not in any meaningful way. I know it's weird, but think about that first kiss we had."

He closed his eyes. "Okay."

"Now, try and subtract you out of it. Think just of me."

"Okay," he said, but sounded less sure.

"Can you tell me one thing you *knew* from that kiss?"

"I knew you wanted me." He opened his eyes, made a face. "As conceited as that sounds."

"No, no, see, that's layering you back on. You're right. I did want you."

"Okay."

"Now, that's a little like what I get, just more intense."

"But names and stuff?"

"I said it was more intense."

"You get it from everyone?"

"Pretty much." She sighed and reluctantly pulled his hand away from her. "So, that's why I probably come across as a little cold. And it's why I have to slow down every so often."

"The whole sitting and being one with the world thing?"

"You're making fun of me, but that's closer than you think." She rolled back again, her breasts entrancing him. She crabbed her fingers, scooped them toward her face. "All this stuff comes in. Sometimes I just need to process it, or garbage it."

"And you do that by sitting?"

"I've learned to make the world go quiet," she said. "When I push everything away, all I feel is the stillness of the ground beneath me."

"Some guru teach you this?"

"No, *I* taught me this."

They fell silent while Zach took all this in. Then he said, "Okay, sorry, I think I derailed you a bit. You were telling me about your family, what happened, then mentioned your thing."

"Right," she said. "My thing." She explained that it just made things harder, because whenever she talked to the investigating officers, she knew they were, for the most part, bullshitting her.

"Bullshitting you in what way?"

"They were pinning the whole thing on an animal attack only because they had no other explanation. Hell, I knew that with*out* using my thing." Zach gave her a look. "Seriously. How many wild dog attacks have you heard of where the entire family is killed and they've come into a suburban house to do it?"

"None."

"Right. Then there was the other wrinkle."

"What's that?"

"They were going on the assumption that my brother was dragged from the scene for a later meal."

"Why's that?"

"Because they never found him."

"Shit." Then, as the information seeped in, he said, "But wouldn't that also kind of, I don't know, make him a suspect?"

"Definitely."

"And?"

"And the cops got nowhere."

"Let me guess," Zach said. "This is where the Rainer I know now kicked in? Started somehow using your thing?"

"Pretty much on the money." She shook her head and Zach saw a tear slip from the corner of her eye and run toward her ear and into her hair. "I had a good husband, a beautiful daughter—"

"You've got a *daughter*?"

"Had, Zach. Her name's April." Her voice low and sad. "But she's not mine anymore."

Zach let it go.

"I had a job. I had a life." Her hands searched the air in front of her, grasping at nothing. "But none of it meant anything. At least, for a while there, none of it meant more to me than finding out what happened to my family."

"What did you do?"

"I became obsessed." She took a deep breath, let it out slowly. "I completely neglected my own family—the one that was still alive and still needed me—to go into some of the shittiest, seediest places you can imagine, just to touch people, read them, to find out what the hell happened."

"And I'm assuming you did?"

"I did. Long story short, I finally managed to touch the right...contact. I found out a hell of a lot in that one touch. That it had been shifters who got them. Still, I guess I got lucky in a way."

"How's that?"

"Had my family just been a meal, I likely never would have found out what happened. I mean, can you remember what you ate last week?"

Zach just shook his head, but kept quiet, allowing her to go on.

"Right. The difference here was one of them had become a shifter."

"One of them?" Zach had lost the thread. "One of…shit, one of your family? Your brother?"

"Yeah," she said. "My brother. Taylor."

Zach felt bad just staring at her, knew it likely made her uncomfortable, but he didn't know what the hell to even say at this point.

She had a brother who was a werewolf.

She hunted and killed werewolves.

"Are you hunting your brother?"

"Yes, I am," she said. "Him and his pack. The pack that Bo once belonged to."

"And when you find them?"

"I'm going to kill them all, Zach," she said. "Every last one of them."

♦♦♦

SHE SAT UP, swung her legs off the bed. "We really should get dressed," she said. "Don't want Sam and Jake walking in on us like this."

She gathered up her clothes and Zach took the time to just watch her as she moved around the room. She sensed him watching her and turned. "What?"

"Just watching you."

"Zach," she said.

"Rainer," he said.

She sighed, but he suspected he knew what she was avoiding. "I know," he said.

"You know what?"

"I know you want to tell me not to fall for you, or get too close to you, or something like that. That you hunt creatures of the night and it's dangerous for anyone to care for you and boogah boogah and blah blah blah."

"It may be boogah boogah and blah blah blah," she said, "but it's essentially true."

"How about we just see where it takes us over the next few days until this shit's over with, then decide what to do from there?"

"Well, that's part of the issue, Zach," she said, grabbing the last of her clothes. "This shit's never done."

She looked at him with an expression he couldn't quite read, then headed into the washroom.

♦ ♦ ♦

SAM AND JAKE came up about twenty minutes later. Instead of going out, they ordered in pizza.

"So, what's the plan?" Jake asked.

Rainer told them that, much as they hated to split up at a time like this, Rainer needed more information and Zach would be able to serve as an extra set of eyes for her.

"What about us?" Sam asked.

"You'll be here," Rainer said. "Jake, you ever used a gun?"

Jake shook her head.

"Knife?"

"Just to cut my steak," she said.

Rainer told her she'd prefer to leave her a gun, but had concerns that Jake may not use it when she needed to.

"You mean if slavering wolves break in again?"

"Basically."

"No problem."

"It won't kill them, and if you don't hit a good spot, you may just piss them off," Rainer said.

"Then tell me how to kill them."

"That's...a really hard thing to do." Rainer stopped, looked hard at Jake. "Don't think of these thinks as normal animals. They look and smell and sound like wolves—goddamn big wolves—but they're not. They're supernatural in the truest sense of that word. They are governed by forces beyond current scientific understanding. They are above and beyond the laws of nature."

"You're saying I can't kill them?"

"I'm saying you'd be goddamned lucky to kill them. But you can make it so fucking hard for them that they maybe reconsider."

Jake thought that over for a moment, looked over at Sam. Then, reaching some internal decision, she nodded. She returned the hard look to Rainer. "Give me the gun," she said. "I'll take the chance. Tell me how to make them reconsider."

Rainer handed her a gun, showed her how the clip and safety worked, got her to dry fire it a couple of times to get the feel of it. Then she ensured there was a chambered round and a full clip.

"Don't hesitate to use it." Rainer pointed to the door and then turned one-hundred-eighty degrees and pointed at the balcony doors. "Anything that doesn't call first before coming through either door, you shoot."

She switched the gun to her left hand, used her empty right to illustrate on Zach. "Aim centre-mass to slow them down, then—if you have a clear shot—a couple to the face. Blind them if you can, but go for the brain. It won't kill them, but it'll fuck them up."

"Got it."

Rainer handed off the gun. Her hand made brief contact with Jake's and she knew she did get it. Rainer nodded to Zach.

"Let's go," she said. "Sooner we get there, sooner we get back."

Chapter Eighteen

THE FED DIDN'T know what the Fed was expecting, but it wasn't to end up chasing this group south to Florida.

Because that's where the Fed was supposed to be heading anyway. The Fed was supposed to meet the Fed's pack there.

The humans were heading toward the Fed's pack. Was it luck, or deliberate? What the hell did this pack of humans know that the Fed didn't?

The Fed followed them to the hotel. The Fed watched the two from the apartment—Sam, the younger girl, and the older, tattooed one. They stayed near the pool the entire time. Far too many people to do anything except watch them.

The Fed didn't like that tattooed one, the way she flaunted her body. The Fed was sure it was likely considered a desirable body, but she'd cheapened it with all the drawings and words. That large black hand on her shoulder made the Fed feel a little queasy for some reason.

But she was a skanky bitch anyway. A woman the Fed's mother whispered in the Fed's ear about. Called her a whore, though she pronounced it "hooer." *She's a wanton woman, Ly-Ly. Just a hooer.*

The Fed knew the Fed's mother was right. She wore a bathing suit that was highly inappropriate for any woman to be seen in. *Far too low on the hips, far too high around the buttocks. And the top is barely more than a couple of small patches, barely enough to…*

The Fed had to stop. The Fed's mother would get irritated if the Fed watched too long.

Instead, the Fed watched the little girl.

What is it about her? Why is the Fed so powerless around her?

Didn't matter. The Fed had a plan. The Fed knew what the Fed would do if the Fed couldn't kill her.

In fact, the Fed had begun to revise the plan a little anyway.

Originally, the Fed had planned to simply kill all four of them and be done with it. But now, with the Fed's mother helping him, the Fed had decided to consider something that, for weaker humans, may be worse than death.

The Fed had decided the Fed would kill the girls, and let the woman and the man—this Zachary Palmer—live a life of failure and pain, knowing they couldn't stop the Fed from doing anything the Fed wanted.

It would put the Fed in the dominant position. The power position.

The Fed's mother approved.

Even better, a few hours later—hours of that hooer flaunting her sex shamelessly before the two of them finally headed back to the room—the Fed's patience was rewarded.

Palmer and the older woman left the hotel.

Left their loved ones open and vulnerable for the Fed to exploit.

How would Zero ever be able to deny the Fed a rightful place in the pack once the Fed finished them?

The Fed's mother whispered to the Fed about maybe having the Fed's own pack very soon. Zero couldn't survive forever, could she?

Of course not.

But the Fed could. The Fed's mother said, *You could, Ly-Ly. You could live forever.*

The Fed could find no fault with her logic.

CHAPTER NINETEEN

THEY PARKED THE SUV on the street. Zach felt his bowels loosening. "Ray, where the hell are we?"

"Northside."

"I'm assuming this isn't the best of areas in Jacksonville?"

"You might make that assumption."

"Is the car safe here?"

"It's going to have to be."

"Where is it we're going?"

"Get out and I'll show you."

The last thing Zach wanted to do was get out. But they really had no choice, according to Rainer. And right now, all Zach could do was trust her and follow her lead. It had gotten her this far, hadn't it?

He closed the door, Rainer hit the remote and the car beeped. Zach was sure that was probably like putting a flashing neon sign on the car that said, "DO NOT STEAL." He came around the front of the car and met her on the sidewalk.

"Okay," Rainer said. "This is going to seem a little weird, but just go with it, okay?"

"You're freaking me out and I don't even know what the hell you're talking about."

Instead of explaining, she just hooked an arm and moved closer to the buildings. Zach followed.

"All right," she said. "Hold my hand and, whatever you

do, no matter how weird it gets, no matter what you see, don't let go until I tell you to, okay?"

The fuck? Then, *Shit, she's probably getting all this. Don't think don't think don't think.* "Okay."

"Yeah, you got it right."

"What do y—"

"Don't think."

Before he could respond, Rainer slid a hand experimentally into a two-inch gap between a pharmacy and a clothing store that was empty and had a *For Lease* sign in the window. Then she pushed her hand in further, up to the elbow.

She leaned forward and put her head into the same two-inch space. Her body quickly followed and Zach was dragged forward into the same space. He watched with widening, panicked eyes as her forearm slipped away and her hand, still firmly clasping his, and both far too wide for the small space, disappeared into the gap. Then his face came closer. *Holy shit holy shit this isn't gonna be good.*

And then he was in the bar. He went to speak, but he felt a tightening on his hand, warning him to clamp down and shut up. He clamped down, shut up, and looked around.

It was a bar. As simple as that. Dark panelled wood, neon beer lights, a long bar along the far wall, mirrored shelves of alcohol behind it, racks of glasses and beer mugs off to the sides.

It was dark, it was smoky, it was loud. It smelled of spilled beer and sweat and cigarettes and a heavier, muskier odour.

Like wet dog.

She turned back to him and raised her eyebrows in a "you okay?" look.

He nodded.

She raised their clasped hands between them and looked at them pointedly, then back to him. Then she released his hand.

Okay, he thought. *We got through that okay.*

Now what?

Rainer moved toward the bar, angled toward the far corner. Conversations didn't stop around them, but they definitely paused for a quick scan of the newest patrons, then resumed. Rainer took a stool that afforded her good sightlines across the large room.

The bartender, all gut and wild Einstein hair and wilder beard, gave her a sour scowl, but brought two mugs of draft in response to her two upraised fingers.

As he slid them across, he said, "I suggest you drink up and get out if you know what's good for you."

"Thanks for the tip," Rainer said. "Here's another one. Don't tend bar if you're a pussy." She took a deep gulp of the beer. "Thanks."

The scowl never left, but the bartender did, moving to serve others.

Zach leaned over. "What are we doing?"

"*We* aren't doing anything." Her eyes never left the tables. "*You* are watching for any potential assholes who want to start something. You're my extra eyes, remember?"

"Got it. So, what are *you* doing?"

"Looking for someone."

"You got something from B—"

She put two fingers to his lips. "No names. No talk."

He nodded and looked around the bar. That's when he realized exactly how many of the patrons were actually staring right back at him.

Shit.

He just needed to remain cool. He figured it was a good plan to figure out where the exits were, in case they needed to make a quick escape. He glanced around.

What the fuck? He looked around, one more time. Slower. More deliberately.

There were no fucking exits to this place. Four walls. No doors. Not even to a washroom.

How the hell does that work?

He looked back to where he thought they came in. No sign of an entrance there.

That's when he felt the worry that had been there all along go up several notches.

When Rainer said, "Found him. Follow my lead, but don't say anything unless there's an attack coming that I don't know about," the worry scaled even higher. *Funny,* he thought. *Didn't think it could go that high.*

He drained the beer, hoping for a small fortification of courage, then followed Rainer over to a table. He watched her hand dig into a pocket, but didn't see what she came out with.

Three men sat around the table, with an empty fourth chair pushed tight to the table. Rainer patted the middle one on the back, then walked around and pulled the empty chair out and sat down. "Boys," she said.

Zach, having no place to sit, chose to stand just behind her and slightly to one side. There were occupied tables behind him that worried the shit out of him, but he fought the urge to turn around every three seconds.

The three men at the table stopped and stared at Rainer. She grabbed a mug, looked in it to ensure there were no butts, turned it upside down to empty the swill in the bottom, then grabbed the pitcher and poured herself half a glass.

This was all observed in stony silence by the three men. It gave Zach a chance to scan each man in turn. One of them was normal-sized, maybe an inch or two taller than Zach. One was quite large and bulging with muscles. Easily a significant span over six feet.

The third man was simply a freak of nature. He was bigger than any human had a right to be. Easily seven-and-some feet tall, easily well into three-hundred pounds, bearded and bushy-haired, with massive growths sprouting above his eyes and from his sideburns. He was damn near a wolf already, without the shift thing going on.

This is like some twisted perversion of the Goldilocks story. Only the choices are much too big, holy shit, and Oh My Fucking God.

"The hell do you and your little bitch want?" the OMFG one said.

"Information," Rainer said, calmly. She took another sip of the beer. "The draft in this place is shit. What is this? Wolf piss?"

OMFG placed his hands on the table, prepping to rise. Much Too Big held out a palm. "Information on what?"

"Zero's pack."

"You want information on a pack."

"Yeah."

"What makes you think you're going to get it?"

"I always get it, Shakes," she said. To his credit, the large guy didn't react to his name, and Zach was getting used to the trick now.

Then she opened her hand and let some small objects patter across the table. Bo's teeth. One of the molars—an obviously non-human molar—still showed the dark centre where a filling was.

"Wow, Buffy," Shakes said. "You bagged yourself a wolf so you think you're some kind of hot shit?"

"My shit's hotter than the three of yours," she said. "But really, that's not your problem, is it? All I want to know is where they're going for their rides. I know they're looking for decent transportation for the Calling. I know it's around here. Just need to know exactly where it is."

The really big one made a grumbling noise that sounded like continents grinding. Zach realized he was laughing.

"Boys," Rainer said, "how about we take this outside? Have a little fun?"

Jesus Christ, Zach thought. *This is the damn restaurant all over again, only this time, I'll be going with her.*

Now the really big one did stand up. Zach wondered whether his head was going to come in contact with the ceiling. It was a close thing, but he had some clearance. The other two followed. Rainer gathered the teeth, dropped them in a pocket, drained the beer, and stood as well.

She made a sweeping gesture to allow the three men to go first. The two smallest went ahead of her, but the giant took up the rear position, leaving Zach and Rainer sandwiched in the middle.

We're so screwed, Zach thought.

They headed to a different area of the bar, a section of wall that had a neon Budweiser sign to the left over a table, and to the right, a poster of a well-endowed blonde with two mugs held up in offering. Someone had scrawled *titties and beer* on it in marker with a sloppy hand. In between, a thin indent ran from floor to ceiling. No more than an inch wide, barely enough room to hide a pool cue in. Zach saw the first man disappear, followed by the second. Rainer's hand slipped back and Zach quickly caught it as she disappeared.

They were outside again, but in an alley. The giant scooched out from an even tighter space than the last one Zach had encountered, barely more than a crack in the wall.

"Give me one good reason why we shouldn't let the Kraken tear you apart."

"The Kraken?" Zach said, before he could filter it. OMFG was called *the Kraken*?

"Oh, the bitch does have a tongue," Shakes said.

"I'm the Kraken," said the giant.

"Okay," Zach said, then resolved to never speak again.

"The one good reason is," Rainer said, "information that might be interesting to you as well. We could consider it a trade. A favour for a favour."

"What the hell could you tell us that would be of any value?"

"You lost a long-time member of your pack about six months ago. Think he went by Fish?"

The small man said, "Fitch."

"What do you know about it?"

"Wanna know who did it?"

"Only if it's you," Shakes said.

"Not if it was another shifter?"

"You lie."

"He went off for a meeting. Probably didn't tell you what it was about. He met with Bo. Bo tried to lay some bullshit story on him about how he could work well with your pack."

"Fitch wouldn't make that decision."

"No, but he could come back and champion Bo if he thought it was a good idea. But he didn't. He told Bo where he could shove his idea. Bo got a little worried then, didn't want this to fuck up his chances somewhere else. Got a little scared Fitch would shoot off his mouth about Bo. Queer any future deals."

She stopped there.

"Okay," Shakes said. "I'm listening. You're not convincing me yet, but I'm listening."

"Bo tore his throat out, then tossed his ass into the river by the zoo. He's weighted down, so I doubt he'll ever surface, but he's down there." She furrowed her brow. "Maybe that's why I thought his name was Fish. Interesting."

"How do I know it wasn't you who did it?"

Rainer reached into another pocket. The Kraken advanced, but she held out a hand. "Relax there, Crackhead. Just pulling out the evidence." She held up a leather wallet inside a Ziploc bag.

"This is Fitch's wallet. The ID's thrown away, the money's gone, but Bo kept the wallet after he tossed the body."

She lobbed it over to him. Zach looked at her, but she seemed to know what she was doing.

Shakes caught it.

"Go ahead," Rainer said. "Smell it. You're going to catch Fitch's scent off it, proving it was his. And you're going to get some of my scent off it, just because I handled it a bit before I could get it in the bag. But you're going to smell Bo all over that." She nodded in encouragement. "You've met Bo before, right?"

Shakes handed the wallet over to the average sized guy. "Tiny has," he said. Tiny pulled the wallet from the plastic bag, held it to his nose. Unfolded it, took a deep breath. Spread the billfold area, drew in another deep breath.

Then he turned to Shakes. And he nodded.

Shakes, the pack leader, Zach figured, looked at the one with the wallet for a long time. Then he turned back to Rainer, who looked very calm.

"This is Bo," he said. "This isn't Zero's issue."

"Right," Rainer said. "Because she kept him so well in line. I'm sure your boys here would do the same."

His nostrils flared.

"You want to know where they're getting their rides? That's it?"

"That's it."

He turned to the one with the wallet. "Tell her," he said.

CHAPTER TWENTY

JAKE SCROLLED THROUGH the channels humming Springsteen's "57 Channels (And Nothin' On)." Springsteen was right. *What the hell is it with hotels? It's like they get their shows from a different planet.*

She gave up and shut off the television. Normally she might have taken Sam for another swim, but Zach and Rainer had been clear about not leaving the room.

"Whaddya wanna do, kiddo?" she said.

"How about we go look at some beleaguered internet porn? I know a good site."

"Why do I put up with you?"

"'Cuz I'm just that goddamn adorable," Sam said.

Jake opened her mouth to reply, but the balcony doors shattered, shards tearing through the drawn curtain. Jake rolled over on the bed, automatically shielding Sam from the sharp glass. Sam's initial yelp was muffled by the pillow as Jake covered her.

When she rolled back, there was a massive wolf in the room.

Sam screamed and Jake scrambled for the gun as the beast lunged.

Chapter Twenty-One

THE FED STOOD in the middle of the blood-soaked room. Someone pounded on the door, yelling that the cops had been called.

They weren't lying. The Fed heard the approaching sirens.

He reached up to his neck and, with a low growl, pulled the sharp chunk of glass from his neck. Nothing to be done about the eye. No time.

The easiest thing would be to simply kill her now and be done with it.

The Fed hunkered down to lunge across the bed at her, cowering in the corner. But just like before, somewhere between thought and execution, something failed. The Fed couldn't do it. Something refused to let the Fed's body do it.

But the Fed needed to do something, and fucking quick.

Leaving her here would accomplish nothing.

The Fed stepped over the tattooed whore's form, paused, and took the precious seconds the Fed didn't really have to change back to human form. Then the Fed gently advanced, no thought of harm in the Fed's head now.

The Fed approached her with no problem. The Fed bent to pick her up and she moved to punch the Fed in the groin. The Fed blocked it, but couldn't retaliate.

Pinning her arms to her side, the Fed hooked her small form under the Fed's arm, stepped back over the other woman, walked across the smashed glass and blood-soaked carpet and out to the balcony.

Making sure the Fed had a good hold on her, the Fed said, "Hold on. The Fed's not going to hurt you."

But the Fed dearly wanted to.

Instead, the Fed jumped over the balcony rail, landed three stories below and, checking to make sure the kid was okay, ran like hell.

Chapter Twenty-Two

Halfway back, Zach was still going on about how they'd just walked out of the alleyway. He'd been sure they were going to die back there.

"You know, as much fun as it is to have my ego stroked by my own personal cheerleader," Rainer said, "don't you think you should phone Jake and let her know we're on our way?"

She pulled the phone out from her pocket and handed it over.

Zach thumbed the number and put it to his ear. "Someday you're going to have to show me how you keep all that shit you carry in those pockets organized."

Rainer smiled.

Zach's smile faded a bit. "No answer."

"You dial the right number?"

He pulled the phone away, checked the number. Read it aloud. "Definitely the right number."

Rainer's face went suddenly grim. "Hotel's just ahead, but dial it again."

He did. "No answer."

Rainer drove past the hotel.

"What are you doing?"

"Not putting my car in that parking lot. If we need to leave again, we might never get out."

She drove half a block away and parked in a convenience store parking lot. They got out and Rainer took his hand.

"If we're asked, we just went for a stroll. New in town, wanted to get some air."

"Right."

In the distance, they heard sirens. "Shit," Rainer said. "We're going to have to do this fast."

They ran back to the hotel, entered through a side entrance, and took the stairs to the third floor. There were a few people gathered outside one of their two rooms. Rainer guided Zach to the other one. Someone was still complaining about the sounds from earlier. Zach swiped the card and they were in the room before anyone could really talk to them.

Rainer ran to the connecting door and opened it.

"Shit."

Zach pushed past her, but stopped when he took in the state of the room. "Let me by," Rainer said.

She bent over Jake on the ground. "Jake?" Zach said. Then, "Sam? *SAM?*"

The room was small. He took in the shattered balcony doors, the glass everywhere, Jake. He ran to the bathroom, heart thudding thickly in his throat, his tongue dry. He swept back the shower curtain.

No Sam.

Zach's mind went blank with fear and panic. *What do we do? What do we fucking do?*

He stumbled back out of the bathroom, hearing the bystanders on the other side of the door. He ignored them.

"Sam?" she said. He shook his head, feeling like his joints were filled with sand.

"Jake?" Rainer shook her head as well. Then she reached out and touched Jake's broken form. Rainer's eyes squeezed shut, then opened again quickly, found Zach's.

"We gotta go," she said.

"Where's Sam?"

Rainer stood and grabbed Zach by the arm. "The wolves

have her. We've got to go. Before the cops get here. Make sure you have your wallet. Leave everything else."

And they ran.

♦ ♦ ♦

BACK IN THE car. Driving out of the city again.

"Rainer, I need you to explain to me what the fuck's going on with my daughter. What happened? What happened to Jake?"

Rainer explained.

♦ ♦ ♦

WHEN JAKE ROLLED back, there was a massive wolf in the room.

Sam screamed and Jake scrambled for the gun as the beast lunged. It was her inexperience with it that worked against her. She brought it around, but the wolf was faster and clamped down on her wrist. She dropped the gun, but brought her other fist around and hammered the animal on its snout. It released her, backed off momentarily.

Enough for Jake to push Sam off the side into the space between bed and wall. Then she reached down and pulled the biggest shard of glass from the bedspread in front of her.

"Come on, you fucker," she said. "You want her, you're going to have to come through m—"

The animal lunged again and Jake brought the shard up and stuck it deep into the beast's neck. It jerked to the side and the glass broke in two, leaving the largest piece in the animal, the smaller piece still in her hand. She looked down to see if it could still be used as a weapon, saw only red and strips of shredded skin hanging from her ruined hand. It had damaged her as bad as the wolf.

It came at her again and she dropped the glass and brought her fist around to pound the spot where the glass entered its neck. It screamed and retreated, trying in vain to twist enough to pull it out with its teeth. It couldn't.

Jake grabbed for the table lamp, lifted it, and jumped off the bed, bringing the base down hard, aiming to bash the animal's skull in, but it dodged and she only struck a glancing blow.

She brought the lamp around again, but left her entire left side open and the beast came in, jaws wide, and tore a massive chunk from her abdomen. Jake reacted and slammed the base into the animal's left eye. She got some small satisfaction from the spray of blood that followed her downswing.

Then the pain doubled her over and the beast was on her. She clutched at the thick fur of its neck, just forward from the first wound she'd given him. It kept lunging forward, jaws snapping, but she held it back somehow. She felt her grip slipping, hands shredded and slick with blood. She waited for it to pull back for another lunge, released, and punched her fist directly into the thing's mouth.

It made a *kak* noise and tried to back off, but Jake kept pushing, feeling its flailing tongue and the sharp cage of teeth that it couldn't seem to clamp down with. She knew her only hope was to ram her fist straight down the fucking thing's throat.

Then it got its feet under it and pulled back more, hacking her fist up like a bone shard, its jaws wide and slavering. To divert it, she slapped again at the slice of glass still buried in its neck and it hacked and howled, whipping its head from side to side. In rage or pain, she didn't know, didn't care.

"Sam!" she said. "You okay?"

"I'm okay, Jake."

"Good girl." She pushed up to a sitting position. She had maybe a second or two at best. The gun was her best hope, but she didn't know where it was. She gambled on it being on the bed, threw herself to the side, her arms questing.

She'd gambled wrong. There was no gun on the bed.

A blur of fur and teeth. A sharp tension enveloped her neck and she was being whipped from side to side. She couldn't get any strength to her hands to pull the animal's jaws off the back of her neck. The whipping kept her off balance.

She heard a loud crack and she knew that was the end. It had broken her neck. It knew it too as all the tension ran from her body with the loss of signal from brain to spine. It tossed her to the floor.

She could just see Sam's terrified eyes over the edge of the bloodied bed. "I'm so sorry, Sam. I'm so sorry."

Sam was shaking her head, eyes wide and red and streaming tears. Her mouth was a round *o* as she said, "No no no no no no no no no..."

The animal heard Jake's apology and turned back to her, teeth bared under quivering flesh. She was completely defenceless.

"Sam," she said. "Close your eyes, baby."

She didn't close her own eyes as the thing came at her again. She watched it come, her penance for failing Zach. For failing Sam.

In her mind, she ignored the pain, just kept repeating the same words.

I'm so sorry. So sorry. So sorry.

♦ ♦ ♦

SHE FINISHED AND Zach said nothing, his face hard, his cheeks shining with tears.

"We have to get to the Farm, Zach."

"She's dead, Ray. You know she's dead."

"I know she's not, Zach."

"You can't know that."

"I never told you what my thing got from her." She took her eyes from the road long enough to meet his gaze briefly, then went back to it again. "She's a special kid, Zach. Special in a way you don't know and in a way I've never seen."

"I don't know what you mean."

"I mean there's something about her that the wolves can't touch."

"What is it?" There was a small hope in him.

"I don't know. I've never seen anything like it. It's like a…a *brightness.*"

"A brightness." Zach considered this. "I don't know what that means. I don't know what you're telling me."

"I'm telling you the wolves can take her, but they can't kill her, Zach." She looked at him one more time, wanting to make sure he got it. "Listen to me: they can't kill her."

She watched as he processed this. Watched his brow furrow. Watched the tears begin again.

The hope grew. "You better be right," he said.

CHAPTER TWENTY-THREE

IN THE STOLEN car.

"Rainer and my dad are going to find you, you know," Sam said. "Then they're going to fucking kill you."

"You're an unpleasant little girl," the Fed said.

"And you're an asshole."

"The Fed should kill you."

"Who's the Fed? Is he as big a douche as you?"

"The Fed is the Fed."

"Yeah, that made a shitload of sense."

The Fed pointed at the Fed's own chest. "The *Fed* is the Fed."

"You mean you're the Fed?"

"Yes."

"Wow," Sam said. "Why the hell can't you just say 'I'? And what the hell kind of douchebag name is 'the Fed'?"

With that, the Fed decided it wasn't worth the effort to talk to the girl anymore and shut up. She seemed to be waiting for an answer. Fine, she could wait forever.

"Now you're giving me the silent treatment?" she said. "Mature."

The Fed kept the Fed's mouth shut. Besides, the Fed's eye hurt like crazy. Once the Fed had gone back to human form, the Fed had been able to pull the glass out of the Fed's neck, but the Fed hadn't had time to properly dress it, and couldn't really stop with Sam in the Fed's care.

The Fed just had to suck it up for a while.

The Fed could do that. Even the Fed's mother said so.

The Fed just needed to get to the Farm as soon as possible.

The Fed didn't like this car, it was bigger than the Fed was used to, but it had been left running in a 7-Eleven parking lot a couple of states back and the Fed's mother told the Fed to never look a gift horse in the mouth.

Now, however, the Fed considered whether the girl should—or even could—spend the time in the trunk. The Fed tested this by asking the Fed's foot to press on the brake, preparatory to stopping to put her in the back. While the Fed's foot was able to brake, it pushed back, resisting slightly.

There was no way the Fed was going to be able to get her back there. This thing, this *whatever it was* with this girl, was never going to let the Fed.

Chapter Twenty-Four

MOONDOGGIE SAW THEM before he heard them. That always fucked him up. They were quiet, efficient, and deadly, doing what they needed to and getting out as quietly as they came in.

So, when the woman and the two men came into the barn, it kind of freaked his shit. That wasn't supposed to happen here.

Shit, man, they're, like, freakin' ninjas with fur. Liking the analogy, Moondoggie nodded his head in time to the Ventures' song playing in the background and smiled. "Right on, dude." Expelling a pungent lungful of marijuana, he tacked an extra "h" sound at the beginning of "right." *Super-fuckin'-natural furry freakin' ninjas.* He was still nodding—his entire body bobbing as though the weight of his shaggy blond dreads bent his spine—when the three moved through the maze of motorcycle and auto parts to come up to him. They were in upright mode, as was he.

"You Moondoggie?" the taller man asked. Moondoggie grabbed a bright orange rag and wiped his hands with it.

"Who's askin'?" Moondoggie responded, and rather wittily, he thought.

The dude rolled his eyes and sighed. All the while his nose twitched, confirming that Moondoggie was indeed a shifter.

"This is Zero, that's Taylor. I'm Syd."

"Righteous." He stuck out a hand. "Moondog," he said.

"But you can call me Moondoggie." No one took it. *Fuck it, man. Their loss.*

"Seen anyone else around here, Moondog?"

"Gee."

"Pardon?"

"Gee," he repeated. "Moon. Dog. Gee."

"Okay, Moondog*gie*. Has anyone else been by?"

"Had a few packs over the past week getting outfitted, but that's about it. Looking for someone in particular?"

"Shifter, goes by the name the Fed."

"A Fed is a wolf?"

"No. Not Fed," eyes rolling. "The Fed. Theeeeeee…"

"Ohhh," Moondoggie said, his upper body nodding again. "Theeeeee Fed. Okay. Okay." He tapped his finger to the side of his head. "Got it, dude. It's like, residing in the temple, man."

"Have you seen—" He shook his head. "Never mind. You haven't." He turned to the chick. Zero.

Zeeeeeee-ro. Quality handle.

"We've come for the motorcycles," Zero said. She wasn't bad looking, but nothing to write home about. If 'Doggie had to describe her in one sentence, he'd say she just missed being pretty. But she was obviously in command. *No shit, a bitch in lead of the pack. Cool.* And on the heels of that came the specific hankering for Doritos. Zesty Cheese flavour.

I really gotta lay off the herb, man.

Moondoggie closed his red-rimmed eyes and focused. He swallowed the saliva in his mouth, and concentrated. Motorcycles.

"Motorcycles!" he exclaimed. "For sure! I got 'em over here!" His arm waved off behind him, vaguely indicating the bikes were somewhere in the west side of the converted barn. He saw them take true notice of the building for the first time then, and he swelled with pride. He had built this shithole up over the past few years into the best shop in the southern US of A. Anything anyone could ask for could be delivered within forty-eight hours. These four wanted Harleys.

And they were damn well going to get them.

"C'mon dudes, I'll—Oh damn, I love this tune!" He started bobbing as he walked to a large tarped area. Though his voice was incredibly off-key, he sang out with no self-consciousness whatsoever. "I got a cruuuhhh-mee jooooob…it don't pay neeeeeeeer e-nuh-huff…"

"Hey!" the chick said. "Focus. Motorcycles. Now." She bared her teeth.

Jesus Christ! Syd thought. *As if I ain't facing enough bullshit.*

Moondoggie, finally displaying some respect, and at the flash of Zero's challenge, ducked his head. A quiet "yes'm" escaped his lips. Sheryl Crow continued to soak up the sun. He moved to the tarp and pulled it aside.

Four gleaming Harley-Davidsons sat, fat and shining, side by side. "I got four. You said you needed four."

"We may yet," Zero said.

The younger dude, Taylor, ignored them, only had eyes for the bikes. "That's what I'm talking about," he said.

Moondoggie shut up then, and just stood back. He loved this part. First meeting of client and machine. Taylor, Syd, and Zero approached the bikes with hushed reverence. Taylor trailed his finger over the Harley-Davidson logo on the gas tank.

As Zero passed the first three, Moondoggie spoke up, though with a lot more respect. "The one on the end's a bonus, like. It's one of the one-hundredth anniversary editions. Softail."

Syd and Taylor's heads whipped first to Moondoggie, then to the end bike. Both their mouths opened.

Zero's eyes flashed. "It's mine," she said.

"Well, yeah," said Syd, his face betraying his disappointment.

"That's what I was gonna say." Taylor punched his arm and gave him look that said he was convinced Syd was full of shit.

"We've got three more bikes from the gang we took them from, but these were the best maintained," Moondoggie explained.

"You got them from a gang?"

"Yeah," said Moondoggie, his stomach growling. "You wouldn't believe these guys! All leather and beards and big beer guts, but Jesus! Try 'n' take their damn rides away, and they're as vicious as we are. Maybe even more viciouser." He shook his head in remembered wonder. "Seven of 'em. It took five of us to finally shut them down." His voice oozed admiration.

"Why didn't you just make them?" Syd asked.

"I wouldn't have minded, but then they would have wanted to keep the bikes, and I knew you guys were comin', so…"

"Yeah," said Taylor. "Good choice."

Moondoggie opened his mouth to reply, but the barn was suddenly vibrating with the thundering roar from the Twin Cam 88B engine. It was a sound like no other on the planet, distinctive as a fingerprint. Zero sat astride the machine, a faraway look of concentration on her face.

She revved the engine once, and caged the beast. Swinging her leg back over, she stepped back and looked at Moondoggie.

"You've done well, Moondoggie," she said.

He bowed his head slightly. "Thanks, man."

Taylor spoke up. "Are there any helmets?" That bought him a look.

Moondoggie said, "Ain't no buckets. You gotta go commando."

"Yeah, commando," said Syd. "Fuck the buckets."

Taylor was going to reply, but the thought was immediately forgotten when the Fed came running in the side door, soaked in blood.

Chapter Twenty-Five

RAINER STOPPED THE car at the side of the road. Zach looked around. He saw nothing but fields, the gravel road they were on, and a small copse of trees off to the east.

"Why are we stopped?"

"I'm thinking we hike the rest of the way," Rainer said.

"What about the car?"

Rainer brought her hand up and pointed to the trees. "There," she said.

Swinging the wheel, and seemingly unmindful of the clearance between the bottom of the car and the lumpy field, she maneuvered the vehicle deep into the copse between two large trees, nose out.

"Jeez," said Zach. "All we need is a sign that drops down when we come speeding out, and we can be Batman and Robin in the Batmobile."

"The last time I was near a car hidden in some trees, I found the remains of what that asshole Bo left behind."

It took Zach a second, but then he made the connection. "Walter's daughter? Sarah?"

"Yes," she said, her tone grim. "Her and her soon-to-be ex-boyfriend, William. Billy."

"Probably bad, huh?"

"Zach," she said, "You have no idea."

His mind flashed to Jake. "I think I do," he said, then felt bad for cracking a joke at a time like this.

"I'm sorry," she said. "You do. I have to remember it's not just me affected by this anymore."

"We're in this together now," he said, then sighed. "Whether I want to be or not."

"I know you'd rather not. Jake. Sam. It wasn't supposed to happen like this." She reached out a hand, took his. "We will get Sam back."

"And make them pay for Jake as well?"

"And make them pay for Jake as well," she said. "Yes."

"I believe you."

"Thank you," she said. "Though, has it ever occurred to you that you may be a little too trusting?"

"Definitely." He had to work at it, but he gave her a smile.

Rainer gave him a look. The moonlight caught her hair and made her eyes sparkle. There was a moment when they said nothing, just looked at each other, that Zach never wanted to end. He took in the beautiful shape of her face, the graceful curve of her cheek, her mouth, lips slightly parted, a flash of white between, the sensuous lines of her neck. It was a brief moment, and his eyes came back to meet hers. He never wanted to ever stop looking at her. He wanted to say so, but didn't know how.

Then the moment was broken by his self-consciousness. *Learn to be still,* he thought. *Actually, screw that. Find Sam. Kill these guys for Jake.*

♦♦♦

IT TOOK THEM fifteen minutes, but they gathered enough boughs and foliage to adequately disguise the SUV. Not a single vehicle passed by in either direction in that time. They got back out to the road and continued on foot.

"What are we looking to find, Ray?"

"A shifter named Moondoggie."

"Moondoggie?" he asked. "You're serious? A werewolf named 'Moondoggie'?" He shook his head. "A person who turns into a dog by the moonlight. Called Moondoggie. Perfect."

"Yeah. They didn't say, but I picked up that he's a surfer. Or was. I'm not sure."

"Great. What do we do with ol' Moondoggie? Bribe him with weed and Scooby Snacks?"

"You're just full of '60s TV trivia today, aren't you?" Rainer asked. "He's supposedly the transportation supply for a network of shifters in the southern US. Apparently, Zero and her pack made arrangements for rides that they were to pick up today. Either we're going to get there too early, in which case we wait for the deal to go down, or we've already missed them. In that case, we pump Moondoggie for any information."

Zach got a flashback of the silo, and Bo. He shuddered.

The two walked a while in silence, their shoes kicking up small plumes of dust in the dry air. Off in the distance, bugs trilled and buzzed about their business. A slight breeze cooled Zach's sweating brow. He looked over at Rainer, gliding along silently beside him, eyes hidden in the night's shadows, her mouth set grimly. She moved with economy, no excessive moves. He wiped sweat from his own forehead. She didn't even seem to sweat, no telltale sheen in the moonlight.

He looked down at her hand, swinging loosely at her side. He tried to imagine all the things those hands had done. How many deaths, how much blood spilled? Then he thought of earlier today, and the way those hands had touched him, held him. It was as though Rainer was some sort of shifter herself. Bloodthirsty, territorial, vicious. But then there was the other Rainer. Warm, caring, loving. He wondered how the two coexisted.

Then, he stopped thinking altogether, and simply reached out and held her hand.

♦♦♦

FORTY-FIVE MINUTES LATER, having seen no cars in either direction, they noticed a dilapidated barn in the distance.

"Get down," said Rainer, and Zach obediently dropped to his haunches.

They slid off the road into the long, dry grass at the side. Zach was grateful that the grass wasn't frost-rimed here. Rainer took the lead, briskly slicing through the grass until she found the driveway. Zach stayed behind her, letting her do her stuff. *Whatever the hell her stuff is.*

Her head turned this way and that, checking out the barn, then the path leading to it, then the road they had just been on. Back to the barn. Back to the path. Back to the road. Leaning forward, her head out of the grass and inches from the path.

Zach was too far back to see anything in the moonlight but the barn and a small house off to the one side. Frayed lace curtains blew through broken windows, making Zach think no one had lived there for years. The barn seemed even worse.

The structure had been added to with no pretense of aesthetics or design. Wood bonded to corrugated metal made additional space. The hoods of several cars now lived out their last days as the roof of a small storage shelter. A large swath of oxidizing sheet metal, the rust black in the moonlight, served as a patch for a section of wall, the rotting boards behind hinting they weren't long for the world.

As he crept closer, shadows coalesced, made more sense. Here and there, mechanical guts were strewn like a child's toys—camshafts, valve covers, distributor caps, transmissions, a tread from either a bulldozer or a tank. Tires, from knobby monster truck-size down to plain old bald ones that would look better hanging from a tree as a swing.

This can't be the place.

"This is the place," Rainer whispered in his ear, making Zach jumped at her sudden, unexpected closeness.

"Jesus," he hissed. She put a calming hand to his shoulder as Zach blinked at her. "How do you figure?"

"A lot of things." She pointed to their left, said, "Check out the road we were walking on. There's a few tire tracks, right?"

"Yeah."

"Well, they all come in here. None seem to pass this place—all in or out of this driveway."

"Okay..."

Pointing ahead now. "As well, the house and barn look pretty rundown, but do you see any holes? In the roof? In the walls of the barn?"

"Well no, not from this angle."

"Not from any angle. I guarantee it." Her arm swept across their field of view. "And check out some of the junk spread around the yard. See that tank tread?"

"You sure it's from a tank? I was thinking bulldozer."

"Tank," she said, leaving no room for argument. "Look at it. It's clean. No rust."

"So..."

"So, this is the place. Moondoggie's." Zach looked again. Taking Rainer's slant on it, the place could have been artfully constructed to look rundown. Had Zach been driving by, he wouldn't have looked twice at the place. And that was the whole point, wasn't it?

Zach looked at her again. She was either brilliant, or she was the most seriously fucked-up person he'd ever met.

Maybe she's both.

"What do we do now?" Zach asked.

"*We* do nothing," Rainer answered. "I'm going to check things out. I need you to lie low for now. It almost got ugly back at the bar, and then there's what happened to Jake and Sam at the hotel. I don't need a repeat of that. I'm going to check out the house first, then the barn. I'll call you if I need you, otherwise, stay low in the grass. I think we beat Zero here, so they're likely on their way."

Zach was going to protest. He surely was, but Rainer leaned forward and kissed him hard, her tongue exploring his teeth and tongue lightly before she broke away. Zach felt his pulse throbbing thickly in his ears.

"Stay here," she said. "Be safe."

And she was gone, running like a lioness through the veldt, barely a whisper to mark her passage.

"I love you," Zach said. He knew it was too quiet for anyone but himself to hear, but it felt important to say it, just the same.

CHAPTER TWENTY-SIX

RAINER TOOK ONE last look at Zach, and headed around the back of the house.

She didn't think anyone was in there, but she needed to get away from Zach. He was beginning to dull her edge. Dammit! *This* was exactly what she didn't want to happen! *This* is was why she had stayed away from any contact up to now. She needed to be tight, to be focused.

Am I brilliant? she wondered. *Or am I just seriously fucked-up? Zach's right, I'm probably both.*

But mostly, I'm fucked-up.

She hoped he was going to be okay in the field. She didn't like his proclivity for falling into shit. And he didn't seem to know when to shut up.

Rainer skirted some debris at the back of the house and tucked herself in beside a rusting furnace-oil tank. *Okay. Put Zach outta your mind. Right now.*

She closed her eyes and closed down on her wildly spinning thoughts. She emptied her mind like she was pushing unruly guests out the door, and settled herself into the silence.

Be still.

One final, cleansing breath, and she was on the move again.

She searched the ground-floor windows, and spied across some tracks imprinted in the dirt that had blown in through the broken glass. It was likely nothing, but she had to check it anyway.

She slipped into the house through a moisture-warped side door and she was in the kitchen. A single, smashed mug lay like broken teeth in the yawning mouth of the sink. No table, and only one chair, overturned.

Into the combined living and dining area, silent as nightfall, Rainer tried to look everywhere at once: in the corners of the room, an eye on the kitchen she had just left, out the windows, the sagging staircase to her right, and the boards at her feet. She moved her head only slightly and out of necessity, her arms out to the side to provide balance as she glided though the room. Nothing here, but tracks led to the stairs.

One final glance out the window. No sign of Zach. *Good, he's staying down.* Then the thought was banished.

Up the stairs, then.

She paused at the bottom, noting which steps would be the troublemakers, calling out to announce Rainer's presence.

That one.

That one, too.

Keep to the far right on that one up there.

She placed her hands, palms out, on the walls and lightly placed her foot on the first riser, ready to pull it back at the first hint of noise. She kept her steps to the far edges of each stair, knowing that's where they were fastened, and where they were the most stable.

As Rainer climbed the stairs, she was strung so tight she was damn near vibrating. Every noise, every creak, every gust of wind she registered, analyzed, and approved before she moved further. She ascended in a sideways crab crawl to better keep an eye both above and below her.

The stairs right-angled. She paused and drew a deeper breath, taking the moment to come off red alert, however briefly. From this vantage, Rainer could see some of the lower floor, as well as the hallway above, and three doors down its path.

One bathroom, two bedrooms. Had to be.

Walk in the park.

She squashed the urge to bolt up the last few stairs and continued on in the same cautious manner. Two steps from the top, she froze.

Rainer angled her head to better catch the sound again. Something was up here.

Time spun out like taffy. She watched the tattered curtain rise and fall in the graceful breeze from the window at the end of the hall. A small voice whispered that it was nothing, that it had come from outside, that it was the sound of her own shoes on the step. A bigger, smarter part of her told her that was so much bullshit.

That was the part she believed. She waited, knowing it would come aga—

There. There it was again. A low, small skritching sound.

Nails on wood.

Fucking shifter.

Rainer picked her way up the final steps, her movements offering nothing more than a sigh. A whispered warning of the pain and death that would be visited upon the owner of those nails. She allowed herself a very small smile.

Glancing at the first bedroom, she dismissed it immediately. It was not the one she wanted. The bathroom was at the end of the hall, and all was visible except the tub. Again, not her target. The second bedroom was coming up on her right and that was where the sound had come from.

She felt herself winding up tight, like cocking the hammer on a gun. Just a little pressure and the result would be swift, painful, and devastating. The door was getting closer, and Rainer steeled herself for the fight. Breathing in through her nose, out through her opened mouth.

At the door now.

One.

Two.

Thr –

A noise from down below in the driveway and the raccoon bolted from the room, scrabbling across the uneven floorboards. It didn't seem to register Rainer, but altered its trajectory to take it in a slightly wider arc around her on its way down the stairs.

Raccoon?

Rainer would have smiled, but there was something going on in the driveway. She quickly covered the three rooms, not worrying about stealth now. Nothing in the bathroom. Nothing in the first bedroom. The second bedroom looked like someone occupied it sporadically. A bedroll, some magazines, wrappers from Hot Rod meat snacks—*probably what had attracted the fucking raccoon.* Two bottles of tequila, one full, one almost empty. Three pictures of surfers riding curls. Then it came to her. Moondoggie.

She ran to the hall window and saw a man. No, a shifter. He moved with too much grace for a regular man. He walked down the path to the road. His movements, with as much animal grace as they possessed, still betrayed the fact that he was not happy.

Deal's gotta be going down right now.

She watched him for a few seconds. He walked slowly, carefully. *Just walking? Or hunting?*

No. Hunting. Definitely hunting.

Shit. She'd get back downstairs quickly and find a good place to observe him from outside the house.

Rainer turned from the window, scooped up the tequila, and headed back to the stairs. She was still cautious, knowing that, while it looked like there was only one out there, the possibility of two or three was high as well. She took the stairs down the same way she came up, sideways, and at one side, avoiding the ones she had noted on the way up. She wasn't about to take chances this late in the game.

She hit the bottom, took a solid scan of the floor and, seeing nothing different from when she left, dropped to a crouch and crossed the room, conscious of every window that looked in on her. No time for sloppy.

She wanted desperately to check his position, but thought it better to wait until she was out of the house. The door was in front of her now, only a few steps away. No windows looking directly in on her, so she stood again and crossed the room. She pushed the door open cautiously, and exited the house.

Grafting herself to the wall, Rainer slid along it like a five-foot snail. At the corner, she risked a look. There were two cars in the driveway. The second had likely just arrived and the first had—god*damm*it—been hidden by the barn. The barn was directly beside her across the path and wide enough that she couldn't see the wall facing the road. But that wasn't what concerned her.

Where the hell is the shifter?

Chapter Twenty-Seven

As much pain as the Fed was in, the Fed felt good. The pain was good because the Fed felt alive, aware. The Fed had discovered it was the closest the Fed got to the feeling of being shifted. When the Fed went over, the Fed was powerful, unstoppable. But as an upright, that didn't happen too often.

And now, the Fed could deliver a package for Zero. Let her kill the kid, make out like that was the idea all along. Didn't have to tell her the Fed couldn't do it.

The Fed had pulled off a little while back at the last gas station, parking well away from anyone else, and trussed the girl up. The Fed couldn't throw her in the trunk, but the Fed could tie her up and toss her in the back seat with a blanket over her.

Then the Fed watched Palmer and his bitch—their faces indelibly engraved in his mind—go by. On their way to the Farm.

This just gets better and better, the Fed thought, and a rare smile creased the Fed's face, then fell off just as quickly. Smiling hurt because of the Fed's missing eye.

The Fed had considered coming up behind them, but instead chose to meet the issue head-on. As the Fed approached the driveway, the Fed had seen something that interested the Fed even more. Yet another gift from the Old Ones.

The Fed had driven straight up the drive, parked, locked the car, and headed off to the side of the barn.

The Fed went into silent mode. The Fed immediately dropped low to the ground, under the level of the tall grass growing to either side of the path. The Fed's carefully sharpened eyes scanned the fields around the barn, the area where the Fed had seen something. *Nothing.*

Then the Fed switched modes. Up to now, the Fed was looking for movement. While the entire area was filled with movement, from birds flying, to bugs buzzing, to the grass bending in the slight breeze, this was all natural. The Fed was looking for something that didn't look right. Something that didn't feel right.

One of these things is not like the other, the Fed's mother sang. *One of these things just doesn't belong. If one of th –*

There. Up against the barn. Low to the ground like he was, and not moving. The Fed could only catch the top part of the person's head. Brown hair, Caucasian.

Palmer.

Meat.

The Fed allowed one more smile to pass over the Fed's lips, then got down to business.

The Fed whispered back down the path, hands and boots barely touching down, mind filtering where each hand and foot should land, storing the immediate topography in the Fed's short-term memory. *The Fed is as silent as a disease,* the Fed thought. *The Fed is as silent as death.*

The Fed drifted up to the corner of the barn, placing the Fed's hands on the wall like a lover, then risked a glance around the corner. And there he was. Palmer. It looked like the loser was spying on Zero and the others through a hole in the wall.

This was going to be fun. And the Fed had him all to the Fed's self. The Fed's very own private stress-reducer.

The Fed watched as the guy bobbed his head up and down and this way and that, vying for a better line of sight. The soft light from inside the barn reflected a bright slash on his face. He was oblivious to the outside world. The Fed came around the corner of the barn, carefully placing the Fed's steps, not touching the barn wall for fear of an unexpected noise. The Fed stalked Palmer cautiously, patiently, advancing slowly, keeping the Fed's body loose but the Fed's muscles on alert. Any movement away from the wall, and the Fed would be on Palmer like Elvis on a peanut butter and fried banana sandwich.

The Fed had ten feet to go when the guy sort of half-stood, but dropped to his haunches again. The Fed stood still, willing the breeze to blow around the Fed. *Nuthin' over here. The Fed's just another tree in the field. The Fed's a rock. The Fed's an island.* Then the guy slid back down to his haunches. Just stretching the legs.

Four more delicate steps, and the Fed was upon him. The Fed's first urge was to reach forward and twist his head until it fell off his body, and drink the juices. But instead, the Fed studied him, the way the wind lifted his hair, the way his back widened and narrowed as he took in air, and let it out again. The distinct and mouth-watering odours of sweat and fear. He was slim—not exactly skinny, but no Stallone, that's for sure—and his hands looked soft.

The Fed leaned over, close enough to catch more of the heady smell of the man, the Fed's nose a mere breath away from Palmer's ear.

"Well, well, well," the Fed whispered. "What do we have here?"

Palmer turned to look, wide-eyed. The Fed watched, fascinated, as his pupil dilated, first from the lack of light, then more with fear.

"Aw, shit," Palmer said.

Chapter Twenty-Eight

ZACH WATCHED HER approach the house for as long as he could, being careful to stay low. She went around the back of the dwelling, and he watched for another couple of minutes. She didn't come out and Zach began to feel overexposed. There was some low ground off to the south and he thought about heading there. It was closer to the barn, but it promised more security.

He wanted to see if he could catch her attention when he heard a low rumble. Dropping even lower, he looked back down the road he and Rainer had walked. He couldn't see any vehicles, but he could damn well hear one coming. There was the ghost of a headlight glow.

He really didn't like being this close to the road. Something was definitely coming.

He had a minute, maybe two, and then he'd be pinned down. *Fuck it,* he thought, and made an executive decision to run like hell for the low ground.

He'd seen many movies of soldiers doubled over in the long grass, running for their lives, but it was a long way from what he was feeling right now. Dust giving everything a dry, papery smell, the long blades whickering past his lowered face, lashing at his swinging hands, his breath ragged in his ears, his tongue dry. A quick glance behind him and he could hear it coming closer, headlights, but still no car. *Good. Good.*

As he ran, he tried to follow the lay of the land, tried to

watch the structures for any sign he'd been seen, and tried to watch the road. Tough to manage just by moonlight. A misstep was bound to happen. He ran, and then there was the footfall that went farther than he'd anticipated, the ground dropping away into the hollow, his body anticipating the ground that just wasn't where it was expected to be. His body straightened, and his arms pinwheeled as he fought for balance, but it was a losing battle. He pitched forward and went sprawling down the hill, but managed to keep his mouth shut all the while.

A little inelegant, he thought as he spit grass and dirt, *but it got me where I wanted to go.*

Apparently right on time, as well. A car turned into the driveway and bounced and bobbled down the weed-choked path to the barn. Zach was lying low, but all the same, he couldn't tell how visible he actually was. He counted on the night to provide most of the cover.

Zach stayed low, though every nerve in his body screamed run. There was no place, however, to run *to,* and Rainer was still around.

He heard the car engine die. That allowed him to hear talking from inside the barn.

Now what do I do? Zach wondered. He was sure Rainer had heard the car come in, but still, he didn't have a clue where she was. What if she was in the barn? What if that was the voices he heard? The thought circled around again, sharper this time. *Oh shit! What if she's in the barn?*

Zach felt panic. *Of course she's in the barn!* If she'd heard the car, she'd try and find a safe spot to hide. It wouldn't be the house, so of course it would be the barn. He had to get a look.

Sucking up all the courage he could muster, Zach dodged around the low hill and sprinted the short distance to the barn, running on his toes, willing his body to be light and agile. His path was by no means straight as he skipped and hopped from one dirt patch to the next, staying away from the dry grass.

Then he was at the barn, his back pressed up to the boards, breathing heavily through his mouth, sweat sticking his shirt to his back. *Now what, Ace Ventura?*

He glanced along the wall and noticed the big, rusty sheet of metal that had been used to patch a hole. It hadn't completely covered the opening though.

Zach slid along the wall, checking both ways, and keeping an eye to the ground for any debris that might make noise and give him away. He brushed aside the sweat from his eyes. And he was there.

The opening started two feet up the wall, and left a narrow, ragged strip about a foot high. Zach bent to look, and found he could see the entire scene inside. Sure enough, four people, and one was a woman. Ray? No, he didn't think so. He shifted his gaze this way and that, trying to see all sides, checking for Rainer.

God, his legs were not used to all this exercise. Standing in a fast-food restaurant was a totally different experience than walking for almost an hour, then running, soldier-style, through fields. And falling down slopes, don't forget that.

He could almost make out their words. He stood, giving his legs a break, but he couldn't see or hear as well, so he squatted again. They were still talking. He turned his head slightly, lending an ear.

"Well, well, well," Zach heard someone say, much to close. "What do we have here?"

Zach turned to look. Standing over him, silent as death, was a man with motorcycle boots and a leather jacket. As Zach watched, he saw thick, coarse hair growing out of the lengths of fingers between the knuckles.

"Aw, shit," Zach said quietly.

♦♦♦

I'M SO FUCKED, Zach thought, not incorrectly.

Ray's gonna kill me. He turned and slowly stood up. He didn't want to make any sudden moves and piss this guy off. Going by the expression on his face—*what the fuck happened to your neck and eye, dude?*—this guy was more than happy to get medieval on Zach. *Maybe Ray's gonna have to get in line.*

The thing that bothered Zach the worst was, aside from his opening comment, the guy hadn't said another thing. He just stood there, grinning like an idiot. But his hands! They were sprouting thick hair. Zach found it fascinating, but it scared the shit out of him at the same time. He saw Bo all over again.

Then Zach made the mistake of looking the guy in the face. The same coarse covering was colonizing his jawline and cheeks. He watched as the man's eyes squinted down, as though in pain. The grin widened as though the pain was enjoyable, pleasurable. Zach saw his teeth, saw the incisors stretch. The guy was drooling, for chrissakes.

What was it about the grin, though? Like it was deliberate—a phony smile for a demented photograph.

Is that how he bares his teeth?

Someone had better say something. Zach pulled off from the wall.

"Look, man," Zach started. "I don't know what you saw, but I—"

"Shut up," the man said in a quiet growl. The grin never slowed.

"Seriously, I—"

"Shut up, Palmer."

He knows me?

The man's hand shot out and Zach felt the punch in the middle of his chest, and, though he expected to be knocked on his ass, it never happened. Zach bobbled back a bit, lost his footing, but never went down. The man still had him by the shirt, but Christ! He must have scooped up a good section of Zach's midriff as well, because it hurt like hell down there.

It had been a good hit. Zach now had a hard time breathing. He wanted to say something to the man, but he couldn't seem to find the breath to do it. He just wanted to say *something*.

Then he looked down.

The man didn't have Zach by the shirt. Zach could only see the man's overly hairy forearm. The wrist and hand were gone, buried inside…

Inside…oh Jesus.

He looked back to the man and, incredibly, the smile widened. The man drew back his hand with a vicious yank, and Zach was dragged forward briefly. A flash of red, then pain.

He knew there was something wrong immediately, something different, but what? What?

His vision started to narrow, and he knew he was passing out. His last look was to the man as he brought his dripping red right hand to his mouth. There was something in it, an oblong, drooling…something. Zach's overstressed brain couldn't grasp it immediately and it wasn't until the man bit down on the fist-sized muscle and the spray of blood told him that he had Zach's heart.

His fucking heart was in the man's mouth, being shredded by those teeth and it was then that he knew he wasn't passing out. He was dying and it finally dawned on him that the wrongness, the different thing he felt was the lack of a pulse.

Ray will be proud, he thought. *I'm gonna learn to be still…*

He had one last thought before the darkness overcame him, then Zachary Palmer was dead.

CHAPTER TWENTY-NINE

RAINER CROUCHED LOW as she sprinted from the house to the car.

The doors were locked and the windows up. She quickly looked in the car.

A pile of fast-food wrappers and a pile of clothes in the back seat. Another quick look around, and she went to the back of the car. Trunk was locked, but she'd expected that. She set the tequila bottles down, one by each rear wheel, out of sight. Might give them a flat if they had to leave quickly.

Choosing her footsteps carefully, she dashed across the path to the barn, stopping with her back to the corner. She could go left or right. Right would take her to the main entrance. Left would take her to the wall facing the road, but also, she was sure, to a patched section that she may be able to peek through to get a better lay of the land.

She went left.

Carefully following the wall, Rainer watched for any peepholes where she might look in, but more importantly, where someone may look out and be alerted to her presence. Up ahead, there was a section of sheet metal patching, the red paint blending into the rust. That was her destination.

Ensuring she was making no more noise than needed, Rainer's attention was split between the wall to her left, and the weedy terrain at her feet. The moon, almost full, cast a rippling shadow on the wall.

As she walked, Rainer cast her eyes downward. She stopped. Looked at a dark patch on the ground. Could be oil.

Could be blood.

She bent lower, hand out to the dirt and grass. Definitely blood.

Head up, she looked ahead to the patch in the wall again. A soft, quiet, "shit" was all that she said, then she was running. As she ran, she felt her guts sinking. She exhaled "no" with every breath.

Zach. Please God let it please not be –

Zach.

He was lying face up on the patchy grass by the wall of the barn. A gaping hole cratered his chest like a blasphemy. His dry, glassy eyes stared unseeing to the stars. His blood covered the surrounding area like the Painted Desert.

Zach was dead.

Rainer's hand shook as she reached out to him, brushing the hair from his eyes. As her fingers made contact with his cooling skin, she was struck with that same sense of knowing. The same knowing she had when she had made contact with Walter back at the gas station. The same knowing she'd had all her life. Most times it worked, sometimes it didn't. Sometimes it failed her when she needed it the most. Like her husband.

But sometimes, yes sometimes, it surprised her.

Like now. Like with Zach.

Her eyes began to fill with tears, and she wiped them violently away. No! She would not cry. Not right now.

She reached out a second time, and it was just skin on skin. It was as though that one thought had held on, like a bubble on the side of a glass, waiting for the right moment to break away and float to the surface.

Like he knew he was going and wanted to leave a final message.

Rainer brought her fingers to her mouth, gently touching the pads to her lips as though trying to get a last sense of Zach's spirit, but again it was just skin on skin.

But in her mind, it would always be there.

Zach's dying thought.

Save my girl. Save Sam.

♦♦♦

RAINER WAS GOING to kill those bastards.

♦♦♦

SHE WAS BACK at the car, retrieving the tequila.

Rainer took the two bottles and poured one into the other until they were even, then she tore two strips of fabric from her shirt and stuffed them tightly into the necks. She upended the bottles to thoroughly soak the alcohol into the material.

Final inspection of the Molotov cocktails completed, she stood and headed toward the entrance to the barn, her legs propelling her forward with purposeful strides. Her mind was blank, not thinking about Zach, the blood, her surroundings, or what she was about to do. She was simply alert to any influencing factors that may stray her from her intended course of action.

At the door, she stopped and listened. Inside, they were talking. Rainer lit one of the cocktails and waited a few moments until someone was mid-sentence, looking for the biggest element of surprise. When the time was right, she cranked back and threw her booted foot into the door, adrenalin and rage accelerating her thrust hard enough to run a splintering crack down its length as it swung wide into the barn.

Without so much as a pause, she bolted through the door and surveyed the situation in a split-second. The one with the blood all the way up his arm and down his front was off to the right, slightly separated from the rest. Him, then.

Her arm was already back, so she adjusted her aim and heaved the burning bottle, taking satisfaction from the instantaneous flame burst. The second bottle followed seconds later, adding its strength to the first, and Zach's killer was separated from the pack.

Seconds later, he'd fully shifted to wolf, but that didn't slow her. Rainer pulled a knife from a sheath at her calf and moved in for the kill. Zach's killer struggled free of his clothes, disoriented and looking to his pack for backup. That gave Rainer the opening she was hoping for. Moving as silent and as nimble as a cat, she came up behind the wolf and beat the shit out of him, never hitting the same place twice, never allowing him to turn and block the blows. When an opening presented itself, she reached around and slashed deeply into his abdomen. Let him feel what it's like to have some body parts fall away. The slick coils of his bowel glistened in the firelight.

That slowed him down. She danced away and behind, always behind him. She buried the knife in his lower back, right in his spine, rocked the blade savagely, and he was down.

"Zee!" he cried. "Syd! Help me!"

Huh. "Me." Not "the Fed." But there was something else at the back of her brain…another thought. *Later.*

He growled and whined and looked past the flames to the rest of his pack, but there was no help there. The other three males had run for the motorcycles. They were saddling the horses and riding into the sunset without Little Joe. All except one. The female—*probably the one called Zero*—stood silently in the acrid smoke and simply stared.

Yeah, well, screw it, Rainer thought. *I'll burn that bridge when I come to it.* Besides, the wolf had his head around, snapping at his back, finally clueing in that there was something stuck into him. She took the two steps over to him and ripped the knife back out, twisting it and feeling the scrape of metal off bone.

"Looking for this?" she asked, her voice a low growl. With the knife came a gush of blood that sprayed her hand, and again, there was the flash. *The Fed. He'd killed Jake. He calls himself the Fed. Federman. That's his real name.* And there was the feeling of blood squirting in her mouth as he bit down on the still-warm heart, and she saw, oh sweet Jesus, she *saw* Zach's face as he looked on, his body not fully aware it was already dead.

He watched Federman eat his heart and he still thought of Sam before he died?

Federman half turned to face her and Rainer was filled with a rage so intense, so complete, that it dwarfed the flames around them.

"I hope this hurts you as much as you hurt Zach, Federman," she cried, and brought the knife down, cracking through his skull and into his frontal lobes. Leaving the blade in there, she swept the blade back and forth in a ferocious sweeping motion meant to turn his brain to soup.

When she finished, the pack leader had followed the other three to the motorcycles. They were yelling to go, but she took one extra second to lock eyes with Rainer through the heat and smoke.

She said nothing, but Rainer understood, just the same. *You and I. We will meet again.*

As the motorcycles powered up, Rainer knew she would never be able to catch them. Instead, she pulled out the knife, grabbed Federman by the ears, registered that he was still alive, and began hacking at his throat. The spine was tougher, but her anger gave her strength.

CHAPTER THIRTY

"FED?" TAYLOR ASKED. "The fuck happened to you?"

The Fed approached the pack, the Fed's hands and face smeared with blood. "Zee," the Fed said, ignoring Taylor.

Zero shot a look that both Taylor and Syd caught. Syd held up a hand and the Fed pulled up short. "Explain yourself. Where the hell have you been?"

"Doesn't matter," the Fed said. "The Fed thinks she's out there. The one who killed Bo."

"She attacked you?" Syd asked.

"No," said the Fed. "The Fed caught some asshole upright spying on you guys through a hole in the barn. Dispatched him."

Zero finally spoke. "I didn't hear a struggle, Fed. What happened?"

"Nothing much," the Fed said. "The Fed just walked up to him, he turned around, and the Fed pulled his heart out and ate it while he died watching."

Moondoggie nodded, his entire upper body bobbling. "Very cool," he said.

"Is he still out there?" Zero asked.

"Yes, but he's not going nowhere."

"So…where's the girl, dude?" Moondoggie said.

"She's got to be around."

Zero was off to one side. Her eyes were far off. "Who was the man?" she asked.

"Shit, Zero. The Fed has so much to tell you. The short answer is, he's with the one who killed Bo. And the Fed's got his daughter."

"What?" she asked, confused. "What are you talking about?"

The Fed laughed, the Fed's teeth red-stained. "The little bitch the Fed visited back before you?...Back on the night Bo died? The Fed tracked them to a hotel not far from here—they followed you here—and the Fed killed her babysitter. Brought the girl for you."

Zero look confused. Syd, Taylor, and the stoner stood back and let him talk.

"This girl," Zero asked. "How old is she?"

"Does it matter?" the Fed asked. "The Fed doesn't know kids. Young. Eight? Ten?"

The Fed watched as Zero turned away. Something had passed her lips, but the Fed wasn't sure what she had said. It sounded like, "just a baby," or something like that. But that couldn't be it. The Fed managed to say, "She—" and that was all. The door was kicked in.

"What the fu—" was all the Fed could get out next. There was a *pop*, and an explosion of flame. The rest was a blur.

The Fed saw a running shape—low, dark, and fast as hell—dodging through the room, bobbing and weaving like a prizefighter. The Fed heard shouts from behind the flames. Everyone except Zee was in various phases of shifting. The Fed shifted as well, automatically, but the damn clothes were snagging the Fed up, slowing the Fed down.

The Fed caught a brief sight of the Fed's pack leader. Zee stood silent and quiet as the frenzy went on around her. The eye of the storm. She looked at the Fed with a sadness so profound that for a moment the Fed forgot the stinging smoke choking the Fed's nostrils.

Then the moment moved on, and the dark shape was on the Fed. The blows to the Fed's body and face hit like bullets.

Something slashed at the Fed's abdomen. There was shocking, lightning-strike pain and rough trembling as his insides turned to jelly. There was an odd slopping sound and the Fed's insides lightened. The Fed wondered if the Fed had inadvertently defecated.

The shape—the Fed had to assume it was the girl—never stopped moving, but stayed maddeningly behind the Fed. Another sharp arcing pain in the Fed's lower back and then the Fed couldn't stand anymore. What had the bitch done?

The Fed felt something new. Panic.

"Zee!" the Fed cried. "Syd! Help me!"

Looking around, the Fed was cut off from the pack by the flames, alone to deal with this slashing demon. Syd and Taylor were gone, lost in the smoke and flames, heading for the motorcycles. Zero continued her inscrutable stare, but the message was clear. She had abandoned him.

The Fed was down now, on his side. He looked down and saw long, roping tendrils that he immediately recognized as intestines. It took a touch longer to identify them as his own. *The Fed's guts...my guts.* Wondering where she was, he took the second of respite to glance behind him. There was something—a knife—jutting out of his spine. With no fingers to wrap around it, he snapped at it with his teeth.

Then it was gone.

"Looking for this?" A low voice, promises of menace.

The Fed looked back around, and the dark shape was now in front of him. She was smaller than he expected. This little girl had done so much damage?

"I hope this hurts you as much as you hurt Zach, Federman," she said, and he had a second to ponder how she knew his real name before the knife plunged down, cracking through his skull and into his brain.

The Fed's thoughts began to scramble as he heard the big Harley engines snarl into life. *They're leaving without me?* he wondered. There was a side to side motion rocking his head, and he was able to figure out the girl was Cuisinarting his brains. Finally, all coherence left him, blowing away like the smoke roiling from the burning barn.

Though the Fed could no longer think, the pain was just as fresh and as bright as his head was separated from his body.

Chapter Thirty-One

THE BARN WAS burning to the ground. There were no sounds of fire engines, no calls of alarm. Just a plume of dust from motorcycles hightailing it.

Rainer left the building and went back to Zach.

She had experienced a lot of death in the past couple of years. Hell, she'd caused a fair portion of it. But she had never approached a corpse with the trepidation she now felt. This was new. This was personal.

This one ached.

The heat from the barn tightened the skin of her forehead as she bent over Zach. She had intended to pull him away from the barn, but as she reached out to pick him up, she hesitated. Her fingers were only a breath away from Zach, and she didn't think she could bear to pick up that same thought from him again. Would it still be there?

Something crumbled and collapsed in the barn, and she closed her eyes. Her hands made contact with Zach and there was nothing anymore. She released the air in her lungs and hefted his body over her shoulder in a firefighter's grip. Zach wasn't a large man, but his weight surprised her. Dead weight.

Initially intending to carry him back toward the car, she decided, painful as it would be, she wouldn't be able to do it. And she didn't want to leave him in the same place as Federman.

The house.

She carried him over the threshold and laid him on the floor of the kitchen, setting his body down as though it was the most precious cargo.

"Ah, Zach," she said. "What are we going to do now?"

She headed back over to the barn at a run, grabbed a piece of burning wood, brought it back, and set anything flammable within the house alight.

She wanted to say something profound for him. For Jake too, but nothing came.

As she turned from the house, she said, "I hope you find each other."

♦♦♦

RAINER WALKED BETWEEN the burning house and the burning barn. The two cars were still there. She should probably search them for anything that might be useful, but she was just too tired.

She walked by them on her way down the driveway.

What the hell is that incessant thudding?

The car?

She pulled her gun, checked to ensure there was one in the chamber, then pointed it at the ground. Crouching, she angled her approach to come from the driver's blind spot.

Something was definitely moving in there.

Staying low and dropping lower the closer she got, she worked back up to the back door post and slid cautiously sideways, gun ready.

As she looked in the side window, two feet came up and pounded hard on the glass. Rainer jumped back, gun up in a two-handed stance and her finger adding a little more pressure.

The feet came up again.

They were small feet.

"Sam?"

Another rhythmic thud.

Rainer ran back to the car and pounded on the glass. "Sam?"

She saw the girl's head pop up.

"Sam!" This time tears did come. "Oh my god, Sam!"

"Rainer!"

And then the memory from Federmen's cesspool of a mind rose up from the depths. *The girl with the boy's name is in the Fed's car.*

Holy shit, how had she missed that?

And there was still something else in the recesses of her mind… Something else.

A glance told her the girl was tied up, so Rainer told her to get back under the blanket while she threw a large rock through the driver's-side window. And then she was out.

Though she stank of smoke, and was covered in the blood of both the girl's father and his killer, Rainer didn't hesitate. She hugged the girl and was hugged back just as hard. Both were crying, both were talking over each other. It took a long while, but they settled down and Rainer was able to hold her out at arm's length and check her over. "You're okay?"

"Yeah, I am."

"He didn't hurt you? You're sure?" She knew he hadn't. Couldn't. But still, she had to ask.

"I'm sure." Sam looked at her. "Where is he now?"

"He's dead, honey."

"You killed him?"

"I killed him."

"Good."

Rainer hugged her one more time. Then Sam said, "Where's my dad?"

♦♦♦

IT WAS THE hardest thing she'd ever had to do, but she explained to the girl exactly what happened to her father. She told Sam how much he worried about her, how much he loved her.

She explained, very briefly, her ability to read people. How she got things from them. Then she said, "And Sam, even as he died, even when he was in pain, I want you to know, the last thought he had was for you." Her eyes filled with tears yet again. "He loved you. More than you'll ever know."

Sam's eyes, already tear-filled, now released a new flood. She looked down. "I know," she said. "Loved him, too."

She snuffled, scrubbed an arm under her nose, reminding Rainer that, despite how she talked, she was just a little girl. She turned her eyes back to Rainer. "You think he's with Mom now?"

"I honestly don't have an answer to that, honey," she said. "I hope he's somewhere where he's as happy as he can be without you."

"Me, too."

"You were his little girl and he would have done anything for you." As she said the words, another name ran through her head. *April.*

For her own sanity, she pushed the name back into the box where it had been for two years.

"Come on," Rainer said. "We've got a long drive ahead of us."

"Okay," she said, accepting it. "You know where we're going?"

"I do." She had known from Bo that she would be going north. It was Federman who let her know how far.

They walked through the dark night back to the SUV. They held hands all the way.

Sam was hers to protect now.

PART THREE
DESOLATION

"The wolf at last stands divested of its sheep's clothing."

THE CALL OF THE CTHULHU
H. P. LOVECRAFT

Last Interlude

THE RAIN CAME down in biblical proportions, instantly soaking her to the skin, making her shiver. She huddled closer to the tiny bundle in her arms, trying to feed her warmth to the cold little body.

Behind her, the front door to her house stood ajar, giving an impression that things were slightly off-kilter. No lights burned in the windows, as it was far too late for that, and any respectable person was safe in their bed, not sitting on the bottom step of their front porch in the screaming rain with their child in their arms.

The front door spoke of things awry, but spoke too quietly regarding the things hidden in its yawning darkness.

Behind her, safe from the rain, in the off-kilter house, her husband lay, still in the bed he'd been murdered in, his body slumped to the side in a position the woman on the front step knew he would never have been comfortable in had he not been dead. The remarkable amount of blood splashed on the bed sang of horrors the vacant doorway only dared whisper.

Down the hall from her dead husband, in the bedroom decorated in bright primary colours, was the body of the one who had wanted her husband and child dead. The face of this second savagely murdered victim betrayed the shock of the actions that led to his death.

On the front porch, the one who had killed both men shivered again and rocked the child in her arms. Water ran from her hair and into her eyes and, try as she might, she couldn't stop it from soaking the child's blankets. There was a small part of her mind that somehow remained rational and asked why she sat there, but it was shouted down by the wild-eyed fear that bubbled up at the very thought of re-entering the house, and the terror that came with the consideration of leaving.

While the majority of her mind stumbled down a path of madness, the small rational part felt relief that the rain was washing the blood from her child's swaddles.

As she raised her face to the sky, the rain mixed with her tears and washed down and into the ragged, open wound at the child's throat, so dark against the pale skin and blankets.

Chapter Thirty-Two

IT HAD BEEN a damn ugly time just after the pack had made their escape from the barn and the insane woman. They hadn't gotten very far—just far enough to find a place to hide, out of sight of the main road—when Syd, Taylor, and Zero dropped the bikes where they'd abruptly stopped, stumbled away, tears and snot and puke bubbling from them.

Unaffected, only an adopted pack member, Moondoggie had stood watch while the three of them went through their digging-a-hole penance for the death of the Fed. It had been some heavy shit to observe, but he shut his mouth and kept watch until they'd clawed their way back to sanity.

Then they got back on the road.

♦♦♦

ZERO AND THE pack had been on the road for a week, travelling ever northward, mostly at night under Sister Moon, and sleeping during the day. Moondoggie didn't dig the cold, it didn't sit well with his aura. Though he'd been stuck in Florida, he'd always been a Cali dude at heart.

Someday, he thought, *I'm gonna get there. Gonna see Cali with my own eyes. Soak up the sun.*

Someday. But for now, he was a provisional member of Zero's pack. And, though he knew it pissed the others off, he couldn't seem to help himself from pissing and moaning about it the farther north they went.

"Goddamn stoner," Syd said to him during one stop. "The Fed's been dead eight days, and you're all bent out of shape on account of the cold?" Moondoggie figured the only thing stopping Syd from bitch-slapping him was because he'd gotten them out of the barn and watched over them after the Fed bought the farm. That gave him some cred.

Well, that, and the whole "pack never harms pack" thing.

But Syd kept saying this would be Taylor's first visit to the Hole and he didn't want to fuck it up. Syd kept saying it was always good to get new blood, but man, what a pain in the ass that new blood could be. Moon figured the "new blood" and "pain in the ass" references were being directed at his person. Might have been that Fed dude, but with him nothing but a barbequed hot dog now, the old boy must have been talking about Moon. Syd kept harping on about the old days with Bo, whoever the fuck Bo was.

Moon noticed he only talked like this out of earshot of Zero. He still had respect for the pack, but he went on and on about what a damn shame it was the pack had been forced to pariah Bo. On and on, the dude whined, like he was doing right now. Disparaging the wrong dude. Moon had hooked them up with wheels. What had this Fed and Bo dudes done? Didn't matter. Old dog was harpin', harshin' Moondoggie's mellow. Again.

Moon sighed, but nonchalant-like, and cocked his head, showing Syd he was paying attention. *Yeah, my dude, I'm smellin' what yer cookin'. Don't care much for the meal, but I'm sniffin' the aromas.*

"Yeah, I still needed to enforce it, and I did," Syd said. *Ah, okay, still goin' on about this Bo dude that got the bum's rush.* "But, goddamn. We had us some times," he said.

"When was that?" Moon asked, just to get Syd's mind from his bitching.

"Two years ago? Three?" Syd couldn't remember. Wolves really seemed to have a problem with keeping time, except for when they needed to get to the Hole.

It could be argued I got chronologically fucked-up. Shit, Moon knew where that was from. *What song?* He needed some Cheetos. Get his brain back in order. Syd was still talking.

"But yeah," he said. "Bo's probably been out three years."

Then, Syd huffed out a laugh. "Bo was a lot of fun with that whole 'Atomic Punk' deal. Man! We'd crash a place, he'd drop the boom box, crank Van Halen, and have the pack in hysterics. To see him out-Roth David Lee Roth—as a wolf no less!—left us laughing so hard we could barely feed. He'd thump his chest like fuckin' Tarzan and go on about nobody ruling the streets but him, the Atomic Punk! Yeah, right."

Moondoggie wasn't up on his Van Halen, so he didn't really know what Syd was talking about, but he nodded sagely, took his word for it.

"Then he had to go and get his sorry ass excommunicated." Syd hung his head. "I still can't figure out why Bo went hunting on his own. You're with a pack, you hunt with the pack, simple as that. Someone always had your back. This time, though," he said, "Bo goes solo, gets sloppy—because the fucking Atomic Punk was *always* sloppy, we *always* had to keep him in line—and brought down some unwanted attention on our pack. When he got back, Zero took him to task on it."

To Moondoggie's ear, she'd done more than that. He read between the lines—Moon was ninja-good at that—and realized that Zero verbally kicked this Bo's ass. "Then what happened?" Moon asked.

"Then Bo lost his fuckin' mind and attacked Zee."

Moondoggie winced. Nothing more needed to be said. *You don't cross that line. You don't break that trust. Pack never attacks pack.* Mic drop.

"Seems like every time some wolf goes solo, some bad mojo hits," Syd said. "Shit, look at the Fed." He hooked a thumb back toward the bikes. "Grabs a girl and it fucks up everything."

Thank the good lord above, or Mayor McCheese, or whomever ran the interior works of this grand cosmic show, that Moondoggie's bike acquisitions numbered four, and the number of escapees had numbered exactly the same when they'd needed to flee the barn.

Then there was that moment when they'd zipped by one of the cars and saw the kid peeking out from the back window. As soon as Zero saw the kid in the back seat, she lost her shit, started screaming at them to get gone. Some fuckery there. *Serious* fucking fuckery.

To be fair, Moon got a little wigged out when he looked at the kid too. Which was weird.

So, they'd cranked the throttles and got gone.

Jeez, Moon thought, *Glad we took the bikes instead of my van. Syd probably would'a started calling it "van Halen" or some such shit in honour of this Bo dude.* The thought gave him pause. It actually wasn't a bad name for a van. Maybe he should get a message to Eddie and Alex on that.

Damn, he could use some Cheetos.

They stayed quiet for a moment, each wrapped in their own thoughts. Then Syd stood. "But Bo...ol' Boris always was an original, though," he said. "He was always a little different from the rest of the pack. Seemed to feel things a little more, experience events a little deeper." He glanced at Moon. "Probably how he managed to get his ass killed."

Syd shook his head, stared at Moon for another moment, then walked away. As he did, Moon heard him say, "Should be the Fed's or Bo's ass in the van, not some fuckin' drug-addled hippy."

Dude's totally *harshin' my mellow,* Moondoggie thought.

And he's probably gonna do it all the way to the Hole. All because he's nostalgic for a couple of dead dickhead pack members.

The Atomic Punk, Moondog thought. *What a moron.*

♦♦♦

THE WIND FELT good on his face. Taylor wished he wasn't stuck puttering along at the speed Zero set. What use was a fucking Harley if you couldn't open it up? *Might as well taken that fucking disgusting Econoline.*

He could just see himself cranking the throttle and letting the bike do the rest. He could almost see himself as that guy on the cycle on the cover of that old Meat Loaf album, *Bat Out of Hell*. The one in red that Richard Corben had painted, with the guy bursting out of the graveyard, seemingly straight out of hell. The exhaust spewing blue-white fire, clots of earth flying in all directions—and there Taylor would be, on top of the screaming monster, wrestling for control, every muscle straining as he clung to the mechanical beast for the ride of his life.

That's what he wished. Ah, reality...shit. Reality was another matter altogether. Zero in the lead, with Syd alongside, and Moon riding alongside Taylor. Moon—Taylor couldn't call him Moondoggie—at least the guy had got them out of the situation at the barn, but as the pack got farther and farther north, he became more and more useless and, besides, he was a pain in the ass. Even Syd, who normally could be counted on for a laugh, was well on his way to hemorrhoidal status himself with all that fucking whining about Moon and Bo. He was even throwing in the odd nostalgic comment about the Fed. And Taylor knew Syd had never really liked the Fed all that much when he was alive, which meant he *really* must hate Moon.

Like the rest of them, Taylor hadn't had a lot of experience with the Fed, but after listening to Moon singing his off-key classic rock and damn near every other line a quote from some obscure goddamn song, he found himself getting a little wistful for the freaky bastard and the way he'd talked about himself in the third person.

It had been fucked-up, but it hadn't been incessant.

Shit, he had to admit, *okay, it was incessant.*

He really didn't miss the Fed at all. *Weird how we suddenly think of the biggest assholes as not that bad once they're on the wrong side of the dirt.*

And then there was Zee. Taylor heaved a big sigh.

Taylor didn't know what the fuck was up with her. Syd had been with her for damn near six years. Longer than anyone. Almost since she'd became a shifter herself. Even he admitted he didn't know what was going on in that pretty head of hers.

Taylor had only been with her about two years, but even in that time, he had been on a lot of hunts, seen things go really well, and seen things go from bad to worse. They had taken on uprights when the odds were horribly stacked against them. Like with the Winnebago in Mexico. Or god, that time in Nevada! The four of them had walked into a bar out off the main roads. They swaggered in all full of piss and vinegar, getting all up in everyone's face, causing enough shit that the weak house band had to stop butchering ZZ Top because everyone was more interested in them. The bar had been packed, and it had been the four of them—Zee, Bo, Taylor, and Syd—against them all, like some scene in a fucking movie. Oh, how they had feasted that night! Taylor smiled again, remembering how drunk they had gotten afterward, out in the desert. And, later that night, Taylor and Zero—both in an alcoholic haze of fuzzy minds and engorged privates—had slid off in the velvet midnight and fucked—hell, *rutted* was probably the more accurate term—like there would be no tomorrow…

Nevada ended up all over the news media. He'd even collected some of the newspaper stories, and probably still had some yellowing, crumpled clippings stashed in a bag somewhere.

But now...that Zee—the Zero who had literally howled at the moon as she came, bucking as she pushed hard against him—that Zee was gone, and now there was only the moody, unreadable Zee left behind. The Zee who froze while one of the pack was attacked. The Zee who ordered them out while one of their own pleaded for help. Zee, the one who never walked away from a fight as long as Taylor—hell, as long as Syd—had known her.

Now there was the Zee who ran from one upright, and made the remaining pack do the same, their tails between their legs.

Like she was fucking menopausal or something. Zee on the rag. It had never bothered Taylor, being in a bitch-led pack, despite some of the comments from the other packs they'd interacted with. But something was going on lately, and it was really beginning to piss him off. Not the fact that she was a woman. The fact that she was turning into a pussy.

Taylor checked up ahead. Zero still sat low in the seat, as though hiding from something. He couldn't see her face, but knew it would be giving away nothing. She was a million miles from here, totally on autopilot.

He remembered her face as the Fed got murdered by that fucking killbot chick.

He remembered her freaking out when she saw the kid in the Fed's car.

She hadn't been right since.

Eight fucking days Zero'd been like this. Not right. Like someone had pulled out her teeth and claws.

What the fuck is it with this little girl? Or the adult one, for that matter, the one who had killed the Fed. He hadn't gotten a good look at her, she'd been a blur of motion. But there was something there…something he recognized.

He shook his head to clear it. *Fuck it,* he thought. *I've danced around it for eight fucking days.* Besides, they had enough to worry about without that shit sidetracking him.

Eight fucking days.

Put it outta yer mind, boy, he thought.

CHAPTER THIRTY-THREE

"RAY?"

Rainer looked over to her passenger. "What's up, Sam?"

"You think...is it okay if I talk to Dad?"

She held up her poker face. "Of course, sweetheart," she said. "You know where it is."

Keeping one eye on the road, she watched as Sam popped the glovebox, pulled out the mobile phone, and pressed the power button.

Sam watched the screen intently as it booted up.

Her fingers danced over the lock screen, entering the code, then she pressed the phone icon.

"You know what you're gonna say?"

Sam shook her head. "No. Just wanna talk to him."

Rainer put out a hand and stroked the girl's hair, and she felt her poker face giving way to tears. The pain coming off the girl was palpable to any human being. But to Rainer, it was so much more intense, the memories transferring from Sam through the contact, and infusing Rainer's mind with images of Zach that she shouldn't have been privy to. Personal, wonderful moments between the two of them.

She concentrated on the road, brushing away the tears as surreptitiously as she could as Sam dialled.

As usual, as soon as she dialled, she flipped it to speaker so they could both hear him.

"Hey Jack! You've reached Zach!" said the dead man. "Cut me some slack, don't give me no flack. Leave me a message and I'll call you right back!"

Jesus, Rainer thought. *He sounds so happy.*

Then Sam started speaking.

"Hey, Dad. Me again." She sighed. "I just wanted to tell you I miss you. Like a whole fucking bunch." She slid her thumbs along the phone casing. *Like she's stroking her father's face.* "Ray's taking pretty good care of me, just so's you know. She's pretty cool. But I guess you know that.

"Anyway, I better let you go. I'm sorry for the cuss word. I'm trying to stop for"—she sniffed, sucked in a breath—"for you, Dad.

"I love you. You were the best dad ever. I miss you."

Then, so quietly, Rainer barely heard it, she said. "Bye, Dad."

She ended the call, powered off the phone, and returned it to the glovebox.

They both watched the road for a long time.

"I see you wiping your face, you know," Sam said.

"Yeah, I see you doing the same."

"Fuck you. I'm not beleaguered crying. *You're* beleaguered crying."

"Didn't you just tell your dad you're not going to swear anymore?"

"No, I—"

"You did," Rainer said, not even trying to keep the laugh out of her voice. "You totally did!"

"If you'd let me goddamn finish, Ray!" She huffed, fighting—and failing—the smile on her own face. "*God!* What I was *gonna* say, before I was *rudely* interrupted, was that I said I was *trying* to stop. Didn't say I was fucking *doing* it."

"Oh," Rainer said. "Okay then. That's a whole different thing."

"Damn right."

Rainer stretched out an arm and nudged Sam. The girl responded by dramatically throwing herself toward the door. Then she came back and did the same to Rainer, who responded as dramatically as she could while still driving safely.

"Gotta ask, kiddo," she said. "Why do you say 'beleaguered' so much?" She totally knew why, but wanted to hear what Sam would say.

She told Rainer the story of her and Zach meeting Jake, and her dad using that word, and her finding out it was a bad cuss word.

"So you just happen to like that particular swear word?" Rainer said.

Sam looked at her. "No," she said. "No, nothing like that. I know it's not really a swear word."

"How do you know that?"

"Because every time I swear…shit, swore…around Dad, he'd always say, 'Sam!' or 'Sam! Language!'"

"Okay."

"He never said that when I said 'beleaguered,' so I knew he was bullshitting me. It's not really a swear word."

"So then why do you still use it?"

"Cuz," she said, but her voice was very quiet. Heartbreakingly quiet. "Reminds me of Dad. And Jake."

And that caught Rainer by surprise. Then they were both crying again, and holding hands again.

"I miss them, Ray," Sam said.

"Me too, kiddo," she said. "Me, too."

The tears eventually slowed, then stopped. But their hands remained linked.

Rainer still felt the pain in the child, but it was pushed down a bit for now. Like it had been wrapped in layers of blankets. Still there, but less urgent.

"We're a tough couple of bitches, ain't we?" Sam said, and Rainer was caught so unaware she snorted with laughter.

"Who you calling bitch, bitch?" she said when she'd finally got herself back under control.

"I'm calling us both bitches, bitch! Tough bitches!"

"Badasses?"

Sam nodded her head emphatically. "Definitely. We're the Badass Bitches Brigade!"

"Right."

"Well, okay then," Sam said. "But if we're both gonna be badass bitches, we gotta get a handle on all this cryin' bullshit."

"Right again," she said, shaking her head, smiling. She was falling in love with this kid.

Then the smile fell away and she tried to keep the worried look off her face.

Oh Zach, she thought. *I'm falling in love with your daughter.* She thought of her own daughter, just a silhouetted sound behind an upstairs bedroom window now. *I don't know if I can lose another one.*

She looked over at Sam, sitting in the passenger seat, watching the scenery flash by. They'd gotten to know each other much better over the past ten days, and the more they talked, the more she saw the spirit of Zach in the little girl. She wished Sam had clearer memories of her mother, but there was so little there, it was hard to glean anything from her. Most of her world was Zach, so of course, he was her main influence.

But she saw something else, too. There was something else there. A brightness. It was like looking at a diamond in dirt, or a particularly bright star. She stood out.

Still, it was more than that. There were ways that others could interact with Sam. If she let someone in, as she had with Zach and Jake and, lately, Rainer, then it became a normal interaction.

But she had to let each person in. She had to give them that permission. Without it, everyone was locked out and could only have a limited interaction. They would only get the surface of Sam, but none of the depth.

It felt like Sam vibrated at a different frequency, and when someone was accepted into her trust, they came to vibrate at that different frequency as well.

Rainer had been puzzling over it all week, and still couldn't explain it any better than that.

But she felt it now. They were at the same frequency, her and Sam. Sam had let her in, and now, Rainer couldn't help but love her, and worry about her. And what was to be done about that?

The solution was simple, of course. She looked over at Sam, put a hand on her shoulder, and gave it a light squeeze. *I won't lose you. I won't let anything take you away.*

On the heels of that thought, another one came up.

"How about we make one more call?" She smirked, then finished. "This time, I'm doing the talking."

Sam popped the glove box with a smirk of her own.

CHAPTER THIRTY-FOUR

TEN DAYS IN, Zero expressed interest in someone else taking the lead bike position. Syd was sick of passively doing fuck all and, against Taylor's weak protests, he pulled seniority to take the lead for a while, hoping it would take his mind off all the bullshit.

On the eighth day, after a ridiculously near-miss with a deer that bounded out onto the highway and somehow threaded the needle between the four Harleys, Zero decided they'd ride through the day. They had decided it over dinner. This was after they'd ditched the bikes at the side of the road and hunted that deer down.

"We're far enough north now that there's not gonna be enough traffic to piss us off anymore," she'd said.

Now, they were day-riding.

They had been on the road most of the day and had just rolled through some tiny-ass blink-and-it's-gone town in some godforsaken northern Canadian territory. Syd knew most of their states were actually called provinces, but then, being weird-ass Canadians, they had to go and call some of them territories. Just to fuck him up.

He'd made the mistake, during a piss break, to mention that to the rest of the pack. Of course, Zero said nothing. That was her standard form of communication now. Non-communication.

Taylor had opened his mouth to say something, but Moondoggie beat him to it. "Wait one, there, my dude. I'm sensing a flaw in the Force, can you dig it?"

"What the fuck is he on about?" Syd said to Taylor. Taylor was smart enough to just shrug his shoulders and look to Moondoggie to elucidate.

"I'm on about your skewed, racist views of our neighbours to the north, my man."

"I'm not being racist. Just saying, this whole provinces and territories thing fucks me up."

"We got that too, my dude."

"What?"

"And we're worse."

"What?" Syd said. "The fuck you say."

"I do," Moondoggie said, rather contemplatively. "I do say fuck. Probably too much. It's a fuckin' problem."

"Jesus Christ, Moondog. Focus."

"Gee."

Syd rolled his eyes. "Fucksake. Moondog*gie*. Happy now?"

"Delirious."

"Then explain your point." Moondog stared at him, uncomprehendingly. "Something about provinces, territories, Canada, and the US?" *God, why do I even let myself get sucked into this shit?*

"Ah," Moondog said, his entire upper body nodding understanding. "Right, right. Okay, so...dig it." He paused for effect, spread his arms, and said, "Puerto Rico, my man."

Syd said, "What?" at the same time Taylor said, "Ohhhhh!"

Fucker was right, of course.

"And that's not even to mention Washington DC, am I right?"

Fucksake.

Syd finished his piss, shook off, stowed his meat, and walked away without saying anything. Because apparently he was racist against Canadians.

It was the kind of week he was having.

Fucking Canuckistan. Fucking Canadians. If they weren't so damn funny, Syd would feed on more of them.

♦♦♦

THREE HOURS LATER, eating Canadians was the last thing on his mind. No, right about now, he was ready to feed on fucking Moondog.

They'd pulled over at a crossroads because the hippie was advocating for a left turn, where Syd knew they needed to keep going straight through.

"Dude," Moondog said, "You gotta listen to the Earth. She'll never steer you wrong."

"You're listening to the fucking *Earth*?" Syd said. "Then why do you have that out?" He stabbed an accusatory finger at the paper map sprayed out on his lap.

"Sometimes you gotta *old*-school it, my man."

"Sometimes, you gotta trust the fucking navigational satellites in geosynchronous orbit, too, you goddamned pothead." This despite the fact that he wasn't really getting any decent information from his horrifyingly expensive and currently useless GPS. But he wasn't going to let the hippie know that.

Moondog looked skyward, clearly ignoring the fact that the roof of the car a couple of inches above his shaggy head was blocking his view. He brought his hands up, cupping his skull. "Negative *waves*, man! Seriously negative *waves*!"

Jesus Christ, I'm gonna kill him, Syd thought. *Rule or no rule.*

"*This* was the right way, dude." He stuck his finger on a point on the paper map. "I'm tellin' ya, we shoulda made a left in Albuquerque!"

"What the..." Syd shook his head. "We were never even *near* Albuquerque. What are you even *talking* about?"

"Literary reference, man," he said. "Bugs Bunny, my man. Any major dude will tell you."

Syd had just about decided to throw pack rules to the wind, and the only thing that saved the dreadlocked moron was when the phone in Zero's pocket buzzed an incoming call and she handed it off to him.

Calls were infrequent enough that, if one came in, Syd typically stared at the unit as though he needed to remember how to answer it. He did this now, then flipped the phone open.

"Yeah?"

"Hey. Syd?"

He answered, "Who's asking?"

"This is Rainer. You might remember me as the one who killed that asshole Fed, and made the rest of you run with your tails between your legs."

Syd kept quiet, feeling all the muscles in his face tighten. The other three straddled their bikes, staying quiet, obviously sensing from his face that there was something weird about the call.

"Anyway, I just wanted you to know something."

"What's that?" Syd said, making his voice drip with menacing sarcasm.

"That we're going to catch up to you. And when we do?"

"Yeah?"

"When we do, we're going to crush you." Rainer's voice also came across as menacing. "You and your entire fucking pack."

"That supposed to strike fear into our hearts or something?"

"No. Just a promise."

"Fair enough. You come along, Buffy. Bring it. I'd love to see you try."

He'd kept his voice calm through the entire exchange. But now, Syd pulled the phone from his ear, disconnected the call.

Then he reached his arm above his head and threw the mobile phone at the pavement, watched it shatter into sharp plastic and glass bits. Then he got off his bike and crushed the bigger pieces under his heel.

"Bitch."

He walked back to the Harley, no one saying a word. He walked right past the ride and up to Moondog. Then he reached out, grabbed Moondog's map, and tore it to shreds, throwing the pieces high to let the wind take the bits.

He went back to his motorcycle, started it, looked disdainfully at the road to his left the hippie had been advocating for, and instead put the bike in gear and headed straight down the road.

The mood he was in, he couldn't give an acrobatic flying shit if the rest of the pack followed or not.

♦♦♦

THREE MINUTES LATER, at their first opportunity to talk to Syd again, no one chose to ask him about the call. As expected, as Syd had pulled away from the intersection, Moondog acquiesced and then the other three were back on the road, heading straight through the intersection, catching up to Syd.

But, three minutes later, Syd slowed the Harley down, first to a crawl, finally coming to a stop, but not bothering to pull off to the side of the road.

Taylor came up on his right. "What are you stopping for?" he said.

"Yeah, man," Moondog said from his left. "What's the deal, dude?"

Zero, to Syd's ongoing dismay, said nothing, choosing to wait behind the three of them. Like she had handed over the reins to him completely. Like she had given up.

"Beer," he answered. "I want beer."

"Works for me," Moondog said. "Probably a good time to tell you that one of my clients told me about a town just off that intersection to the left back there. Not on the map, but they got a bar."

"Fucksake," Syd said. He dropped his head. Breathed in. Breathed out. Then growled out a "fine. Lead the way, Moondog."

"Righteous," Moon said. "Any major dude will tell ya."

"Moondog?"

"Yeah, Sydster?"

"Shut the fuck up and find me some beer."

"Sure, Syd."

"A lot of beer."

"Right, Syd."

"An ocean of beer."

"You got it, Syd."

CHAPTER THIRTY-FIVE

MOONDOGGIE U-TURNED AND the pack followed him back to the intersection, and they took that turn. To the newest pack member's credit, he led them to an even smaller blink-and-you'll-miss-it town, but he led them straight to the promised watering hole.

Yes. They could blow off some steam. They parked the Harleys and Zero told them they needed to get some beers in them, maybe start a fight, maybe get laid. They needed to forget the past few days for a while.

That's what she told them. They needed to forget the past few days.

She knew they were thinking she was talking about all four of them.

But there wasn't enough beer, fists, and dicks in the world to get her to forget the past few days.

Or that little girl.

♦♦♦

THE FOUR OF them—Syd in the lead, and Zee bringing up the rear—entered the drinking establishment. It couldn't be classed as a bar, at least as far as Syd was concerned. There was no real indication that it was a drinking establishment of any kind. Just some fucked-up sign over the door. No neon beer lights, posters of booze ads, no sports memorabilia. This place didn't even have electric lights.

Syd caught the smell as he walked through the door and first stepped on the rough-hewn planks of the floor. Lanterns. The place was lit with old-style lanterns, for chrissakes.

Even that shithole in Nevada had been outfitted better than this. Not even a damn jukebox.

It was four walls and a roof, some mismatched tables and chairs. And, from the looks of it, some hardcore regulars. At the bar, a young man with long brown hair pulled back into a ragged ponytail, most of the hair managing to slop back out again, served the drinks.

Hardly looks old enough to drink, Syd thought. *Ah, hell, what do I know? He could be forty for all I know.*

There was a table toward the back. Moondog gestured toward it and Syd nodded. Zero was back to follow mode. As Syd passed the boy behind the bar, he held up four fingers.

"Four beers. Draft," he said and kept walking.

"No draft, buddy."

"No draft?" Syd stopped and stared at the kid behind the bar. *What kind of a fuckin' bar is this?* "What the hell do you mean, 'no draft'?"

The bartender, who really was a boy now that Syd got a good look at him, leaned over the bar, a nasty rag still clenched in one hand. "Do I fucking stutter? I said, no…fucking…draft. Pick something else." He pointed to the bottles lined up behind the bar, like they were the menu.

Syd immediately felt the hackles rising on the back of his neck. He tried breathing through his nose and counting to ten.

The Fed dead, Zee in la-la land, assholes on the cellphone, a girl we can't kill, a week and a half on the road, and now some pimpled punk all up in my grill. Syd was really trying to keep his composure, but he wasn't being too successful at tamping it down.

Moondog sauntered over. *Oh yeah,* he thought, *and a fuckin' hippie beach bum riding shotgun, how could I forget that?*

"Dude, you gettin' the beers, man?"

"Go away," Syd said through clenched teeth.

The punk still there, leaning on the bar. Despite the implied challenge, Moondog didn't leave.

"Was just gonna help you bring 'em—"

"Moondog," Syd said, his voice dropping lower. "Go away. I'll deal with it."

Moondog backed off, his hands held in front of him, placating. "Negative waves, dude, negative waves."

Syd turned back to the bartender.

"Beer," he said. "Just get me four fucking beers."

"I don't think so."

He didn't—

"WHAT?"

The bartender's tone was confident and even. "Jesus, *dude*, get your hearing checked," he said, stabbing a finger at his own ear. "I'll keep it to single syllables: I...don't...think...so. Want it put another way? How 'bout, 'no'?"

At this point, two lumber-jacketed regulars scooped their beers and sidled over to an unoccupied table. The bartender continued.

"Even easier, this even you should be able to understand: *Fuck off*."

To Syd's credit, he didn't explode on the spot. "What's your name?"

"Why?" said the bartender. "You gonna write a letter to the management?"

"No," Syd said, baring his teeth. "I wanna be able to tell my pack who it was I killed."

Syd was beginning to shift. He could feel it coming, and didn't try to stop it.

"God*damm*it!" The barkeep slapped the top of his bar with a damp hand. "Cocksuckin' *were*wolves. I fuckin' *knew* it." It was the next comment that actually gave Syd pause for a second.

"Fuckin' Stinky Pete and his fuckin' predictions."

It only stopped Syd for a second. The shift completed with a wet popping of bone and the syrupy sounds of muscle sliding over bone. Syd was ready. He lunged at the kid behind the bar, allowing his fury to scale up to eleven. His claws dug into the rough flooring and his powerful muscles launched him in a trajectory that would take him over the bar and right at the kid's throat.

Syd was in the air, his senses focused to the single pulsing vein in the kid's neck, anticipating the dark, warm spray—

The kid's expression hadn't changed. He simply held up one finger, as though to scold a child.

Then Syd stopped.

Just...

Stopped.

He was in mid-launch. His hind legs stretched fully after the jump, his front legs extended out, ready to grip the boy, his mouth open and already salivating. No part of him was touching any surface. He was in mid-flight, but he wasn't going anywhere.

The bar went quiet, the only sounds coming from the scrape of a chair, a subdued cough, and the pattering of Syd's saliva on the floor.

The kid dropped his rag and came around the bar. He passed the two lumber jackets. One of them hooked a thumb at Syd. "Hey guys, look! Fuckin' air-wolf."

"Ah doan know..." said the other. "He's mighty quiet now. Hush-puppy?"

"Actually, in that pose," said another, "he looks just like Superman's dog. What was 'is name?"

"Krypto, wasn't it?"

"Yeah! Krypto!"

I'll kill them all, Syd thought. *All of them.*

The kid ignored the exchange. He ambled calmly over to the wolf, as though something frozen in mid-air was a common occurrence, grabbed a solid handful of Syd's snout, and walked him the length of the room. Syd was incredulous.

This skinny shit put his hands on him? And he was leading him to the door, and Syd could do nothing about it because he was still in the fucking air.

"Red, can you open the door so I can throw this shit out?"

"Yup."

The door was opened and Syd felt a remarkably strong push and he was sailing through the air—as he had planned to do all along—and landed about ten yards from the bar entrance. He leaped to his feet and in three bounds was back at the door. He threw his entire weight at it.

And stuck.

Again, he was mid-air, bunched up and bracing for an impact that never came. He had stopped less than an inch from the door. With some experimenting, he found if he slowly eased his limbs, at least this time he could move.

With some maneuvering, he was able to get himself unstuck, though it meant him dropping on his ass most ungracefully.

The door opened one more time, and three more wolves were tossed unceremoniously into the muddy street.

Now! While the door's open!

Syd hurled himself at the entrance, putting everything he had into it. He was going to take out that scrawny motherfucker if it was the last thing he did.

Until he got stuck again, this time about three feet away from the door. He was in the same place, but this time the door was still open, and the barkeep was standing there, a look of disgust riding his face like an old friend.

"You're one dumb son of a bitch, you know that?" the kid said. "Try it again and I'll stop doing what I'm doing now, and instead, I'll kick your bitchy little ass. Now get out, and stay the hell out! You can tell the rest of your goddamn pack that none of you are allowed in this bar."

Syd was sure that, after the door closed, he heard the kid mutter, "Werewolves. Goddamn werewolves."

That was when he looked at the sign above the bar for the second time.

Abandon hope, all ye who enter here.

No fucking shit, Syd thought, bringing a half-shifted arm—more paw than hand—to his face to clear a gobbet of mud. He flicked the offending crud away with disdain.

"Dude!" Moondog said, the word coming out *daewd.* "What the hell just came down? That was one righteous bitch-slapping we—"

"Shut up," Zero said, her voice a whisper in the twilight.

"That fuckin' bastard!" Syd said, his fists—now they were closer to fists—clenching and unclenching. "I'm going to burn this fucking place down to ash!"

"Shut up," Zero said, the volume raised half a notch.

"Ha!" laughed Moondog. "Dude! You sound just like the three little pigs, man! 'I'll huff an' I'll puff an' I'll *blow* yer—"

"SHUT UP!" Zero roared. When Zee let loose, it was biblical. Syd thought he felt the ground move under him. And he thought *he* was filled with righteous fury. Maybe he was, but Zee was Mount fucking Vesuvius.

Moondog and Taylor literally went so far as to drop to the ground again and present their bellies. Moondog may have pissed himself, but Syd couldn't tell with all the mud.

Syd wasn't going to debase himself like that. He had more dignity than that, and both he and Zero knew it.

As they stared at each other, at an impasse, the door opened "...hah! No shit, Willie! 'Bout the only thingy missed was the rolled up newspaper on the snout, eh? Haha! Bad doggie! I'm thinkin'..." A lumber-jacketed man—were there any males in this town who weren't?—was looking behind him at the other patrons still in the bar as he exited. Finally, his grey head swivelled on his whiskered neck and his eyes came around to four sets staring coldly into his, teeth bared, hackles raised. His next step faltered, inches from the step.

"I'm thinkin'...uh...I'm thinkin' I could use another beer or two before I call it a night." With that, he backed into the bar he had just walked out of, his eyes never leaving the four wolves that waited not ten feet away. Syd entertained ideas of stringing his intestines around the bar like twine, of throwing the man's still-warm skull so hard that it punched a hole through the tissue-and-spit wall and landed on the bar, a grinning reminder of the fate that awaited them all. They couldn't stay in there forever, and the bartender couldn't keep an eye on every one of them once they left.

It was going to be a good night after all.

"Let's go," Zero said.

Syd swung his head around in surprise. "What?"

"Let's leave," she said, her voice back down to that low whisper. "There's nothing left to do here. We're beat, no two ways about it. Now, we leave."

"But there's gotta be a dozen guys in there!" Syd said. "We can nail them as they come out!"

"You really think anyone's going to come out in the next couple of hours? Get a brain! They're going to be in there drinking their faces off just to forget what they're *imagining* is waiting for them right now. Nobody's coming out of that bar tonight." It was the most that Zero had said in days. And it wasn't what Syd wanted to hear right now.

"Doesn't matter, Zee," he said, trying to keep any pleading tone out of his voice. He was getting pissed with himself because he normally wasn't a pleader. It pissed him off and made him feel inadequate. "We can wait 'em out. We've done it before. Remember Daytona? We—"

"We aren't in Daytona. We never got our asses handed to us in Daytona. And we aren't here to waste our time waiting out a bunch of fat, drunken old men who'll likely piss themselves or puke before we can get the first bite in." She dropped her head to look at the mud. Paw prints everywhere. "I've made my decision and it's final."

She looked back up, squarely into Syd's eyes.

"We leave for the Hole. Tonight. Now." There was no arguing with her.

What a goddamn time for Zero to assert her authority again.

CHAPTER THIRTY-SIX

OVER THE COURSE of their travels, Rainer got in the habit of asking, at every stop, if anyone had seen a scruffy group of biker types with a shitty disposition. Some had. She wasn't far behind. A day at most.

Then there was the day she rolled into a town that was more a collection of buildings than an actual place where people lived on a continual basis. The streets were rutted pathways of permanent mud, slowly migrating out of town on the tires and fenders of the rusted, decades-old vehicles that bounced along their length.

"I'm just going to try and figure out where we are, okay?"

"No problem," Sam said.

She parked the car at the end of the row of wooden structures, half expecting to see some sort of hitching post. She leaned over, popped the glove box, and pulled out the map, having learned a few days ago that GPS was useless here.

She got out of the car for some air and spread the map on the hood of the car. Her finger traced the path she had taken and paused briefly at each recognizable point of reference. Then she traced the long distance to the next one, easily a couple of hundred miles beyond where they were right now.

"Hmph!" she said, looking up at the town. "Place either doesn't exist or doesn't have a name."

"Or the mappin' guys ain't *heard* of us yet." The statement had been delivered through a cigarette-sharpened voice behind her. "Hell, we only *been* here seventy-odd *years*. Only *bad* news travels fast, eh?"

Rainer turned, a little miffed that she hadn't heard the man coming up behind her. Then again, maybe he had just been standing there all along, part of the landscape. He was short, his grime-encrusted hunting cap levelling off around Rainer's chin, which qualified him for hobbit status. Long, white-yellow hair hung in dirty clumps under the cap, clawing their way into his collar and arcing over the front of his padded nylon vest. An unlit cigarette—partially smoked—hung from his lower lip as though it had been affixed there permanently. He could be in his late forties, or his late seventies. Rainer honestly had no clue. The rough and scratchy whiskers perfectly matched his voice.

"Where am I, mister…?" She left the last word open so he could fill in the blank.

"Dink."

That couldn't be his name.

"I'm in a town called Dink?" she asked incredulously.

The man broke out in a hoarse laugh that sounded like a smokers' hack. Still, it was a full-on belly laugh that most people reserve only for special occasions. And this man threw it out there for all the world to see. One hand on his knee, the other wrapped around his spacious belly, he truly enjoyed what he had heard.

It took him a minute or two, but he finally got a grip on his jocularity and was able to answer her.

"Dink ain't the name a' no *town*!" he said. "That'd be just *dumb*!" A few low chuckles slid out between breaths. "*I'm* Dink. Dink is *me*! *My* name is Dink!"

"Oh, I'm sorry mister—"

"Dink. Just call me Dink."

"Okay…Dink." The sound rolled out like she had shit on her tongue. "Where am I?"

"Lost, by the sounds of it."

Rainer made a face. *Christ! I've killed for less than this!*

"Okay, okay, pretty lady," Dink said. "Truth is, *ain't* no real name for the place. More'n anything, it's jest a collection of *buildin's*."

"Surely to god it's called something. How do you get your mail?"

"Ain't a lot of mail worth *gettin'*, most times bills an' such. But anythin' we *do* get comes from the *next* town over."

"That's two hundred miles from here."

"Yup."

"So—"

"*Mostly* we jest call it No Hope."

That stopped her for a second. *My god, what a bleak name for a town. Even one here in the middle of nowhere.*

"It's sorta the name of one of the *places* here," Dink continued. "Closest anything really *has* to a name, 'round abouts."

With that, Rainer looked up from her map and began to see the town. And then she began to understand the not-rightness of the place. Then it struck her.

No signs.

There wasn't a sign to be seen. Small buildings of various sizes and shapes. Paths—streets, she guessed—going here and there. But no signs. No street signs. No business signs. Not a one.

"Well," she said, putting on a smile. "That's going to make it a bit more difficult to navigate."

"Yup," Dink said cheerfully.

"First things first," Rainer said. "I'm looking for a bar. The local watering hole, where all the animals come to drink."

"'All the animals'?"

"Yeah. A place that serves the locals, but maybe a few stray passersby, such as myself. Maybe some place me and my little girl can get some food, too."

"Well," Dink said, scratching his head as though to excavate the knowledge hidden there. "There's only one bar 'round here that suits that description," he cocked an eye toward her. She noticed the other one tended to drift off to another direction altogether. It reminded her of those lizards that could look in two directions at once.

"Don't know if it's such a good *place* for a pretty little thing such as *yerself*, though," Dink finished. "*Definitely* not for a little *girl*. And you prolly won't be gettin' no eats, there, neither."

"Don't you worry about us, Dink. I can hold my mud pretty well. Well enough for the both of us."

"Betcha can, betcha can." His scraggly head bobbed in agreement. "No offence."

"None taken." She smiled. "Where can I find this place?"

"Funny enough, it's about the only *place* with any sort of sign around here. See that *street* over there?" Dink pointed.

Rainer looked at the muddy path he angled a crooked, cigarette-stained finger toward. "Yes, I see it."

"Head down *there* a piece. 'Bout your third or fourth place on yer *left*. Got a *sign* above the door. Y'can't miss it."

Rainer waited a beat for him to tell her what the sign was. When he didn't, she figured it was the fact that there was a sign at all was landmark enough for him. In a place with no signs, though, it rubbed against her curiosity. She had to ask.

"What's the sign say?"

"Oh!" Dink said. "I guess I jest *fergot* to letcha *know*! It's one a' them old *quotes*."

He scratched at his head again, excavating more information.

"Says, 'Abandon *hope*, all ye who *enter* here.' But, like I *said*, mostly we jest call it No *Hope*. It's sorta the name of any of the places here. Closest *anything* really has to a name."

"Dink," Rainer said, putting on her friendliest smile, "feel like a drink?"

"I usually try not to *imbibe* before six—"

"Well, it's 4:37. But I'm buying," Rainer said, looking at the capillaries sitting prominently on his nose.

"Okay," Dink said. "I could probably bend the rule *slightly*, just to make sure you *find* the place okay. *Especially* with the little *girl* an all."

"Okay, you just hold up for a moment, Dink, and let me get Sam."

Rainer went back to the car and opened the door.

Sam looked up at her, the bemused expression on her face betraying her thoughts on the man named Dink. "Listen, we need to get some information, and I think this is the place to do it. Apparently it's a bit of a rough place, but you're with me and I'll protect you, okay?"

"Okay," Sam said, not one iota of worry in her voice.

They headed off on foot to the bar with the sign above the door.

Abandon hope, all ye who enter here.

♦♦♦

"HERE," DINK SAID. "Let me show you *'round. Innerdooce* ya to some a' the *regulars*."

She stopped short of the steps, staring down at the muddy ground.

"Watcha lookin' at?" Dink asked.

"Paw prints," she said in a low voice. She looked up at Dink, her eyes squinted down so he couldn't see more than a dark slit. "You know anything about this, Dink?"

"I know there was some *excitement* here a couple of days ago," he responded as she dropped to her haunches. Then, more thoughtfully, "...er mebbe it was yesterday?" Her fingers stretched out and delicately traced the hardened divots imprinted in the mud. "Let's go *inside*. I'm *sure* someone can tell you *more*."

"Okay," she said absently. Standing back up, she brushed the stray dirt from her hands. "Lead on. I want to talk to someone about this."

CHAPTER THIRTY-SEVEN

THE DOOR OPENED and Theo began his long swim up out of a twenty-year sleep.

As he set glasses in the proper cubby under the bar, Theo heard the squeak of wood on wood and the chunk of the door being pulled shut. He looked up to see Dink lead the way into the bar, but it wasn't him who caught Theo's eye. It was the woman who stepped confidently in behind him.

Theo watched as she crossed the threshold. She passed under the sign he had hammered into place so many years earlier, her eyes tracking it as though it was going to jump off the wall at her.

Theo watched as all the eyes came up when the door opened, registered Dink, but stayed up when they caught sight of the woman behind him, holding the hand of a young girl. Her confidence was the first thing that struck Theo. This was a man's place. A hard-drinking, trash-talking, fist-fighting man's place. A sanctuary from the outside world. A boy's club—no girls allowed.

Theo watched her face. No fear. She had an expression on her face that said, *I can work with this.*

She moved in close to Dink's hairy ear, and Theo wondered what she thought of the amount of wax and dirt built up there, and spoke a few words. Dink spun around, his eyes bright with hope. "Really?"

"Really."

Dink moved to the centre of the room, his chest puffed out with obvious pride at having been the one chosen to deliver his message, though he was blushing furiously at having been thrown in the spotlight. But from the pep in his step and the sparkle in his eyes, Theo figured no little embarrassment at being thrown in the spotlight would stop him. He was excited as hell about something.

He pulled off his coat as he reached the core of the room, and raised it above his head.

"Hey everybody," he said in a raised voice. "Listen *up*! My new *lady* friend over there...uh..."

"Rainer," she said quietly.

"...Rainer, right, she says she's *buying*." There was a cheer. Dink smiled and waited patiently for it to die down a touch. Then he said, "She's buying for the rest of the *night*." Oh, how the eyes came up at that one, some of the inhabitants obviously questioning whether they had heard the older man correctly. Dink nailed it with the next line.

"Drinks are on *her*, boys, so belly up to the *bar*! *Yeee-HAWWWW!!!*" he yelled, swinging his jacket around above his head. Now Theo understood why Dink was able to suffer through the embarrassment. Normally, he avoided attention. But the promise of free drinks for the night would certainly ensure that a little extra attention wouldn't stop him. Not to mention the bragging rights this would afford him. This would be a story that would be repeated for years, and grow each time in the telling.

Almost like a naked man running in the streets, Theo thought, and began setting the drinks up.

♦ ♦ ♦

RAINER SAT DOWN with Dink at one of the corner tables, got the little girl situated, and one of the guys actually went a couple of shacks over to bring them both back some dinner. "Least I can do, seein' as how you're gonna pay to get me hammered tonight," he said.

And then she held court for the next few hours as the liquor flowed and the place got louder. The few men in the bar all got up and took the time to thank her at one point or another. Even a morose-looking man named Red who, Rainer found out when she shook his hand, generally said nothing more than "yup." She was also rather surprised to find out he was rich enough to buy the booze for the guys every night for the next decade and not even notice the deduction from his multiple accounts. She realized she'd seen a couple of shows, and read multiple articles on the disappearance, several decades back, of this captain of industry.

Huh. You never know who you'll bump elbows with in a bar.

♦♦♦

THEY WERE BOTH busy over the next few hours. Both Theo and the woman—Rainer—in the corner. For her, it was talking to the parade of men coming over to thank her. Hell, it looked like even old Red broke his one-syllable rule tonight. It likely didn't hurt much that she was a looker.

Theo was kept busy over those few hours pulling and popping caps off beers—these boys could *drink*—but he was practiced at running the booze. Twenty-odd years in this shithole town had at least provided him with one skill. *I traded my demons for spirits.*

Theo still managed to grab quick, surreptitious glances at the woman and girl as he grabbed beer after endless beer from the warm cases stacked along one wall. He'd hand off the beers over the bar as chilled as if they had just been pulled from a frigid mountain stream, and he would watch as this confident woman chatted up the customers. His customers. Guys who didn't really trust anyone.

When the cases got low, Theo made a bit of a show heading into a back storage room—which literally held a broom and a dustpan and absolutely nothing else—to get more beer. He'd reach in and pull out three cases at a time. Somewhere out there, there was a bar manager who was going to be scratching his head at the loss of several cases of beer. Theo used to worry about that, but he'd stopped decades ago. *Needs must.*

As he transferred the borrowed beer from the closet to behind the bar, he watched her and wondered who this woman was, why she was in his bar, and why she was getting all the guys liquored up and sloppy. She had to know this was going to cost her a good chunk of change. There weren't too many reasons any woman wanted to be surrounded by a bunch of drunken men. She didn't look dumb, and she wasn't drinking anything but water.

She was obviously looking for something. And that got Theo's spider-sense tingling.

The majority of the dozen or so men were experienced at the craft of alcoholic consumption, and they were also well-versed in the rules of the No Hope bar. If they were going to get sick, it would be down the road. Most of the boys were apt to pass out first, their bodies falling back on the only emergency measures they could deliver under the present circumstances—total mental shutdown.

When Theo noticed three of the boys approaching that state, it was time to roust them out and close up. It was barely past nine, far too early to close the bar on a normal night.

Then again, this wasn't a normal night.

"That's it, boys!" he yelled over the general din that, despite the level of customer intoxication and general merriment, immediately quieted down. "Time to go home to those who love you." *And let them hold your head over the toilet,* he thought.

There was some grumbling and griping. One brave soul begged incoherently for last call. Theo ignored them all. A few began to suit themselves up for the chill that would have invariably set in since the sun set. When Theo came around the bar, everyone sped up. Those who were now challenged due to alcoholically-impaired coordination were given an assist by those who were only slightly less so. But everyone knew…when Theo came out from behind the bar, things could happen. Fully grown men turned to animals and got stuck in mid-air, for instance—that was only a night or two ago. Or some overly drunk patron might try and take a swing at the bartender. That happened last week.

Though he was a slightly built man—looking more like a boy of twenty or so—every man in the room deferred to him. He carried an air of *power* about him that even drunkenness could not ignore. The room cleared in minutes.

Theo shut the door behind him, not bothering to lock it. Not having, in fact, a lock with which to do so. Cases and cases of booze in the joint, and only one person had ever attempted to steal from Theo. When the locals found him the next day, it hadn't been hard to figure out what had happened. There had not been an incident since.

He turned, intending on extinguishing the propane lanterns around the room, when he realized two more people still occupied the room.

Shit! he thought. *Didn't even remember she has to settle up the bill.*

"Sorry, bar's closed," Theo said. "I gotta ask you to settle the bill and leave."

"I'm not really looking for another drink." She held up her plastic bottle of water. "I've still got lots here." He glanced over to the girl—her name was Sam, he'd caught that at some point over the evening—but she had swaddled herself in both hers and Rainer's jackets and was burrowed in to sleep on the bench seat.

"What can I do for you, then?" Theo asked.

"What I really need is information. I need someone to talk to." She eased a chair out with the toe of her boot. "Can we sit and talk for a few minutes? I imagine I owe you for a rather large bar tab."

Theo leaned against the bar, preferring for the moment to keep his distance. "I'm listening."

"Well, see," the woman said, "that's the problem. I've just invested a large amount of money in your bar here, and all I really got for my largess was a bunch of guys who were more interested in listening than talking. I'm looking for more give and take."

Theo chuckled. "I could have saved you an awful lot of money if you'd just asked me that back when you came in with Dink. I could have told you these guys wouldn't be much help."

The woman leaned back in her chair, rocking it back on the hind legs. "And that's exactly why I'm here: everything I did hear pointed me to you. Though, I've gotta say, *no*body seems to know your name."

"Isn't that interesting?"

"Mm-hmm," she said. "They don't know a hell of a lot about you beyond whispers and conjecture.

"Huh," Theo said.

"I'm Rainer, by the way," she said as she held out her hand. Theo had an awkward moment when her outstretched hand sparked a memory. The last time he had shaken a hand was…

Thirty years ago, give or take.

The Toad. When he'd said goodbye to him. He'd already lost Laura, and within a day, he would also lose Marcia.

He shook his head to dispel the memory, crossed the floor, and stretched his hand out as though he was sticking it into a snake pit.

Their hands met across the air.

And out of the blue, Theo was awake. Wide awake for the first time in two decades. Everything he had experienced was a dream, and *this*—this woman in front of him—was real.

Their hands met, and with a dizzying snap, he was inside her head. Right inside her, wading through the minutiae that comprises a person's memories and experiences. Growing up. School. Friends. College. Dave, her husband. April, her daughter. The death of her family. Wolves. The painful collapse of her marriage. Stalking wolves. Hunting them. Killing them. Zach. Sam. Jake. The Fed. A cellphone. Dink. He saw through her eyes as she walked into the bar, noting the sign as she crossed the threshold, surprised and delighted at the warmth of the yellow glow spilling through the opened door.

And weirdly, Theo felt Rainer feeling him. A strange, doubled back loop of experience with no solid originating point. Theo or Rainer? They were feeling it together, sharing exactly the same thoughts, feelings, and references, her experience becoming his becoming hers.

Once the initial shock wore off, Theo somehow found his way back into his own mind.

For a moment, they simply stood, staring at each other.

Theo's overwhelmed brain screamed, *Holy Christ! What just happened?*

CHAPTER THIRTY-EIGHT

HOLY CHRIST! WHAT just happened? Rainer's overwhelmed brain screamed. She was used to getting a buzz from people and had prepared herself for this guy. She hadn't bothered asking his name, or anything else. She knew a quick handshake would have provided her all she needed. But then *BAM!* and goddamn, she received so much more than she had bargained for.

She had a weird feeling, like she had just come out of a long period of sleep—as though her husband and family and Zach had all been a bad dream.

God! she thought. *If that was only the case!*

What she wouldn't have given right then and there to wake up in bed beside her husband and know it was all a dream. The whole soap opera cliché. But no, Zach's daughter—the girl Rainer had sworn to protect—had her head in Rainer's lap, a visceral and tangible reminder that that strange dream she'd just woke up from was not a dream at all.

Rainer knew, though, that no matter what happened going forward, she would always measure her life in terms of before or after that handshake with Theo.

Also, the information she had received from Theo—*Theo! His name is Thelonious, but he goes by Theo*—made her realize that nothing had changed. Hell, if anything, her world had just got a lot more complicated.

There were more than werewolves in the world. That scared the shit out of her. She felt the same feelings emanating from Theo as well. Though his fear had been an ongoing thing for so much longer than Rainer's situation had even been an issue. The things he had seen and done!

Christ Almighty, she realized, *he looks like a teenager, but he walked away from high school and came here when I was seven years old.*

Then more realization bombs. *He looks young, but he's forty years old. He doesn't even know how old he is. He doesn't even know what year it is. That demon – Swlabr? all'Gueroth? – messed him up.*

The demon, but also the Book. It had been gone for decades. Almost since he'd arrived here, yet still, It had a hold on him. It wasn't here, yet still she felt It worming at the edges of her mind, prying at the boards, looking for a weak spot that It could peel back and crawl in. Its greed, Its hunger was enormous. It hadn't been physically here for decades, yet still, Theo had kept Its profane desires and demands tamped down for twenty years.

Shit, Rainer thought. *I thought* I *had problems.*

"You do."

What?

"You do," Theo repeated. His words had seemed to desecrate the bond between them, the holy union cheapened by mere speech. Speech was so…primitive. Tin cups and string when you could use a phone. Crawling on your belly when you could fly.

Their hands were still clenched together. Rainer reluctantly loosened her grip, sensing Theo doing the same thing, though neither of them truly wanted to break the connection. But there it was: their fingers fell away from the shared grip and the light in Rainer's world went out.

Theo's mind had been filled with so much ugliness and filth, but it had also carried such hope and care. It was a drug and Rainer wanted more.

"Your problems are deep and immediate," Theo continued. "This must be finished."

"Yes," she said. The only word she could get out. She sipped at the water to freshen her dry throat.

"They were here, you know," he said.

"Yes, I know they were," she said, finding her voice once again. "I saw the paw prints as we were coming in. Then I saw them when we…"

"So then you know that your…" His eyes were soft, empathetic.

"Yes, I saw him, too." She didn't even want to think about it, though she understood exactly what he was talking about. "He's something I'm going to have to deal with as well," she finished, rather weakly.

The place was silent and they both sat, unable to look away from each other. The wind was picking up outside, and the old building groaned in sympathy.

"You need a place to sleep," Theo said, not needing to explain.

"I do." She glanced over at Sam, still sleeping. "We both do."

Without another word, he held out his hand—though, to Rainer, it seemed more hesitant than the last time—and her hand connected with his. There was still a jolt, there was still a flood of light, a flood of information, but both were expected, less impactful this time around. It affected and joined them both, but they were not overcome. The taste, so shocking to them the first time, had now been acquired and was now welcomed.

He gently pulled her to her feet and said, "Let's get you both set up." Then, with incredible care, he lifted Sam and nodded his head for Rainer to follow him.

♦♦♦

THEO LED HER, though it wasn't necessary, upstairs to his apartment above the bar. He took Sam to the spare bedroom. There was no bed—the room was quite empty save for some old paperbacks—and it was cold when they entered, but Theo squinted his eyes a bit and the room warmed almost immediately.

Rainer veered left, went unerringly to a closet—stopping only for a moment to consider how weird it was that she knew the place as thought *she'd* been the one living there for the past two decades—and pulled a small pile of blankets out for a makeshift bed. Then she followed Theo into the room.

The blankets smelled of disuse and dust until she entered the spare room. Theo was still holding Sam in his arms, but looked up when she came in. He wrinkled his nose, said, "Sorry," squinted his eyes again, and the blankets smelled clean and freshly washed. It could have been her imagination, but they also felt softer as well.

Rainer laid out three folded blankets for the bed, then Theo gently settled Sam in. They removed her shoes and covered her with another blanket.

As they left the room, Rainer said, "Think she'll be okay there?"

"She'll be completely fine," he said. "She's completely safe, and she won't wake until morning."

They made their way down the hall toward his room. She had already seen it, lived it. Still, she was struck by the overwhelming feeling of *home*. It was something that Theo had not felt in the three decades he had been here. It wasn't home, instead it was a place to lay his weary head and wait for the Book to return and sing to him. But tonight, she knew, tonight was different.

Tonight, it was *their* home. There was no awkwardness, no question they would share a bed. Tomorrow? Well, tomorrow would come and be dealt with tomorrow. Tonight was the only moment of importance.

But tomorrow, she—they—would plan for the Hole.

♦ ♦ ♦

THEY WERE PLEASANTLY surprised by the shared intimacy when they made love. Theo couldn't have asked for a better way to lose his virginity. It had been forty years, but it had been worth the wait.

And for the first time in over two decades, Theo didn't think about the Book for one blessed evening.

CHAPTER THIRTY-NINE

SAM WOKE UP the next morning in a jumble of blankets. She dimly remembered something about being carried upstairs by the man then, nothing but after that, nothing but the whispering.

She'd dreamt that someone was whispering to her. Almost singing, weird as that was. It kept telling her terrible things, but in a way that made them sound less terrible.

No, that wasn't right.

~...oooohhhh the thiiiinkssss yyyyooooouuuu can thiiiinnnnk...~

It made them sound fun. Like they'd be really good to do.

~...oooohhhh the thiiiingssss weeee can doooo toooogetherrrr...~

What was weird was, when Sam finally woke up, she realized it wasn't actually a dream.

Because that someone—actually, she knew it was a some*thing* now...a Book—kept up the steady stream of suggestions and promises.

She found it...

...interesting.

But she wasn't ready to tell Rainer or the man yet.

She found the bathroom, did her business—she would likely always think of it as doing her *bidness*, because that's what her and her dad used to say—and went a little farther down the hall to the other bedroom. He was in there, and so was Rainer.

Her lips curled into a smirk. *She boinked him.*

Sam wasn't completely aware of what that involved, but she knew it always meant no clothes and a bed.

She walked up to Rainer's side, her feet silent in her socks on the wooden floor. Rainer's hair was a mess, and her mouth was slightly open.

Sam leaned forward, up close to Rainer's face, and said, "Hey, who do I have to kill to get some goddamn breakfast around here?"

Rainer cracked an eye that floated around before settling on her.

"Yo," Sam said. "I'm a child. I'm helpless and fucking hungry! Feed me!"

"Have I told you lately how much I love you, kid?" Rainer said in her most obvious sarcastic voice.

"Say it with eggs."

"Whoa," the man said from the other side of the bed. "Tough room."

CHAPTER FORTY

"WHAT EXACTLY IS this 'Hole' anyway?" Theo asked, sipping his coffee. It steamed mightily in the early morning darkness. Not that it would be getting light out any time today. This was the land of the six-month night. Oh sure, it would get a little lighter, enough to fake an uninformed mind into thinking that maybe everyone was wrong, and the sun really did come up. Another one of those Canadian myths, like that everyone spoke French, or that they all lived in igloos in snow twelve months of the year and rode their polar bears to work, all while saying "sorry, eh?" and pronouncing "about" as "aboot."

He took another slurping sip of the coffee. It was damn good, but damn hot. Theo didn't think he had ever enjoyed anything so much as the bacon, eggs, and home fries he had just inhaled. Rainer and Sam too, for all of that. Theo had commented that they both looked like sharks in a feeding frenzy. A wood stove and cast-iron pans had delivered manna from heaven to their plates. Or maybe it was just that Theo finally had someone to make it for.

"You really need to ask that?" Rainer asked, bringing him back around.

"Well, yeah, I kinda do," Theo said. "I mean, yeah, I've got your knowledge of it, but you have to realize, you've had your normal life processes in place to slowly discover the information, process it, form your thoughts and opinions…basically digest it." He set the cup down on the table and reached out for her hand.

"I, on the other hand, just got the entire thing dumped on me as one big chunk. I've got to chew it a bit before I can swallow it." He cocked his head to one side. "You know what I mean?"

"Yep," she said. "I can smell what you're cooking."

"What?"

"Dude," Sam said, canting her head to the side. "Seriously?" Then she crammed another piece of bacon in her mouth. He smiled. Damn, it had been a long time since he'd smiled.

Rainer shot a look at Sam, then turned back to Theo. "I smell what you're cooking. I'm picking up what you're putting down. I understand what you're saying."

"Oh. Okay." He drew that last word out, saying that he wasn't sure but he'd let it go for now. "I know a fair amount about the wolves," he said. "About fifteen, maybe twenty years ago, not too long after I landed here, a strange group of people came through the bar." He paused, putting his other hand on top of Rainer's, sandwiching hers between his. Her hand was warm and pleasant. "You have to understand, while I had gone through a shitload, it was *my* shit. I, like everyone else on this damn planet, thought I was the only one with problems. That only I had ever seen any supernatural shit." He swiped at his hair, pulling it back from his face.

"Lately though, and more and more, I am beginning to hear weird stuff coming from some of the people who came through the bar."

"You think it's the Book that draws them?" Rainer asked. Sam stopped chewing and watched the two of them.

"That's something I've thought about a lot. And the answer I'd give is, yeah, the Book draws them. Like flies to shit. Like fuckin' Elvis to a pork chop."

"You're so full of interesting expressions," Sam said, "I can learn from you."

"Oh, fantastic," Rainer said, the sarcasm hanging dryly between them.

"Why, thank you, little lady," Theo countered. "It's a holdover from my school days. Anyway," he continued, "fifteen-odd years ago. This weird group comes through the bar. They hung out with each other, way off away from the others. That in itself wasn't anything unusual—I see a lot of that, but this group was different."

"It was the first pack you'd ever seen," Rainer said.

"It's like you're reading my mind." Theo smiled. "Yeah. It was. They were totally antisocial and intent on picking a fight with anyone who would take the bait. Damn thing was, nobody was biting."

"Pardon the pun," Sam said.

"Right. Anyway, that in and of itself set off my spider-sense. I figured werewolves would come in looking like Wolverine from the X-Men, or at least something damn close to that."

"For someone who doesn't go near any electronics or media of any sort, you're sure up on your movies," Rainer said.

"Movies?" Theo was confused. "What movies?"

"Spider-Man and the X-Men."

"They're *movies*?" he asked. "I'm talking about the comics I used to read thirty years ago." He shook his head. *Modern technology. Damn!*

"Anyway," he continued, "long story short, they were assholes, they got kicked out, and I started to do some research." Theo knew Rainer understood he was talking about the Book.

"I found out enough to know they're miserable bastards," he said. "But nowhere did I get any info on the Hole."

"Not surprised," Rainer said. "It's not something they really share." Holding her hand, Theo picked up the unspoken added part: *like Mormons with their underpants*. He had no idea what that meant, and didn't ask as he watched her face cloud over and again. Theo knew her thoughts. "Unless they're really stupid."

"Tiny?"

"Tiny."

"What the hell is tiny?" Sam said. "And why are the two of you talking in some kinda code?"

"Tiny is a who, not a what, Sam. He's a werewolf who gave us…shit, he gave me—"

"You and Dad?"

"Yeah, kiddo. Me and your dad. Sorry."

"S'okay."

"He gave us some information. After I was able to convince him."

"You kick his hairy ass, Ray?"

"Something like that." Rainer smiled. "Anyway, the Hole…"

Chapter Forty-One

There's an ancient legend that tells of a time when Brother Wolf walked with Sister Moon. Though they were brother and sister, over time, they came to love each other more deeply. A deeper love that should never blossom between siblings.

They came to feel the unbridled passion of lust.

Their hunger for each other remained unconsummated, however, for fear of the wrath of the other spirits that governed the heavens and the Earth. Each night, however, the wolf and the moon would walk, barely managing any distance between them, torturing themselves and each other by remaining close, but never touching, two paths in parallel, never crossing. And each night, Sister Moon would have to leave and Brother Wolf could be heard to howl his frustration at the heavens.

After much time had passed, finally Brother Wolf could no longer hold back his desires. Asking Man for help, he was told of a place far away, where the wolf and the moon could go and never be found.

So, Brother Wolf and Sister Moon crept off to the faraway land and let their passions run free. For days they made love. Each night, the ground trembled and the mists rose from the heat of their lust, finally unleashed.

But the governing spirits noticed that, each night, there was no moon in the sky. They noticed that each night, the long, mournful sound of the howling wolf was not to be heard.

Curious, they asked Man if he knew where Brother Wolf and Sister Moon had gone. Man was treacherous, and jealous of Brother Wolf—for Man, too, harboured a desire for Sister Moon—and he betrayed their location.

The spirits found the forbidden lovers, and were angry. How could they allow this incestuous relationship to go unpunished?

Brother Wolf was sent back to the land of Man, and Sister Moon brought back to her home in the sky. Owing to the treachery of Man, the Wolf considered him a mortal enemy.

Sister Moon soon became swollen with child, and both she and Brother Wolf waited anxiously for the spirits to render judgment.

When Sister Moon was ready to birth the children she and Brother Wolf had made those many months before, she cast down a rock to that same faraway forbidden place, making a bed for her newborn. But when her beloved offspring were birthed, she and Brother Wolf soon understood the judgment the spirits had made. Their children were grotesque combinations of man and beast.

The spirits explained that Man had initially helped, then ultimately betrayed Brother Wolf, so a fitting punishment would be to forever gaze upon their children and see their betrayer. The wolves would be cursed to walk upright as Man, but walk as a wolf with the night.

Though the offspring of Moon and Wolf hated Man, they had been cursed to coexist with their betrayer. However, their one love would always be their mother, the Moon.

CHAPTER FORTY-TWO

"LET ME GUESS," Theo said. "That bed Sister Moon made is the Hole?"

"You got it," Rainer said. "Near as I can figure, it's a crater from a meteor that hit thousands of years ago. It's not that big, but it's deep."

"And it's—"

"According to the maps I've been able to lay my hands on, and from what I got from Tiny, and that other fucker"—Theo knew immediately she was talking about the Fed, the shifter she'd killed in Florida—"it's about two hundred miles northwest of here." Neither seemed to mind the constant cut-offs and interruptions. They now shared the same mind. Though they both found it amusing watching Sam ping-pong between them, trying to suss the gist of the conversation.

"We can head out whenever you're ready, but I'd suggest we—"

"Get some supplies first." Theo chewed on a thought for a moment. "There's a lot of terrain that's gonna be on foot, right?"

"Right," Rainer confirmed. Neither questioned the 'we' aspect. Theo knew Rainer would have been more apt to cut off an appendage before picking up another sidekick, but this was different. They were part of each other now.

"What about..." *Sam.*

"She comes."

"I could likely find someone to watch over her."

"I made a promise, Theo. She comes with us."

"Yeah, *Theeee*-o," Sam said. "The kid comes too."

He wasn't completely cool with it, but he knew enough about the two women sitting across from him to know that if anyone could handle themselves, it was these two.

"Fair enough," he said, dropping his voice to a semblance of military machismo. "We ride together. No one gets left behind."

The moved in unison to clear the dishes. It was going to be a long day. And the shifters already had a two-day lead.

CHAPTER FORTY-THREE

THEO PARKED RAINER'S SUV at the end of the last trail, beside four road-dusted Harleys.

While he moved to the back to pull out the packs, Rainer examined the motorcycles.

"Zero's pack?" he said.

Her mouth was a grim line as she said, "Yeah."

They both shouldered their backpacks. "You gonna lock it?" Sam said, looking at Rainer's SUV.

"Nope," Theo said. "I can't imagine the last time any actual human beings were out this way, so either we come back to it, or..." And here, he trailed off.

"Or the wolves do," Sam finished. "Either way, it won't matter."

"You're far too smart for your age," Theo said. "What are you, thirty-five?"

"What are you?" she said, smirking. "Nineteen?"

"Okay," he said, fist bumping her. "Good one. Touché."

♦♦♦

THEY'D WALKED FOR several hours. It had been mostly quiet, each lost in their own thoughts, only the sounds of the wildlife and their own breathing to disturb the silence.

They had just over another hour to go, but it was getting on night. They found a well-secluded spot in a deep gutter that may have once been a river and set up camp. No fire. They huddled down into sleeping bags and ate cold meat and bread.

In the dark, muted, non-threatening night sounds. And off in the distance, the sound of a hell of a lot of wolves, howling in unison.

"What are we going to do once you catch up with the pack, Ray?" Theo asked.

"I honestly haven't a clue," she replied.

"Yeah you do," Sam said.

"I do?"

"Yeah. You told them on the phone we were gonna crush them."

"I did say that, didn't I?"

"Yeah, you did."

"Sounds like a plan," Theo said.

Rainer had no idea how she was going to do that. She only hoped, with Theo's residual powers held over from the Book, that they'd be walking back out of here sometime soon.

She figured it was a slim hope. Still, she'd put together an extra pack for Sam. The wolves wouldn't hurt her, couldn't hurt her. There was the chance she might walk out of this, even if Theo and Rainer didn't. It was also a slim hope, but it was something.

♦♦♦

EARLY AFTERNOON THE following day. The last few hundred yards toward the lip of the crater took longer than the last couple of miles. Despite Sam's protests that there were no wolves on watch, Rainer and Theo picked their way carefully, using whatever cover they could find to ensure they weren't spotted.

Sam found herself getting a little impatient because the whispering had come back and told her they were fine. All the wolves were in the crater.

They'd been doing this for so long, they didn't worry about anyone crashing their stupid werewolf pyjama party.

She was impatient, yeah, but Rainer had been pretty cool, and had saved her, and held her every time she cried about losing her dad or Jake, so she was willing to shut up and let her go slow.

And Theo was actually a pretty cool guy, too. He'd seen some bad shit, she knew.

She knew because the whispering had told her.

So, she just listened to the whispering.

~…soooonnnn weeee will crusssshhhh themmmm…~

♦♦♦

RAINER HAD INSISTED on silently checking their entire area before they could relax. That took another couple of hours. It was early evening when the three of them finally crouched at the lip of the crater.

"Shit," Theo said.

"Yeah," Rainer said.

"There's gotta be hundreds of them down there," Sam said.

"Thousands."

"Shit," Theo said again. "We need a new plan."

"We need a *plan,*" Rainer said. "*Any* plan. We can't do this alone."

At that moment, Rainer, Sam, and Theo heard the moist sound of intestines slopping and shifting around to new places, and the low-knuckled crunch of bone sliding and re-socketing and reforming into cartilage.

Son of a bitch, Sam thought. *Rainer checked the whole fucking area. Where'd they come from?*

Then they were the only humans standing. Surrounded by wolves.

Surrounded by shifters.

Stupid fucking whisper, Sam thought. *You told me we were safe!* And then she thought, *Fucking lying-ass Book. Fuck it.*

She stood to her full height. "We're here to see Zero and her pack. Take us to her so we can crush her."

Sam knew they wanted to kill the three of them. But instead, she pushed out a radiance that they didn't like much. She felt them shying away from it. The wolves instead frog-marched them into the crater.

With Rainer on one side of her, and Theo on the other, Sam heard him say, "You got some balls, kid."

♦♦♦

TWENTY MINUTES LATER, they were standing in the middle of several thousand werewolves. Rainer had to admire Sam's bravery, but they were dead. She'd failed to keep Sam alive.

Another family lost.

The wolves glanced back, then moved to allow a path. Through the path came Zero, Syd, Moondoggie, and Taylor. Even in their full wolf forms, Rainer knew them.

And without any further movement, without conscious thought, the entire scene shifted and the focus narrowed down to two individuals. Rainer and Zero stood across the barren crater from each other. One set of human eyes staring with deadly malice into a set of cursed wolfen eyes. Despite all the wolves from hundreds of different packs, all backed off, creating an arena of sorts, sensing this was Zero's fight.

Zero stood, and Rainer watched as the fur pulled back into the skin and her entire form shifted, hind legs straightening, then bending forward, the barrel chest flattening and widening, breasts appearing, the nose pulling back into the skull, teeth retracting.

She stretched and flexed and Rainer heard bones pop and crackle. Then Zero, naked, stood before them in human form. She spared a quick glance at Sam, then looked straight into Rainer's eyes.

"What brings you here, upright?" Zero said. Rainer heard the command in her voice. There was a potency there that was undeniable. But there was an undertone there as well. Something she couldn't quite identify.

Rainer pointed to Taylor. "I'm here for him," she said. "I'm going to kill him. And I'm here to kill you as well."

"Crush you," Sam said, then fell silent when Theo put a hand on her shoulder.

"Really?" Zero said, her confidence overwhelming. *Why wouldn't it be?* Rainer thought. *We're surrounded, with no hope of escape.*

Zero continued. "And do you expect us to be as easy a kill as Bo and the Fed?" She looked around at the other shifters. "Do you expect the others to sit back and let you get away with it?"

"I'll take the rest on—"

"*We'll* take the rest on," Theo said.

Rainer looked over, grateful. "Right. *We* will. All three of us, and we'll likely die. But I'll promise you now," Rainer said, hate rolling off her tongue, "you'll be gone before me. And a hell of a lot more of you will be digging a hole for your fallen pack members."

"I sincerely doubt that. But please, tell me more about Taylor. Why would he hold your interest so raptly?"

As the words left her mouth, Rainer watched Taylor begin his own transformation. *I hope it fucking hurts you*, she thought. *Hope it hurts every goddamned time.*

"That piece of shit?" Rainer said. "He's my brother." The effect of her statement rolled through the packs. Even Sam looked shocked.

Zero's confidence seemed to slip for a space of a heartbeat and she glanced over at Taylor, now standing just behind and to her left.

Rainer allowed sufficient time before going on. Zero turned back and met her eyes once more.

"About two years ago, three people were savagely murdered and eaten," Rainer said. "An older woman and man, a seventeen-year-old girl. The only body never recovered was my brother's." She nodded toward the wolf who sat just off to her left. "Taylor."

"And now you've come for the grand reunion and the Hollywood rescue," Zero said, and the surrounding wolves snorted and pawed the ground, their humour at the situation evident. Taylor stood very still, betraying nothing.

"Somewhere along the line, you infected him, Zero." Rainer's voice came out in a throaty grumble. She was aware she was clenching and unclenching her fists. "You initiated him. Made him take out his entire innocent family."

She felt the tears come then. She hated them for showing her vulnerability, but she refused to wipe them away. "Didn't you?"

Taylor remained standing, not responding. *The scared little puppy.*

"DIDN'T YOU, YOU BITCH?" Rainer spat, her voice raw. *"ANSWER ME, YOU SHIT."*

Zero turned to Taylor. "Is your life here so horrible, brother Taylor? Tell your sister how terrible it is to be a shifter."

Taylor squirmed, then stepped forward. "Ray…" he said, and then the words seemed to sputter and die on his tongue.

"Fuck you," Rainer whispered.

He tried again.

"You have no idea of the thrill…" Taylor's fingers clenched and unclenched as he searched for the right words. "The *intensity* of the feeling. Your bones crackle and vibrate as though they are charged with electricity. You feel your guts squirm and shift, sliding inside you to relocate. Your flesh prickles and itches as coarse hair sprouts and grows.

"You want to sleep," he said. "You want to run. To *scream*.

"You want to *kill*."

"YOU KILLED YOUR OWN FUCKING PARENTS, TAYLOR!" Rainer howled. The sound echoed off the walls of the depression and bounced back at her, multiplying her torment. She took a moment to breathe. "*My* parents. *My* sister." She couldn't let them break her like this or she *would* lose. *But Jesus! He killed our family!*

She had to calm down. Then Sam took her hand and said, "God, you lost all your family too, Rainer?"

She looked down at the girl, and saw her own tears tracing lines down her cheeks.

"I'm so sorry, Ray."

Slow down, Ray. Breathe. Be still. Deep breath.

She let the breath out slowly. *Thank you, Sam.*

"You killed your own mother, father, and sister, Taylor," she said, her voice much lower. "They"—she pointed to Syd and Moondoggie and Zero—"told you to kill, and you did." Keeping the calm was a struggle, but she held the line. "And you would have killed me, too, had I been there. Wouldn't you?"

"Ray, don't ask me that."

"You *would* have, *wouldn't* you?"

"Ray—"

"Wouldn't you?" Her voice tighter, but the emotion still under control.

"Yes. Of course."

Of course.

The words hung in the air, but the only ones uncomfortable with the answer were Rainer, Sam, and Theo. And yet, when Rainer looked to Zero, was she not squirming a bit? Did she not look uncomfortable?

Zero spoke up.

"That's in the past, Rainer. Taylor is a shifter now. He is reborn, and cannot go back to his old ways. There is no 'cure.'"

Rainer smiled, showing Zero her teeth. She let go of Sam's hand.

"Sure there is," she said. She did the next thing exactly as she had seen herself doing it ever since she found out the truth about Taylor. The fluid movements practiced so often in her mind, in her daydreams, in her fevered nightmares. The act so familiar to her, it was more instinct and muscle memory than actual thought.

She drew her handgun—the one that had so freaked Zach so short a time ago—aimed, and shot Taylor through the chest.

Rainer felt as though time had spun down to a short but extended series of moments. She could have sworn that she actually watched the bullet of silver explode slowly from the barrel through a quick burst of flame and spiral across the short distance. She was sure she saw the ripple of Taylor's skin as the bullet pierced his flesh, the silver working its profane, unknowable effect on his body as it singed a dark hole around the sudden opening, cracked through a rib and, blunted now, shred through the soft tissue of his heart before exiting out just below his right shoulder blade, taking a good chunk of flesh and bone with it. The fleshy divot carried on for several yards before landing at the base of a large boulder. The bullet, now far smaller as the silver interacted with the supernatural flesh of the wolfen shifter, executed far more damage with its infection than with its velocity and path.

Taylor looked at Rainer, his eyes registering shock. The same shock he must have seen on his family's face two years previously. He slumped to the ground, and died without a word.

"Bastard," Rainer said, and spat.

The sound of the gunshot echoed around the rocky walls of the Hole. Thousands of wolves sat squinting, their ears flattened against their heads. The bullet had killed Taylor, but Rainer knew there was still the possibility of a resurrection. If they somehow managed to get out of this, she'd have to decapitate her brother.

All she would have to think about was her parents. Or better yet, her little sister, dead now two years. Ensuring Taylor's death would be revenge, but it would never take the pain away.

Just like killing the Fed never took away the pain of losing Zach.

The shot still ringing in her ears, Rainer turned to face Zero again.

♦♦♦

"YOU'RE FIGHTING IT, aren't you?" Rainer said to Zero but gesturing to Syd, tail between his legs, fruitlessly scratching at the ground, the dirt darkening with his piss. "You're fighting that urge to dig yourself a hole and hide."

Zero looked severely uncomfortable, a sheen of sweat on her forehead, her upper lip, across her breasts. Rainer was sure she could see a slight tremble in her arms and legs. She watched the woman's lips curl back in a rictus of agony for her fallen pack member.

Looking down at Taylor's body beside her, his still-warm figure steaming in the cold of the darkened day, Zero said to Rainer, "Bo, the Fed, and now Taylor. That's three of my pack you've killed."

Yes, your voice is shaky, too, sweetheart, Rainer thought, then said, "I'm not quite finished yet."

Zero asked, "What do you feel right now, Rainer?"

Rainer had to give her credit. It had to be a bitch, fighting instinct, but she was doing it.

"Nothing," she finally answered, suddenly feeling her own weariness. "Cold. Tired."

"Then I feel sorry for you," Zero said. "Try to imagine feeling the motion in the ground beneath you. To *feel* the grass growing. To *feel* the planet spin on its axis, and to *feel* the movement of the Earth orbiting the sun. To *feel* the insistent tug of the other planets as they flow in their own paths.

"We feel that." She looked down once again to her dead pack member. "Taylor felt that." She stabbed a shaking finger at the body. "You say you feel nothing, yet I feel the passing of his essence.

"But in addition to all of this, running deeper and richer than all the rest, like a mantra of strength, to feel the *moon,* wherever it may be, a watchful mother always looking out for her pups. Nurturing them, sustaining them.

"And to see it! Full and glorious, as it pushes the blood through your body, giving you the will, the power, the strength, and the instinct to hunt and survive.

"What's the connection?" Zero asked. "I don't know, nor do I care. I only know that I'm bound to the moon and she is a devoted and dutiful mistress."

"Yeah," said Rainer in that same world-weary voice. "But sometimes the old lady is a bitch." The gun in her hand came up once again—

And was knocked flying through the air to land a short distance from Zero's feet. Another wolf stood behind Rainer, his tongue lolling out of his mouth.

"Fight. Fair," the wolf said, pushing the guttural sounds out of a throat and mouth not up to the task. He wasn't gearing up for an attack. None of the wolves seemed to be. His actions stated that he'd only intervene to keep it fair. Zero didn't have any weapons beyond fangs and claws, so Rainer would not be permitted one either. Rainer caught the faint nod between the two creatures.

How the hell did Theo miss him? she wondered. *Ah well, fuck it. In for a penny…*

"Gonna make me do it the hard way, are you?" she asked.

"The only way," was Zero's growled response.

"The only way." She huffed out a laugh and touched Theo in warning. "And what's so fucking fair about three or four of you attacking a single human?"

"We—"

Zero's response would never be heard. Theo stepped behind Sam to shield her as Rainer launched herself at the woman, hands out, going for the throat. She knew Zero could shift at any time, so she was bound and bent on keeping those fangs away from her own throat. Her fingers made contact, burying into the thick muscles of her neck, her skin a conduit to Zero's mind.

They both froze, Zero's arms stretched wide for the attack that never would come, Rainer's hands pushing against a force that had been leashed.

With the contact of skin and skin, Rainer was plunged deep into the misery of Zero.

Chapter Forty-Four

It had begun raining earlier in the evening, just after Nancy and Jason had gone to bed, but sometime later, Nancy had been pulled out of an exhausted sleep by the sound of torrents of water pounding the roof and furiously sluicing down the eavestroughs. Long, fluid shadows dripped down the wall of her bedroom. She lay there, not quite awake yet nowhere near sleep. The rain was a low, comforting roar outside the house. But wasn't there another sound there as well? Some foreign noise?

No, she didn't think so.

But she was awake now, and thirsty.

Nancy was reluctant to get out of bed. It was warm, she was comfortable, and Jason looked so cute with his head snuggled up to her pillow. He'd been such a help since Emily came along, letting Nancy sleep while he fed her, never complaining, seeming to relish the quiet, private time he got to spend with his newborn daughter. Now that Em was sleeping through the night—if getting them up at five in the morning was truly sleeping through the night—Jason had seemed almost disappointed.

Nancy was worried about walking down the hall to the stairs. She would have to pass right by Emily's room, and she might wake up. *Why don't I keep a glass of water by the bed like I always see on TV?* she wondered. *Because it would be room temperature and I'd never drink it.*

But her tongue was practically sticking to the roof of her mouth, and now that she had thought of water—*Oh, wait! Grapefruit juice!* – she had to make the trip. Emily's soft, regular breathing was coming through the monitor and she sounded about as out as Jason was. With exaggerated slowness, Nancy slid from the bed and tiptoed down the hall to the stairs, making sure to avoid the squeaky floorboard in front of the bathroom.

She slipped barefoot down the stairs by the glow of the hallway night light, her shadow magnifying her image the farther she got. She still felt fat even though she had lost all but three pounds of the weight Em had put on her. Another ten pounds would do it.

She rounded the landing and navigated by the light shining through the stair railings. The ceramic tile was cool under her feet, and made her long for her warm bed. Just a quick drink and she'd be back there. She came into the kitchen and opened the cupboard door with one hand and reached for a glass with the other. The edge of the door scraped against the inside of her right arm and she pulled it back quickly. The skin there was tender. Nancy carried the glass to the refrigerator and opened the door. The fridge light allowed her to examine her arm, and she saw four distinct ragged gashes there, already beginning to heal.

What the hell?

Nancy had no concrete memories of getting the wound, only a slight flicker of memory—early Christmas shopping, carrying several packages to the car, feeling the impact of something sharp, and what sounded like the skittering of nails on pavement as she dropped her parcels. No memory of cutting herself, or of any pain.

Yet, three days later, she was just noticing it for the first time. Very strange.

She shook her head and wondered, as she had numerous

times before, how having a baby changed everything in your life. *What did I do with all my spare time before Em?*

Nancy poured some grapefruit juice, drank it back, and winced at the tartness, loving it nonetheless. One final tip of the glass and she drained the last of the juice. She took a couple of steps toward the dishwasher to place the glass inside, but as the refrigerator door closed, there was a large shape behind it.

A wolf.

Nancy wanted to run, to yell for Jason, to protect her child. She wanted to do *something*, but she was frozen in place. The wolf was huge, sitting on its haunches, the top of its head easily reaching Nancy's shoulders, and she wasn't a short woman. As she stood there a strange tremble began in her, and something was also going on with the wolf. She was still very much afraid, and the forgotten glass trembled in her hand, but there was a newer, different feeling beginning to pervade her. A sense of *thrill*, of *adventure*.

And the wolf… He—she knew it was male, but she didn't know how she knew it—was changing, growing. Then the word popped into her head: shifting. Yes, he was shifting. She heard wet noises and hard, crackling ones that were strangely comforting and exciting to her, and Nancy watched as the animal became a man.

Nancy's trembling increased. Be it fear or excitement, she couldn't tell. But the sounds and the sights got to her, and the glass she had forgotten was even in her hand slipped from her loose fingers and began its descent to the ceramic tile.

"Ceramic tile's great, hon," Nancy recalled Jason saying in a conversation from a couple of years ago, before Emily was born. "But there isn't any give. You drop a glass, it's gonna break." They had been standing in one of those massive "big box" depots—and wasn't *everything* becoming a depot now?—and, having found a tile that would perfectly complement the colour scheme of the new house, Nancy had turned on those big brown eyes of hers, knowing Jason could never say no to them. And, of course, he hadn't. He'd just pulled his wallet out with a chuckle and a shake of his head.

Now, his point was going to be proven as gravity accelerated the glass to those tiles, which even now were so cold on the bottom of her feet.

Nancy's body tensed and she jumped back, trying to avoid the anticipated shards of flying glass, but they never came.

Instead, a large hand shot out and deftly caught the glass, inches from the floor.

"You dropped your glass, Nancy," the man/wolf said. "Please accept my apology. I did not mean to startle you." His voice was low, glottal, as though spiced with an accent. German, or perhaps Scottish. He kept his tone low and intimate.

"Who are you?" Nancy asked, looking way up into his eyes, her voice trembling much less than she had anticipated. "What do you want with me?"

A deep, chesty, rumbling laugh from the man, and she felt something tingle between her legs. He was naked.

"You ask questions you know the answers to. I notice you asked what I want with *you*, not mentioning Jason and little Emily, both asleep upstairs." Again, Nancy was surprised, but not as much as she'd expected. *How does he know all our names?*

"You are easily read, Nancy." The man smiled and she was once again plunged into a strange dichotomy—revulsion and…what? Thrill? No, not strong enough. The only term that came close was lust. A quivering, sweaty, aching lust, such as she had never felt before. But for all that, it was not a sexual thing. No, she didn't have a handle on it yet, but it was an ache for…something.

"You are now finding strange feelings and desires are beginning to surface, yes?" She nodded, mouth too dry to speak. "Yes, this is normal with the shedding. The old ways are falling off, to be replaced by the new."

Old ways? New?

"Your arm," he said. "The scar."

Nancy raised her arm, where the scar had been minutes ago. It was now gone. Her confused eyes came up to meet the man who towered before her.

"Who are you?"

"Zeion."

"How do you know so much about me?" Nancy asked. "Do I know you?"

"We met once, briefly," he said. "Three days ago. In a parking lot."

"The parking lot…" Nancy said softly, touching the inside of her arm where no scar showed.

"That's when I set you on a glorious path," Zeion said. "I sensed something in you—a spark that has been noticeably absent in the others who I have made." As he spoke, Zeion set the rescued glass on the countertop without a sound, and gently enfolded Nancy's hands in his larger grip. Nancy's knees were very close to buckling.

"I have made some unfortunate choices, and I have lost all those who would run with me," he said. "I must start over, and you will be the first of my new pack." Nancy heard a hint of both melancholy and excitement in his voice.

"To answer your other question," he continued, unleashing a smile that set off fireworks in her brain. "I've come to help you in the shedding of the dregs of your current life. There can be no collusion between your old life and that which you will become.

"You must break the bonds that tie you to the world of Man."

He dropped his hands from hers, and Nancy let out a sigh of disappointment. His touch, his very tone of voice, was addictive. She felt a sheen of sweat coming over her, soaking her nightgown.

"Why?" she asked. "How?" She didn't feel she was capable of full sentences.

"Take my hand." She did willingly. "Now…close your eyes, concentrate. Can you feel the moon? Can you feel the drawing of her, making you lighter, stronger? Feel the warmth of her glow, palpable even as the clouds hide her. Feel the energy she gives freely! Feel the protection she offers! The strength! The power!

"Can you feel it?" Zeion's voice hissed in her ear like a lover in the throes of passion.

"Yessssss," she said, her eyes still closed.

"Now, slowly, open your eyes. Look at me," he said.

Nancy's eyes came up and before her was the wolf again, sleek and shiny, his eyes aglow. And she felt different! Powerful, full of strength, hunger, agility, like she had only been running on some half-power up to now. Like someone had reached inside her and turned up every dial she had!

"I…feel…wonderful!" she sputtered.

"You look magnificent," Zeion said. "You have shifted. You are almost one of us." Nancy heard the wolf in front of her. He was growling and softly barking, but she could understand him. It was just dawning on her that she was responding the same way.

"Almost?" she asked. "I'm almost one of you?"

"Now, you must shed all vestiges of your past."

"How?"

"Ah," said Zeion. "We simply initiate your newfound powers, now that they have manifested. Come."

With that, Zeion turned and loped down the hallway and stood waiting for her at the bottom of the stairs.

Nancy stood, noticing her nightgown pooled on the floor, and padded cautiously to where Zeion waited. It was such a strange feeling, to be walking on four legs, yet so very comfortable. She could feel the untapped strength in her now, and the agility that could steer and direct it.

This is what I was craving! This incredible feeling of power.

They stood side by side at the foot of the stairs. Nancy looked at Zeion, but he deliberately turned his gaze from her to the top of the stairs. She knew exactly what he was telling her, and she lightly bounded up the stairs. Zeion followed very close behind.

At the top of the stairs, she turned left and padded down the hall, in a very different form than when she had first climbed out of bed a few minutes ago. She paused at the door to her bedroom, her front paws just over the threshold, and looked back.

Zeion's intent glare seemed to drill into her skull.

This is the shedding, she thought. *Go on, girl, get it done.*

Jason had rolled flat on his back, as usual. He had always slept that way, unless he was curled into her. She walked to the foot of the bed. Zeion somehow very close behind again. He nudged her with his snout, and she knew it was now or never. Readying herself, Nancy then leapt onto the bed and stopped, staring down at her husband. Jason's eyes had popped open in surprise, and his head immediately pushed back, as though trying to bury himself in the pillow. Nancy's head shot forward, and her teeth clamped down hard on his windpipe. She felt the first gush of blood spray into her mouth, a feeling that made her sick, yet electrified her at the same time. She bit down harder, feeling things tearing and rippling on her tongue. Then she pulled back, taking a large chunk of Jason's neck with her, some of the skin peeling up off the musculature in a flap under his chin. His eyes were frantic, watering and wide with panic. His hands grabbed at her fur, but weakly, weakly. As she stood over him, she watched as he turned his head on what was left of his neck and his left arm stretched out across the bed.

He was…

Oh my God, he's looking for me! He's trying to save me!

Blood was jetting from his neck, making black leopard

spots on the sheets. The bed was rocking as he fought to hold on, and Nancy didn't notice Zeion as he hopped to the bed.

"Finish it," Zeion growled.

Nancy looked down and she felt a deep thudding in her chest as she watched her husband feebly trying to stem the flow of blood from his neck, his hands black and sticky from his own fluids. She didn't know what to do.

"Finish it," Zeion repeated. "Break his fucking neck!"

Nancy hesitated only a second, then she shot her head forward, bit down hard on Jason's torn neck, and, with a vicious whip of her head, heard a grinding crack that felt satisfying as it reverberated through her teeth. Then, Jason was still.

She let go and tasted the blood and gobbets of flesh as they slid down her throat. The force of her killing blow had turned Jason over so that he appeared he was sleeping on his side.

"Excellent," Zeion said. "Now. One other to remove."

Nancy backed away from him, and slipped unsteadily from the bed. As she tumbled backward, that feeling of power disappeared. The taste of Jason's blood did not. She hit the carpeted floor and saw the white skin of her legs. She was human again. She turned and vomited. Small chunks of Jason slopped on the carpet.

"The first kill is always the hardest," Zeion said, sitting comfortably in human form as well. "It is better that it was a loved one. You can show some mercy."

"He was..." She spit blood. "He was trying to save me."

"Yes, poor, misguided soul." Zeion sighed. "But come! We can disseminate the issues at a later time. You have one more to take off the board." He held out his hand.

Nancy ignored his offer as she wiped her mouth with the back of her hand. Small tendrils of vomit arced from her chin to her wrist. She reached over and pulled the covers—bought with wedding money three years ago—and wiped herself clean.

She was stalling, and they both knew it.

Through the baby monitor, Emily heaved a sigh. Both sets of eyes turned to the little radio, its faint red LED blinking like a homing beacon. *I'm coming, honey,* she thought, and terror made her shiver.

When Nancy turned back to Zeion, he was crouched in front of her.

"It must be done," he said. "There are few laws amongst the packs, but this is one of the two most sacred. Of course, you know the other one as well."

No wolf shall cause harm or death to another wolf, she thought, the rule popping into her head like a bubble breaking the surface of a lake.

"You are fortunate," Zeion continued. "There are wolves out there who had very large families! You have only two." He smiled. "I had to kill twelve. Eight family members, and four of the help staff."

Then, he actually chuckled.

"Come," he said, once again extending his hand. "Delay it no longer. You will feel better once the final deed is done." Nancy sat still for a moment longer. The only sounds in the room were of rain, of breath being drawn, and of her heart pounding in her ears.

She reached out and took his hand. He pulled her up lightly, as though she weighed nothing. She stood before him, naked, covered in her husband's blood. The only light was from a streetlight outside, and the walls still dripped with shadow rain. He reached out a hand and ran it delicately down her throat to her breast, stopping at the nipple. She was distressed to realize they were hard. He brought his finger to his lips, and licked Jason's blood from it. Then he smiled.

"Let's get the other one." His voice was husky and betrayed his own excitement. As did his erection.

Without a word, she walked past him and padded down the hall, retracing her steps of only a few minutes ago. This time, however, instead of turning for the stairs, she turned to face the door to her daughter's room.

Affixed to the door was a small porcelain plate, with hand-painted flowers and leaves framing the ornate script. "Emily's Room" it said brightly. Nancy remembered Jason becoming more and more frustrated as he attempted to centre the plate, to get it "just so." She remembered coming up behind him, putting her arms around him—and how good it had been to be able to do that again, now that Em was born and the baby belly was gone—reaching up to kiss his neck. He had turned his head absently and she could see his tongue poked out one side in concentration.

"Finally got the angle of the tongue just right, tool man?" she had asked with a giggle.

"Do you mock me?" he had said, laughing in return. He finally had it straight. It was perfect. Emily had been perfect. They had been perfect.

Nancy felt a warm hand on her cool skin. "It must be now," Zeion said, louder now, his hands seeming to become more familiar with her flesh.

Nancy reached out and turned the knob quietly, ever so silently. If she was going to do this, she would ensure that Emily would have no clue.

The door opened on the room, the bright primary colours scaled down to shades of grey in the night. The crib was a few feet in, right beside the change table. The room smelled of baby powder and fabric softener, and that smell that only babies had: clean, pure, sinless. The blankets had all been kicked to the bottom of the crib, as she did every night, and Emily lay on her back, one tiny fist up beside her head, the other fist just under her chin. Jason always called it her Freddie Mercury pose.

The only sound was Emily's breathing. Nancy quickly realized hers and Zeion's breathing was as quiet as a morgue. Nancy rested her sticky hands on the side of the crib, all blond wood, matching the other furniture. Disney characters cavorted around the room, and Sesame Street characters hung from a mobile above her bed. Emily had already taken to Elmo. Perhaps it was the bright red.

She looked down at her daughter, and her vision blurred as the tears began. A voice in her ear: "Do it now! Take her! Shed the past!"

"NO!" she screamed as she lashed out her hand. She had Zeion by the throat and, somehow, she had claws—sharp claws that tore his throat out, faster and easier than she had thought. Emily was awake, and screaming as blood spattered the change table, the crib, the walls, her baby. Zeion reacted instantly, reaching out for her, but she grabbed a fistful of hair and yanked his head back. Her mouth came down on his ruined neck—thicker than Jason's—and she clamped down on it, feeling the bones of his spine grating at her teeth, poking the roof of her mouth. With a clawed hand still in his hair, the other at his shoulder, she pulled and twisted, hearing the sharp crack, and still not releasing, still refusing to believe he might be dead, holding and biting, loosening only to reposition for a better grip and bearing down hard, Emily's wailing a grim, high-pitched soundtrack, and she ripped and tore and shredded until she felt a different taste in her mouth, down her throat, and though it was new, she realized it was spinal fluid as his head finally separated from his body.

The two separate pieces of his body dropped to the floor. She stood trembling above him and pointed a shaky, claw-tipped finger.

"No!" she said, her voice quivering with anger. "No! Not my daughter!" As though his dismembered head might still be able to hear and understand.

She turned to pick up Emily, still wailing in her blood-soaked crib, the screeching like needles in Nancy's ears, and as she bent lower she reached out her arms, knowing Em would reach up, of course she would, this was Mommy.

Then Nancy saw her arms. The arms that reached for her little girl were dark with coarse dark hair, her fingers ended in thick black claws. Emily didn't reach up to be comforted. Instead, she shrieked in an impossibly higher tone that bored straight through Nancy's head, her eyes squinting down in pain and she felt—yes, she *felt*—her ears flatten out against her head.

Trying to ignore Emily's squealing terror, Nancy slid her hands under the child—*Oh she's* soaked *with his blood!*—and brought her up to her shoulder. There was no consoling her, however, Emily's senses telling her that this wasn't her mother, that all was not right in the world.

Nancy tried to shush her, tried to make comforting noises, but all that came out were whines and low growls. She didn't seem to be able to come back to fully upright—*No, human. The term is human.* Her arms were still covered with fur, she could see her snout, and she couldn't help breathing through her mouth.

And Emily wouldn't shut up.

Nancy wouldn't put her back in the crib, and she couldn't go back to her bedroom. It was pissing down rain outside, but suddenly, the rain seemed like the best idea.

Emily howling in her ear, Nancy ran down the steps, resisting the temptation to forget the child and drop to all fours. Down to the cool ceramic tile and across the small foyer to the front door. Her claws slipping on the doorknob, slick with blood, not able to get traction on the brass-plated ball. Trying, trying, and Emily would not shut up, shut up, *SHUT UP*!

Suddenly it was absolutely imperative to get out of the house. *Fuck it, drop the kid.* Emily was set on the floor—*Too rough!* – and while her crying didn't stop, it seemed to change gears. Still, the keening wail was a sonic acid, how could she think with that infernal noise?

Cleansing rain! She needed to get them out into the rain. The rain would wash away the blood, the fear, the sin. She gripped the doorknob with both paws and squeezed and turned and still the door refused to cooperate.

The deadbolt! Of course! Her low, nervous chuckle was a rough counterpoint to the high shrill spiralling out of Em's piehole. She cranked the latch and went back to the dented, misshapen knob. This time the door popped open and the roar of the rain flooded her senses.

As much as it pained her, she picked up the wailing thing once again and pushed aside the screen door, letting it slam behind her, Jason somehow never getting the chance to decrease the tension on the damn thing. The tension had been wound up in the thing too long. *Too long, dammit!* If it kept up, it was going to break. *Yes, definitely break if the wailing kept up and then the rain would get in, yes it would pour through that hole, that wound, that gaping ragged wound, damn him, damn them all, damn the uprights with their squalling pups, they need to be silenced. to be shut up shut up sh* –

The rain was beating on her head, slicking down her hair. She was sitting on the bottom step of the porch, naked and finally human again. The white step she sat on showed swirling darkness as the blood was sluiced from her body, but try as she might, she couldn't shield Emily from the rain, to not let it soak into her blankets. But Emily was so quiet now, so still.

Nancy looked down at her daughter, still trying to shield her from the rain with her own head, and she gently pulled the blankets away from Emily's face. But here, the blanket was torn, the loose threads dangling and dripping rain, and dark – *Too dark!* – and suddenly Nancy couldn't get the blankets away from Em's face fast enough. Em's eyes were open, and water pooled in the hollows without any movement from her to blink it away. Then Nancy pulled the blankets lower and saw…

As Nancy raised her face to the sky, the rain mixed with her tears and washed down and into the ragged, open wound at the child's throat, so dark against the pale skin and blankets.

She had killed her husband, her child, and her life. There was nothing left.

She had broken the sacred law of both humans, and of wolves.

She had nothing left anymore.

She *was* nothing.

She was Zero.

CHAPTER FORTY-FIVE

THEY HAD BEEN frozen, Zero's arms stretched wide for the attack that never came, Rainer's hands pushing against a force that had never come.

Rejecting the contact of skin and skin, Rainer forcefully pulled herself back from the misery of Zero.

♦ ♦ ♦

RAINER'S HANDS FELL away from Zero's—*Nancy's!*—throat, and she stood up. Zero swallowed hard. The two stood staring at each other, breathing hard.

"What happened?" Syd asked, confusion evident in his voice. *When the hell did he shift?* Rainer wondered. He stepped forward, closing the distance between himself and his pack leader. "She just stands there! Zero, kill her! Take her now!"

Zeion's last words echoed in Rainer's mind, as she was sure they did in Nancy's.

Syd was still ranting when Rainer spoke up.

"Syd," Rainer said. "Shut up. It's over."

"What?" This from Syd, Theo, Sam, and several of the others. She realized no one else knew what she now knew. That only she and Zero knew.

As far as everyone else was concerned, it hadn't even started.

Zero dropped her head.

"I will not stand by as you give up again, Zero," Syd said. "I will lead this pack back to glory!" With no hesitation, he leapt at Rainer, leaving the ground even as he changed, coming at her with teeth bared.

"Syd! No!" Zero yelled, but too late.

Halfway through the ten-foot distance between himself and Rainer, Syd once again found himself suspended in mid-air. All eyes turned to Theo, who stood at the same point he had been through the entire ordeal, both hands raised. The wolves standing closest to the circle did not move, did not so much as twitch. It was obvious who held control here.

Sam whispered a soft "cool."

"I suggest you all hold your ground. I believe Rainer has something to tell you all," he said. "Am I right, Ray?"

Rainer nodded, no joy on her face, no relief at being spared another wolf attack. Instead, she quietly approached Syd, still hanging in mid-air, one hand stretched out as though to allow him to sniff her palm. It was obvious she was attempting to show the others she meant no threat, no harm. She stopped, inches from his mouth, her trust in Theo complete. Lifting her hand, she rubbed along his snout and back to the top of his head, her hand between his ears. Once there, her hand stopped, and seemed to press down. She inhaled deeply, and tensed.

Syd's body tensed, convulsed once, and a low whine came from him. It lasted only seconds, and as she pressed on the top of his skull, he gently dropped to the ground, as light as a cloud. His body relaxed as it settled to the earth. Slowly, gently, she took her hand from his head and stepped back.

"Now Syd," she said. "If you still want to take me on, fine. But I think right now it's more important that all the shifters here understand exactly what happened when Zero was made. Don't you?"

Syd snarled, but said nothing. Nor did he attack. Instead, she figured he was weighing his options.

The wolves were getting edgy with all the silence and the waiting. Finally, Syd looked up.

"I think she needs to tell it," was all he said. It was growled out, but Theo translated it for Rainer and Sam. With that, Syd got to his feet, glared at Zero for the pause of one breath, then turned and stood beside Moondoggie, his only other pack member now.

All eyes turned to Zero. Rainer could feel the weight of their stares as a palpable force. Zero—*Or is she just Nancy again?* Rainer wondered—hugged herself, sagging under the force of the combined expectant gazes of her brothers and sisters, and she began to weep.

Again, time stretched out as the silence dragged on. The wind picked up slightly and Rainer shivered, but held her ground. There was no challenge as Theo and Sam moved to stand beside her.

"Tell it," Rainer said. She reached out for Theo's hand and, upon contact, he let out a soft breathy "oh" of understanding. She did the same with Sam. Sam said only, "Whoa."

Nancy raised her head and her lips parted, but no sound came forth. She looked to Rainer, and Rainer, in turn, stared coldly back at her. She would get no sympathy from either camp.

Sighing, she tried again.

"I was made by Zeion. Rather than killing my daughter, my…my Emily…I killed him." The sounds came out flat and cold in that dark place. The reaction was immediate. With those words, she had condemned herself.

Some howled their complaint, others their grief, for Zeion had made them as well. Still others lost control and pissed where they stood, low whines coming out as a funereal dirge.

"He wanted me to kill my daughter!" Nancy yelled, as though it would explain all to the packs. But these were wolves. They all knew. They had all participated. They had all shed their human lives and their former loved ones to be here in this place and on this night.

"You dare speak this in our most sacred of places?" one asked.

"We should kill you ourselves!" another joined in.

With Rainer holding both Theo's and Sam's hands, Theo's translation of the maddened yips and barks flowed across all three of them.

"We cannot," Syd spoke up. "*No wolf shall cause harm or death to another wolf.* She will be banished from all packs. She will be a pariah. A Rōnin."

The wolves encircled Nancy, sitting close, contempt and hatred roiling about her naked flesh. As they moved forward toward Nancy, Theo knew they'd been forgotten for the moment and pulled Rainer and Sam back. They eased through the ever-tightening crowd until they could make their way up the side of the crater.

A scrabbling of shale and dirt warned them of an approaching wolf. Syd.

"You don't think you can leave here unharmed, do you?"

"You don't think you can stop us, do you?" Theo asked. "You know you can't. I've stopped you too many times now for you to be that stupid."

"Go back to your pity party," Sam said. "Bitch."

Rainer tightened her hand on Sam's to shut her up. "I think what we're trying to say is, you stay out of our lives, we'll stay out of yours."

With that, the three of them turned their backs to the shifter and climbed out of the Hole.

♦♦♦

THEY TOPPED THE ridge of the crater, and Rainer asked, "We're not just going to let them go, are we?"

"No," Theo said, looking back down the path they had just taken. "You know me better than that."

"What are you going to do?" Sam asked. She looked up at Theo and Rainer saw his face soften slightly.

Rainer realized she really liked his face. She stood silently, waiting for Theo's answer.

"I thought you said we were going to crush them, Ray?"

Rainer continued to watch Theo, waiting for his reply. Sam wasn't as patient. "So…" she prompted, drawing the word out.

Theo smiled at her impatience.

"So," he said, "I've still got enough juice from the Book to confine them to the Hole. They won't be able to go beyond the perimeter—right here—without experiencing a violent reaction."

"Whaddya mean, 'violent reaction'?"

"You're gonna like this, Sam," he said. "If they go past the edge of this crater, they'll puke so bad it'll eventually start tearing their insides out." Rainer knew Theo had had first-hand experience in that area. "And nothing will be able to get in until every last one of them is dead."

"There's nothing down there but rock," Rainer said, pointing. "They'll have to…"

"Exactly," Theo said. "They either feed off each other, or they die. Let's see how long their sacred law will hold up under death by starvation."

The three of them stood, looking over the Hole, seeing the animals below them.

"Are all the wolves here?"

"Not sure what you mean, Sam," Theo said.

"I mean all the wolves from everywhere in the world. Are they all here?"

"No," Theo said, and his brow creased.

"Then they won't *all* die," she said. "Not *all* of them."

"No."

Rainer didn't know what to say, and it was obvious Theo didn't either. They stood watching a little longer, then Theo turned to Rainer and said, "We've got a long walk back. We should get started."

Rainer started to nod, but Sam cut her off. "No," she said.

"Why not?" Rainer asked.

"Because it's not enough," she said.

"What's not enough, honey?"

"Them." She pointed downhill to the wolves. "That they will live here for a while, but others are still alive in other places."

Theo dropped to his haunches in front of Sam. He looked up at her. "Sam, I know it's not easy to understand. But sometimes you just need to walk away from evil. Live to fight it another day."

"But that's not right," she said. "Walking away from it."

"I know, I know," Theo said, his voice soothing. "And I wasn't much older than you when I learned that myself." Rainer watched his eyes darken. "I thought I'd beaten my particular evil, but then I found out it wasn't gone."

He held Sam lightly by the shoulders. "I didn't want to walk away, honey. But I had no choice."

Rainer saw Sam's head nod.

"I get that," Sam said. "You couldn't do anything. You were still learning."

Still learning? Rainer thought. "Still learning what, honey?" she asked.

"Still learning how to use the Book."

Rainer saw Theo tense.

"But if you still had It, you'd know how to use It now, Theo."

"Sam," Rainer said, "what are you—"

Sam put out both palms. And then the Book was in her hands. "But I have It now. And I know how to use It better," Sam finished.

All was quiet, all was still. Theo remained where he was, looking into Sam's eyes. Sam returned the look calmly. Then she narrowed her eyes, and Theo felt the Book flex the air around them.

Then the howling began.

Rainer looked to the source of the sound. Down in the crater. The Hell Hole.

Theo remained frozen, staring at Sam. Try as he might, he couldn't coerce the Book, couldn't pull It from Sam.

Rainer saw what was happening. She couldn't figure out what she was looking at, but she could see it. The figures there, proud, beautiful animals despite their inherent evil, writhed and twisted on the ground. Their feet kicked at imagined attackers, their jaws snapped at invisible targets.

She turned back to where the little girl still stood, her hands clenched around the massive Book, Theo crouched in front of her.

"Sam!" Rainer said. "What are you doing?"

Theo remained still as the two of them locked gazes.

"She's killing them," Theo said, his voice barely a whisper. "She's killing them all."

"Jesus Christ." Sam looked up at her. "Honey?" Rainer said.

"I have to," was all she said.

Rainer reached out a hand and cupped the back of Sam's head, feeling her fine hair, soft against her hand. But underneath that hair, the thoughts that swirled in that skull…

♦ ♦ ♦

KILL THEM KILL them all, they killed Dad they killed Jake, they kill and kill and kill but they can't kill me but I can kill them I can crush them like we told Zero we would and she didn't believe us but I still scared her and then she thought maybe I could crush them, I can I can and I will I'll crush them and squeeze them until their guts spray out of their mouth and their eyes and their ears and their asses and there's nothing left of them and I can still crush them crush them crush them

♦♦♦

…THEN RAINER PULLED her hand away.

She is, Rainer realized. *She's killing them. Her and the Book.*

She walked a little way from Sam, not knowing what to even say to her right now.

Rainer had seen a lot of things in her life. She'd seen death and life occur in front of her. And she'd seen men change into wolves and wolves morph back into men.

Still, she had a hard time understanding what she now saw. A little girl. And the massacre of an entire species. Her eyes and ears took it in, but she didn't get it.

The animals stood, heads bowed down, legs shaking and straining as they fought desperately to stand yet were forced inexorably down. Tails slipped between legs. These powerful beings pissed themselves in fear as they were forced to lower themselves to the ground, as though the fist of a vengeful god reached down from the heavens, making them kneel.

And then she realized, looking back at Sam, *That's exactly what's happening*.

A vengeful, nine-year-old god.

Every wolf in the area had dropped to the ground. Sam had made each one bow to her.

Then, almost as one, they rolled to their side. Rainer watched as some, in their fear or panic, morphed back to human form. The ground was littered with thousands of the shifters, all prone on the ground.

And still the downward pressure continued.

Howls increased in both volume and intensity, then faded as the lungs that supplied the breath were crushed under an unrelenting pressure.

Then Rainer heard the cracking.

Loud, gunshot cracks, louder than the now-muted mewlings of the beasts as their bones were compressed against each other. She watched as bodies jerked and writhed, but none stood. None raised their heads. They remained pinned to the ground.

Fur rippled and skin stretched and bone tore loose.

"Sam…" Rainer said.

Theo and Sam remained as they were. Sam working the Book, Theo horrified at what she was doing.

Rainer didn't know how to feel. Her brother was down there. The murderers of her family—hers and Sam's and so many others—were down there. Those animals had murdered wantonly and without regret. Still, the sight of them, the sounds of them dying…

It was horrible. She wanted it to end. Not necessarily to stop, but to end.

She couldn't bear to watch it any longer, and moved back to where Sam and the Book and Theo were. They still hadn't moved.

But tears rolled down Theo's cheeks.

"Sam…" she said again. She reached out to touch the girl again, but thought better of it and pulled her hand away.

The snapping and popping continued, increasing in frequency, reminding Rainer of popcorn, starting slow, then coming faster and faster. With this, a low moan rose, raising the hairs on her arms and neck. Then she realized what it was.

The last of the air in their lungs pushing past their vocal cords. A low, involuntary sound. A death dirge.

And still the pressure continued.

By now, the ground had turned red with the spraying blood of the broken bodies. It ran in rivulets and commingled in pools.

The bodies continued to flatten under the pressure, bones grinding to dust, bodies distending and stretching like flesh balloons, before finally bursting with a moist *puh* sound that actually made Rainer's stomach turn once again.

And still the pressure stayed on.

Stayed on until the bodies were crushed flat and began disintegrating. Even the blood stained out wider than was possible on the cold ground.

She's crushing them completely, Rainer thought. Then another thought came to her, this one from Sam's mind from long ago. *Atoms.* She remembered the poster in Sam's room from that first night, so long ago. The Periodic Table. *She's breaking them down to atoms.*

Then finally, when it got down to nothing but the sound of wind, Sam and Theo broke their connection and it was done.

"Sam," Rainer said one last time. Sam turned to look at her. "What have you done?"

"I killed all the werewolves," she said simply. No anger, no emotion whatsoever. Just a flat statement of fact. Then she loosened her grip on the Book and spread her hands as though to let It fall. Instead, It vanished.

What is she?

Rainer couldn't bear to face the girl and instead looked out across the red-stained plain. Out of the corner of her eye, she saw Theo stand and do the same. It looked exactly the same as when they came in, simply devoid of the shifters. No rocks had been crushed. The landscape remained untouched. It was simply the shifters that had been affected.

"Did she really—"

"Yes," Theo said. "She reached out through the Book and crushed each wolf."

"Did the Book..." Rainer's voice caught, stricken with fear.

"Did It choose her?" Theo asked. "No." He looked down at Sam. He reached out a hand and smoothed an errant lock of hair down. "No, It didn't. She bent It to her will."

"I got the impression that was impossible."

"Ten minutes ago," he said, "I would have said the same thing." He looked at Rainer. "Sam exists outside the Book's influence." She saw the tears still standing in his eyes and didn't know what they represented.

Okay, the Book doesn't have her. Which means the Book still does *have Theo.* She shook her head. *But Sam used the Book.*

She pointed out across the plain. "She killed them all?"

"She killed every one," Theo said.

"All of them," Sam said.

"I don't think you're getting it," Theo said. "She killed *every* one of the werewolves. On the planet." He swept his arm across the plain. "What happened here? It happened everywhere."

"They're all...?"

"She found every one. No matter where they were. And she did the same thing to every...single...one." He looked down at the girl and Rainer saw equal measures of fear and respect in his gaze. "She wiped them off the planet."

"Every fucking one," Sam agreed. "They killed Jake. They killed my dad. They killed your family." Sam looked up at Rainer. "They had to go."

Rainer wanted to back away from the girl. She wanted to get as far away from the girl as she could. Instead, she bent and hugged her. "I'm so sorry about Jake and your father," she said.

"I'm sorry about your family. But this is why the wolves had to die," Sam said. "It means you don't have to hunt them anymore."

Rainer just held the girl. Theo dropped back down and looked at Rainer.

"You and Theo can be together," she said. "And maybe..." But she didn't finish.

Theo laid a hand on Sam's shoulder. "Maybe what, kiddo?"

"Maybe we can...sort of...be a new family?"

Rainer and Theo's eyes met again. Rainer read his gaze and saw her own thoughts echoed there.

Sam scares the shit out of both of us.

"I think that's a pretty good idea," was all that Rainer said.

AUTHOR'S NOTE

SO, *BLOOD LOSS*. Some fun, huh, Bambi?

I mentioned in my notes after the last book, *Out for Blood*, that I'd made a resolution to start writing after years away from it, and that I'd even signed up for a creative writing course to get my ass in gear.

So, while I was still trying to figure out what the hell I was doing with that weird story idea I had been calling *School is Hell* and eventually ended up as *Out for Blood*, I attended my first writing class, and on the first night was given an assignment. I don't remember much about the parameters around the assignment, but I do remember what I wrote.

See, the weekend before, I'd bought a crappy, old, shit-brown Toyota Corolla off my brother—and the less said about him, the better—and he'd left a bunch of tools in the trunk. After work on the Saturday night, I said I would make the half-hour drive to his new place to drop them off. He couldn't come to me, because, well, drinking, driving, loss of licence, you get the picture.

I thought I'd remembered the way, having been there about a week before, but I got all twisted up and lost. So I pulled into a gas station to use the telephone booth to call him for directions. And while I was waiting for the guy in the booth to finish his call, another guy came walking by my car with a three or four-foot section of wood. Probably four inches by four inches. And while I watched, he opened the door to the phone booth and drove that chunk of wood right into the other guy's head. I'd been standing outside the car, maybe twenty feet away, and I quickly looked around. Surely someone was calling the police, or doing something. I mean, I was a skinny young guy, and the wood-slinger was a mountain. But as I looked, I saw one guy pumping gas, studiously looking exactly one-hundred and eighty degrees away from the very loud men. And the guy manning the booth at the gas station? He was looking down, with a hand over his eyes. Nope, nothing to see here.

I literally didn't know what to do, and was frozen to the spot, until the guy with the wood stopped kicking the ever-living shit out of the guy from the booth, turned, looked at me—apparently the only guy stupid enough to look at the scene—pointed at me, and said, "You're next, motherfucker."

Thank god I left the car running.

Long story short, I blew out of there, hit up the next gas station I could find, called 911, told them what I'd seen and where, then hung up and got directions so I could drop the shit at my brother's and get the hell out of crazytown.

I drove by the first gas station on the way to my brother's place. No cops. No wood-wielder. No broken phone booth guy. I have no idea what ever happened to them.

So, when it came to the writing assignment four days later, it was top of mind. But I wondered if I could twist it up a bit. Then I had the line, "No, we're gonna kill him. But we're gonna do it right."

I had no idea what it meant, or where it would lead, but that's the scene I wrote. Oh, and Rainer? Yeah, he was a dude in that first draft. Not on a date. Just out with a friend.

And, for the longest time, that was the opening to this novel. Eventually, I messed around a lot with the story, figured out the werewolf angle, and that opening kept getting pushed deeper and deeper into the story, until it became the seventh chapter. But yeah, most of that shit? It really happened.

Hey, a writer takes their inspiration where they can get it.

Speaking of openings, there's a line in Chapter 32: "Like with the Winnebago in Mexico." Just a quick, throwaway line about an unexplained bit of excitement from before. Well, actually, that was the original second opening for the novel. I wrote this whole scene of these wolves trying to cross back over the border from Mexico into the US, and shit goes pear-shaped. Unfortunately, I could never get it quite nailed down. Now it's a deleted scene sitting on some hard drive somewhere.

So this book is the oddball of the series. It's the second one in the series that I wrote, and I came at it with all confidence because, when I sat down to write it, I'd already finished up the first draft of *Out for Blood,* so I was all, *Hell, I'm experienced at writing novels now! This'll be a cinch!*

Heh. Ha ha ha.

Right.

This one, like the one that came before it, and damn near every one that came after it, went through a ton of different permutations. Or iterations. Or false starts. Pick your poison.

Initially, Bo was going to be cast from the pack due to him contracting the one disease the wolves could get: AIDS. And the secret that Zero would have carried was that she had it, too. And Theo was going to spread it to all wolves.

But…it didn't work.

It was also going to end with Theo locking the wolves down in the Hole. That was the end. Apparently Sam had other ideas, as you read.

Also, initially, I had the wolves escape in Moondoggie's van (which I would have absolutely called "the shaggin' wagon"), because I also put Sam in the back of that van. And, truth to tell, I literally wrote her in, then out and with Rainer, then back in, then back with Rainer, at least five times.

God's honest truth, I'm still not sure I picked the right path on that one. There's a particular scene with Sam and Zero around a campfire that I flat out love, but it had to go. Banished to that dastardly cutting-room floor.

The other oddball thing about this novel? The reason it's a bit more of an outlier? This is the only one that doesn't occur in or around my fictional cursed town of New Hope. Yes, it has a former resident of the town in Theo, but still.

Nope. Instead, I created the new fictional town of Laughlin, which is a heavily fictionalized version of my hometown of Oshawa, Ontario. For those who have never heard of it, we're about an hour east of Toronto. Laughlin, of course, is taken from one of the biggest patrons of the town, R. S. McLaughlin. Seemed only right.

Changing gears a bit, I think what I like the most about this novel—aside from the nastiest violence I likely ever have, or ever will write—are the characters. These characters were not planned by me. No, instead, they kept knocking on the inside of my skull, demanding that I shut up and let them take over. I'm glad I listened.

Rainer, as I said, started out as a male character. After that first scene for the creative writing course, our second assignment was to take one of the characters and put down everything we know about them. And that's when I figured out he was a she. Dude looked like a lady, and who was I to argue? I absolutely adore strong female characters, both in my fiction and in real life, so why not in one of my stories?

Once I had Rainer, I began to figure out Zach. Poor old Zach managed to get my old manager's job from when I worked at Arby's way back in the day. So, again, that whole scene in the Second Interlude? Rainer kicking the asses of the guys in the fast-food joint? Yup. That happened in my store.

Only it was a skinny little guy that came in for free coffees, not vanilla milkshakes. We got to be good friends for quite a while, that guy and me.

And then there's the Fed. Oh god, the Fed.

In my second (and last) corporate job, very early on, there was this operations manager who, thankfully, I only had the misfortune of working under for three months. I won't disclose his real name, but somewhere in that last name were the three letters F-E-D. And instead of saying "I" or "me," he would refer to himself in the third person. Yes, he truly called himself "the Fed." I'll never forget the first time I heard it. I was in a boardroom with about twenty other members of my team. Pizza had been brought in. And as the meeting was going on, suddenly, we saw two hands grasp the doorjamb, then this silly little man's head popped into the room. And he said, "The Fed smells...pizzahhhh!"

A couple of months later, I was briefly supported by the Fed, and it was a most unpleasant experience. I knew he was going to show up somewhere in my writing.

At a writers' conference, many years ago, one of the speakers told the story of attending a posh event where a few authors were speaking. Turns out there was one author—yes, I know who the author is, and no, I won't tell you—who was dreadfully boring. Torturously boring. And our intrepid speaker, and the big Scottish man he sat beside, got to the point where they were so desperate for this author to shut up that the only thing keeping them sane was the knowledge that, once the author finished, there would be a break where they could dash to the bar and down a couple of heavily alcoholed beverages.

The author finally did shut up, the break was announced, and the two guys ran for the bar. Turns out everyone else did too, and the line was enormous. As luck would have it, they just got to the bar as the lights flashed to signal the next speaker, and that break was over. The bartender spread his hands, and apologized that he was no longer allowed to serve.

Our speaker was obviously angry, but his mate, the big Scot, was absolutely incensed. He reached over the bar, grabbed the poor bartender by the front of his shirt, dragged him forward, and growled, "Whut's yer name?"

"Charles," the bartender said, sheepishly.

Still holding Charles with one hand, the Scot pointed his finger at the man's nose with intent, and said, "Well then, Charles, YEW are goin' t' die a fookin' HORRIBULL deeth in my next NOOVEL!"

The funny thing is, I heard that story at least five years after I'd last dealt with the Fed, but when I heard it? It clicked, and I knew I was going to give the Fed a fookin' horribull deeth as well. And I knew exactly which novel to do it in.

The Fed? If you're out there? I hope you hated my tribute of you.

Moondoggie? Yeah, he was another surprise. I was just going to have a generic mechanic hand over their bikes and die. But then I heard Sheryl Crow sing "Soak Up the Sun." And then, in the back of my mind, this tall, skinny, blond-dreaded stoner started first bobbing his head along with the tune, then he started singing it in his off-key, kush-roughened voice. And I couldn't ignore the crazy bastard.

The two other characters I want to talk about briefly are Sam and Jake. I'd very quickly decided that Zach was going to have a daughter, but that's literally all I knew about her. And yes, you'll find this and subsequent novels follow my somewhat-unconscious trend of giving my female characters female names that get squeezed down to guy's names. Sam. Jake. Ray. Lex. It's a problem. I'm working on it.

Anyway. I had an amorphous daughter character named Sam. And then I knew I'd need someone to be watching her while Zach was out discovering the wild and woolly world of werewolves. In came Jake.

I know I based Jake, at least her profession and somewhat visually, on an internet personality that had her own website back in the '90s, with paid subscriptions for nude photos. No porn, no crotch shots. Just very tasteful nudes. Think I can remember her name now? Nope. Not even Google could help me with it.

But that was the visual aspect. I will say that, when I finally threw Sam and Jake in a scene? Yeah, I just shut up, backed up, and let the two of them take over. I didn't plan it. I didn't have a clue what they were going to say, or how they were going to say it. But hot damn, I will say I created two of my absolute favourite characters.

Which, of course, makes me feel worse, considering what I did to both of them by the end of this novel.

But that's what I was going for with this one. Blood loss. Yes, bleeding, but also, the loss of your family, your blood. Everyone in this damn book has lost someone, by accident, disease, tragedy, or design. I've had many people in my past that professed to love me. And every one walked away. I wanted to capture some of the pain of not losing blood, but hemorrhaging family.

Family is important. Never take your loved ones for granted. Because when you do? Yeah, there's real horror in that.

Finally, one last note. Back before I took a break from social media, I talked to a few authors and befriended some of them. One of them, a very witty, interesting, and somewhat tortured guy named Ed Kurtz? Yeah, he was the one who first used the term "Canuckistan." I absolutely can't take credit for that one. I stole it from Ed Kurtz. Ed, wherever you are? Thanks for taking a chance on me, and I hope you like what I did with Canuckistan.

And that brings us to the end of the third part of this six-part monster.

As usual, I hope you dug it.

ABOUT THE AUTHOR

TOBIN ELLIOTT HAS written for most of his life. After some unfortunate incidents with walls and permanent markers, he switched to safer things like pens and paper, and later, typewriters and then computers. Though science fiction was his first love, horror has always had a powerful hold on him, even back before he wore big-boy pants. He likes to have the shit scared out of him, and he likes scaring the shit out of others. Somehow, it always comes down to shit with Tobin.

Tobin spent his formative teenage years in a small town about four hours northeast of Toronto. Those experiences, and the magic and wonder of that place, never left him, though he left the town through no fault of his own. He currently lives within a three-hour drive of the place, and occasionally gets back to top up on his sense of wonder and nostalgia.

Based on that town and surrounding areas, Tobin has written several novels in his Aphotic World series.

Along with those writings, Tobin has been fortunate enough to have had three horror novellas published, as well as seven stories in various anthologies. He has been a board member of both the Writers' Community of Simcoe County (WCSC) and the Writers' Community of Durham Region (WCDR), and, for five years, was an annual participant in the Muskoka Novel Marathon, a 72-hour writing marathon to raise money for adult literacy programs.

Finally, he also taught creative writing for two different continuous learning programs. Tobin writes ugly stories about bad people doing horrible things, and it was his pleasure to show other people how to do the same thing for almost twenty years.

If you're interested in more ramblings by Tobin, well, he's not much into social media. He sees it as a blight on humanity of almost Bookian proportions. And yet, still, he's on there.

Facebook: The Horror Guy (/tobinelliott.horrorguy)

Twitter: @TheHorrorGuy91

Instagram: @tobinelliott.horrorguy

♦♦♦

I HOPE THAT this book captured your imagination, and I hope that this series will turn you into a loyal reader.

Because loyal readers are an author's secret weapon. They can influence other readers…how?

Through reviews.

If you loved this book, and yes, even if you hated it, please also consider leaving a review on the site where you purchased it, and/or Goodreads, or anywhere else. You can also drop me a line at TheHorrorGuy91@gmail.com.

As a reader, you have an immense power to influence others.

Please, use that power.

Made in the USA
Middletown, DE
05 September 2024